Monarch Beach

Monarch Beach

Anita Hughes

 St. Martin's Griffin ⚏ New York

MONARCH BEACH. Copyright © 2012 by Anita Hughes. All rights reserved. Printed in the United States of America. For information, address St. Martin's Press, 175 Fifth Avenue, New York, N.Y. 10010.

Design by Anna Gorovoy

www.stmartins.com

ISBN 978-0-312-64304-1 (pbk.)
ISBN 978-1-250-01584-6 (e-book)

First Edition: June 2012

10 9 8 7 6 5 4 3 2 1

To my mother

Chapter One

The day my life changed forever started like any other Tuesday. I liked Tuesdays. My appointment book stayed blank on Tuesdays. Sometimes I wondered how the other days filled up so quickly. You'd be surprised how ladies' auxiliary lunches, PTA committee meetings, and library fund-raising can occupy your time. Not to mention the karate lessons, piano, and chess club Max had after school. Like many stay-at-home moms I was a full-time chauffeur for my son and fund-raiser for his school. Tuesdays were mine. I started the day with a yoga class, usually followed by a fresh strawberry muffin at the Lemon Café. But this Tuesday, the Lemon Café was out of strawberry muffins, so I did something different. I made an unexpected visit to my husband's restaurant and found him in the back room with his pants down and his legs wrapped around Ursula, his new chef. He tried pulling his pants up before I swung open the door, but it was a glass door. I had seen what I had seen: my tall, dark French husband sticking it to his blond Scandinavian chef. I thought, how cute, they had matching ponytails: Ursula's was a long blond plait down her back, Andre's was a short black ponytail I had always found very sexy. Apparently, Ursula did, too. I slammed the glass door so hard I heard it shatter behind me. I jumped in my car and tore away. Black Tuesday changed everything.

I didn't drive far. My hands were shaking, I was afraid I would lose control of the wheel. While I wanted to kill Andre, and possibly Ursula, I didn't have a personal death wish. I pulled into the parking lot at the post office, threw my purse under the seat, and started walking. I was still in my yoga clothes, so I looked like any other mother going for a morning hike. I left the parking lot and took long strides till I reached the lake, a walk that usually took me half an hour. That Tuesday I made it in sixteen minutes. I sat on a bench watching the ducks and took deep breaths. It was a beautiful spring day. The sun was warm, the sky a pale blue, and beds of purple and white daisies surrounded the lake. I often brought Max here on Saturdays while Andre worked. We tossed stale bread to the ducks. Max threw stones in the water and we would both be quiet so we could hear the "plop" sound when they landed.

That Tuesday the only sound I heard was my own sobs. I sounded like a stuck pig. And I felt like a complete idiot. What a cliché I was. Married for ten years, mother to a fantastic eight-year-old son, never suspecting that when Andre went to the restaurant on Tuesdays to "do the books" he was also doing the chef.

I tried blaming myself. I should have protested when Andre

wanted to hire a female chef. Ursula was a former sous chef at the Palace Hotel Dining Room in Montreux and she specialized in fondue. Andre's restaurant specialized in fondue: cheese fondue, salmon fondue, chocolate fondue. But if he hadn't hired Ursula I may have found him in the supply closet with Yvette the hostess, or Marie the cocktail waitress. I couldn't even blame Ursula. Andre was thirty-five. He had olive skin and green eyes. He looked like a European film star, and he was her boss. Ursula had only been in California for six months. Maybe she thought it was part of the job description. The only person I could blame was Andre.

I closed my eyes and remembered just a few nights ago, breezing into the restaurant on Andre's arm on our date night. We had been to the movies and seen *The Proposal*. I loved romantic comedies where the couple overcame all sorts of obstacles on their path to happiness. We sat in the back of the theater and Andre slung one arm over my shoulder, and played with the hem of my skirt with his free hand. I slapped his hand away, pretending to focus on Sandra Bullock and Ryan Reynolds, but I loved Andre's attention. I loved knowing that after ten years together, he still wanted to put his hand up my skirt.

I remember seeing Ursula fleetingly while I waited for Andre to give directions to his staff. Now I thought maybe the direction he gave was "kiss me harder," while I politely discussed the savory flavor of fondue with one of the couples dining in the restaurant.

My sobs became hiccups and I recalled the last time my life changed in a single day. I was eighteen, and I had arrived home from school to find four envelopes addressed to me on the marble table in my parents' foyer.

"Good afternoon, Miss Amanda." Our housekeeper swept up my backpack. "Your parents had to go out. I prepared a snack for you in the kitchen."

"Thanks, Rosemary. I'm not hungry. Please let me know when Mom and Dad come home." I grabbed the envelopes and climbed the staircase to my bedroom. I sat on my bed looking at the view from the bay window. My bedroom was on the third floor of my parents' house. My friends rolled their eyes when they came over and called it "the palace" under their breath. It had a full-sized ballroom where my parents held parties with seven-piece orchestras. In the basement there was a separate kitchen and living room for the staff: housekeeper, cook, laundress, gardener. I had the third floor to myself. My bedroom took up half the floor. It had a four-poster bed and a huge desk where I did my drawings. And it had the most amazing view of the San Francisco Bay. On clear days I watched hundreds of boats zip under the Golden Gate Bridge. My father had made his money himself. He wasn't ashamed to spend it, and I refused to be ungrateful for the luxury that surrounded me.

I held the envelopes printed with their college insignias and tried to decide which to open first. I hesitated. Should I wait for my parents to come home and open them together? I was their only child, and they were as excited as I was to know where I would spend the next four years. But I didn't know where they'd gone, or when they'd be back. I opened the envelope from Stanford first. I read the letter carefully. I had been placed on their wait list. I took a deep breath and opened the envelope from Rhode Island School of Design. It was a long letter on dark gray stationery saying I had been accepted.

I hugged it to my chest. My dream was to be a fashion designer: not a very popular goal at my college prep school. I had to beg my advisor to let me apply to RISD. I breathed a sigh of relief and opened the envelope from UC Berkeley. I had been accepted there as well. Not surprising, since the campus was dotted with benches and playing fields donated by my father.

The last envelope was from Parsons in New York. I held it and closed my eyes. For the last two years I had dreamed of attending Parsons and interning for a fashion designer, being in the center of the fashion universe. I slit the envelope and opened my eyes slowly. I was in. I had been accepted at Parsons. I fell back on the bed and looked at my beautiful hand-painted ceiling. I felt my life was lining up perfectly like the gold stars painted on a night sky above me. There was a knock on the door and Rosemary poked her head in. "Excuse me, Miss Amanda. Your mother phoned. Your parents are almost home and they would like you to meet them in the library."

I gathered my college letters and ran down the two flights of stairs to the library. I sat in one of my father's leather wing-back chairs and debated how to tell my parents the news. They would hate to see me go across the country, but they would be thrilled. I had inherited my love of fashion from my mother. I spent countless afternoons and weekends as a child sitting in my mother's closet and sketching her evening gowns. As I grew older, I would take the sketches back to my room and make small changes; erasing a shoulder strap here, adding an ivory bow there, until I created my own fantasy dresses.

"Amanda showed me a design today that rivals Coco Chanel," my mother said one evening to the ladies who arrived for a Junior League meeting.

"Mom, nothing rivals Chanel," I replied, secretly glowing.

"Coco Chanel was once a young girl, too." My mother poured my hot chocolate while the ladies drank tea in fragile porcelain cups.

After I made polite conversation, and my mother dismissed me with a discreet nod of her head, I ran up to my room and looked at the sketch, wondering if it really did resemble Chanel. I vowed I would sketch and sew, and read and learn everything I could about fashion. One day my label would be found in Neiman's and Bloomingdale's and in chic boutiques on Fifth Avenue.

🦋 🦋 🦋

I clutched my acceptance letters, thinking that day was coming closer, but my parents walked in looking like they had seen the grim reaper. My mother entered the room first. She wore one of my favorite outfits: a pale pink St. John suit with gold cuffs. I looked at her face, usually so artfully made up that she glowed from across a room. Her cheeks were white and her eyes were swollen from crying.

My father staggered in behind her. He was over six feet tall. He had white hair and his forehead was lined, but he usually moved with the confidence of someone who had come from nothing and created his own empire. That day he looked like an oversized schoolboy: scared and weak and wanting to hide behind his mother's skirt.

"I have the best news!" The words popped out of my mouth.

"Your mother has some news," my father said softly.

"It's not my news." My mother shot an imploring look at my father. My parents had been married for twenty years. They met late in life: My father was busy building his empire and "forgot" to get married. My mother was a self-described "debutante left on the shelf." They found each other at a symphony gala and married six weeks later. I could not remember them ever looking crossly at each other. I never heard them raise their voices in anger or hurt. My mother glided from room to room of our house like a fairy godmother, sprinkling good taste and serenity on everything she touched. My father worked long hours but returned at night to scoop her up and take her to dinner and dancing. I would sit at my window, watching them roar away in my father's latest sports car, content to be left alone, happy to have parents who idolized each other.

"Grace, please."

My mother looked at me seriously. "We've been to see Dr. Galen. Your father has liver cancer. Dr. Galen said . . ." She paused. I had never seen my mother without a perfect French manicure. I had never known her to smell of anything but Chanel No. 5. And I had never heard her unable to finish a sentence. My friends called her the "Queen of Polish." She was a legend in San Francisco for her witty fund-raising speeches. Invitations to her Sunday evening "salons" were hugely coveted.

"Dr. Galen said"—my father took her hand—"I have nine months to live. A year if I be a good boy and stop drinking and smoking." His broad face broke into a smile. "But have I ever listened to what anyone said? I can't die. I have to see you graduate from high school and college."

I crumpled my college letters into tight balls. My eyes filled with tears. We just stood there like three department store dummies. My parents and I, who had ridden camels in Egypt, who had stared down lions in Africa, we could beat this together.

"Simon," my mother said quietly. "Dr. Galen is our second opinion."

I looked at my father, hoping he would tell my mother she was wrong. When he looked at me, his eyes were wet. "The only person who has ever made any sense in my life is your mother. I guess she's right then."

I remember turning away and studying the wall of books as if they held the answer. It wasn't surprising my father had liver cancer. He was of the Rat Pack generation. Like Dean Martin and Frank Sinatra, he worked hard, played hard, and felt immortal. Every night for as long as I could remember, he and my mother would start their evening with a cocktail. Dinners in our long formal dining room included a bottle of fine wine; a tall brandy followed dessert. The nights they went out with friends, or to social events, I knew he drank for hours. But I had never seen him drunk. My father was a gentleman and I adored him.

"What's your news, honey?" my mother asked.

"I, ah, I got my college letters," I said. I dropped the crumpled letters on the floor and watched my future roll away. I could not miss the last year of my father's life. New York would have to wait.

"Don't keep us in suspense." My father smiled.

"I got in to Berkeley," I said. I could go to Berkeley, and spend weekends at home. I would be close when anything happened.

"That's fantastic." My father beamed. He loved his alma mater. We used to prowl Telegraph Avenue together on Sundays. Sometimes we would hike up to the Lawrence Laboratory and look at San Francisco from across the bay.

"I thought you wanted to study fashion, honey. In New York." My mother looked at me sharply.

"Well, sure, later. But UC Berkeley is a great university. And I love the campus," I faltered.

"Amanda, did you get into Parsons?" she asked.

"Yes, but I don't want to go," I replied stubbornly.

"Amanda, you've been talking about Parsons for two years. You can't put your life on hold for us. I'll be here with your father."

"Your mother is right," my father said, nodding.

"I'm not going to Parsons. I want to stay right here. " I fled upstairs. My parents may be pillars of strength, but I was an eighteen-year-old girl about to lose the only man I ever loved. I locked my bedroom door and cried until it was dark.

I sat on the bench by the lake, wishing I could ask my father what to do after I discovered Andre and Ursula glued together with shrink-wrap. When I was nine my father and I went on a ski trip, just the two of us, to Aspen. My mother had twisted her ankle doing the foxtrot at the Asian Art Museum Winter Gala, but she insisted my father and I keep our reservations and go without her.

I remember the heady feeling of boarding the plane, the flight attendants gushing over my father, so tall and handsome with his steel-gray hair and his easy manner.

"Can I get you anything, anything at all?" A blond flight attendant leaned close while she adjusted my seat belt. She seemed to be sending my father a secret signal, a discreet flutter of her eyelashes, the way she ran her tongue over her lips, which I didn't understand.

"I've got everything I need right here," my father replied. I saw his face close down, and he spent the rest of the flight asking me about my drawing classes, and guessing what my mother would do in our absence.

We stayed in a rustic chalet on the side of the mountain with three other families from San Francisco. One night, after a long dinner where the children were relegated to a table in the kitchen and the adults kept flitting in and out, popping open bottles of wine, I watched one of the women take off her fur coat and drape it over my father's shoulders.

I stopped in my tracks, about to join him in the dining room, and heard the woman giggle, "Nothing feels better than fur on naked skin." Even before my father saw me, he took the jacket off his shoulders, steered the woman back to her husband, and said he was going outside to get some fresh air.

I joined him on the balcony, and put my hand in his pocket to keep warm.

"Why did Mrs. Graham give you her fur jacket?" I asked.

"Alcohol affects people in different ways," he explained slowly.

"In bad ways?" I moved closer to my father. It was twenty below zero, and I was wearing leggings and my favorite pair of socks with toes.

"Sometimes, but then you just gently redirect them."

"You mean, Mrs. Graham got confused and thought you were her husband," I said, pondering the possibility.

"Something like that." My father nodded and led me back inside.

The next night my father invited me to eat with the grown-ups. With his wife absent, I was his shield to keep away interested females.

I wiped my eyes and plucked a handful of daisies. I knew what my father would think of Andre. He hated weakness of character.

🦋 🦋 🦋

My father defied the doctors' prognosis and died two weeks before I graduated from Berkeley. I spent almost every weekend of those four years playing games with him in his library overlooking the bay. He taught me chess and backgammon and how to never lose at tic-tac-toe. They were wonderful weekends. My mother would greet me with hugs and little presents: a pashmina she picked up at Neiman's, a pair of Tod's driving shoes she thought would be excellent for walking around campus. Then she would mumble something about a committee meeting and leave us alone.

I learned how to relax. I wanted time to stand still so I could always be looking at my father wearing his "at home" clothes: a silk robe over cashmere pants and leather slippers. I wanted to be able to hear his voice saying, "You can do anything you want, Amanda. Just make sure you know what that is."

When I stood up with my graduating class on a foggy afternoon in May, I promised myself I would listen to him. Now I would go to New York and start my life. But I looked at my mother clapping furiously as I received my diploma and realized I couldn't leave her either. She looked perfect in her black Dior suit, but she was thin as a stick and she was smoking two packs a day.

I moved home for the summer and got a job at a boutique in Presidio Heights. I would help my mother heal and in the fall I would move to New York. I pictured walking the avenues of New York and drinking in the winter clothes in the windows of Bergdorf's and Bloomingdale's.

I met Andre on July Fourth and by the end of the summer I was engaged to a sexy Frenchman who had been in America for ten months and didn't know why everything was closed on the Fourth of July. My dreams of becoming a fashion designer came to a halt. I had only myself to blame. No one forced me to fall in love. I could have said no when Andre appeared at my mother's house just before Labor Day with three dozen red roses and a box with a small, square diamond ring. But I was twenty-two, and drunk from a summer of long evenings holding hands and walking along the bay. Maybe I was trying to replace my father. Maybe I just adored having Andre whisper *"J'adore"* in my ear.

I remember the evening I first walked into Andre's bistro. My friends all had big Fourth of July plans but I didn't feel like celebrating. It was our first holiday since my father died, and by evening I desperately needed to get out of the house. My mother was trying to keep herself together. She filled her days with philanthropy but at night she sat in the library and smoked. I couldn't get her to stop. If I told her she was killing herself she would look at me knowingly and nod. If I suggested we go out to dinner or hit a movie she would say she was tired and go to bed.

I asked Rosemary to watch her and I headed out to Sacramento Street. I needed to get some fresh air. Sacramento Street was deserted. All my usual haunts were closed. I kept walking, hoping at least Starbucks was open and I could get a hot mocha before I went home. I saw a tall man with a black ponytail lounging outside a restaurant.

"*Allo,* beautiful," he said.

I turned around. There was no one else on the sidewalk.

"I am talking to the beautiful girl with curly brown hair," he said as I walked closer. "That's you." His face broke into a wide smile. He had very white teeth and a Roman nose.

"Hello," I replied.

"Come inside and have something to eat." He motioned to the doorway. He wore dark blue jeans, a white apron, and white sneakers.

"Are you open?" I asked.

"*Mais, oui.* Why wouldn't I?" he asked.

"It's the Fourth of July," I replied.

"So?" He shrugged his shoulders.

"America's birthday. You know, a national holiday."

"Bastille Day is my national holiday. I am Andre Blick, this is my restaurant." He held out his hand. I shook it awkwardly. I had been so busy worrying about my father during college I hadn't dated. Every now and then I would get pizza with a group of kids, but mostly I kept myself apart.

"Okay, I am hungry," I agreed finally.

"Excellent, you are my first customer this evening." He escorted me to a table, his arm lightly touching mine.

I turned out to be his only customer. He cooked for me and served me himself, his waitress having gone home early. Eventually he sat down next to me and opened a bottle of wine.

"I don't drink," I said, pushing away the wineglass.

"You have to drink, it's a national holiday." He filled my glass and poured one for himself.

"I thought your holiday was Bastille Day," I said.

"I am in America now, with a beautiful American." Andre clinked my glass. "To national holidays; may we celebrate many more."

I knew he was flirting. No one had ever flirted with me and I didn't know how to respond. He was handsome, like the Roman gods we had studied in mythology. I concentrated on my crepes and let him talk.

"I have worked in a kitchen since I was this high." Andre placed his hand four feet off the floor. "My father was a chef in Toulouse and he let me stir the sauces and chop vegetables when the owner of the restaurant was away." He paused and sipped his wine.

"When I was nineteen, I hitchhiked to Paris and became assistant chef at a bistro in the Thirteenth Arrondissement," he continued. I liked the way he moved his hands around when he talked.

"Last year an American came in every morning and ordered my crepes. He said he was opening a French restaurant in San Francisco and asked me to be his chef and partner."

"You left your family?" I asked. I couldn't imagine living an ocean away from my mother.

"America is the land of opportunity." He flashed his perfect white teeth. "I could not refuse. I moved to San Francisco and voilà. Crepe Suzette was born," he finished his story, refilling our glasses and moving his chair closer to mine.

"Who's Suzette?" I asked.

"My partner's wife. Ex-wife now. She didn't like the long hours he keeps at the restaurant so she's divorcing him for a stockbroker who is home at four p.m." He shrugged. "You Americans are funny. In France you get married, you stay married. Affairs, long hours, doesn't matter. Marriage is for life."

"I can understand long hours. Affairs would be another story," I said.

"See, Americans. Very puritan." He shook his head. His English was almost perfect. And he was so beautiful, his features chiseled from stone; I had to stop myself from looking at him. He was only twenty-four but he seemed older.

"Your crepes are wonderful. I have to go." I fished my credit card out of my purse.

"Do you have a boyfriend waiting at home?" Andre leaned on the table, his elbow pressed against mine.

"No boyfriend. My father died recently, I am staying with my mother. They were married a long time and she really misses him."

"Love. There are no happy endings. That is why we must live now." He touched my face with his fingers.

I pulled back. "I better go. What do I owe you?"

"Dinner is on me, in exchange for your beautiful company." Andre shook his head.

"Your English is very good. But you say 'beautiful' too much."

"One can never say 'beautiful' too much if it is true." He didn't get up or remove my plate. He just sat looking at me.

"I need to pay, please. I don't want your night to be a complete waste."

"I will let you pay if you let me take you out to dinner on my night off," Andre said.

"Okay. Agreed," I said.

I handed him my credit card and he got up and walked over to the cash register.

"I need your phone number," he said, placing the bill in front of me.

I wrote down my phone number and gave it to him. I opened the bill and signed my name. He picked up the bill and studied it closely. I remember thinking maybe I shouldn't have tipped him; it was his restaurant. He handed me back my credit card and touched my shoulder. "When we get married you won't have to change your initials, Amanda Bishop."

I should have seen the warning signs, I thought, kicking a handful of pebbles into the lake so the ducks lifted their necks and shook their feathers. Andre had told me stories of wealthy women who propositioned him when he worked at the restaurant in Toulouse. How he lost his virginity in the giant fridge with the wife of the local judge. Andre had the morals of an alley cat and I had been blinded all these years by his declarations of love, and by the way he put his hand on the small of my back.

In my parents' circle, at the highest rung of San Francisco society, infidelity was not tolerated. Families lived in mansions at the top of Pacific Heights and their morals were as lofty as their real estate. My father had been a member of the Bohemian Club and every summer he had spent a week at the Bohemian Grove, a private enclave in the redwood forest visited by heads of state, where women were denied entry. One year as he was leaving for his week's retreat, one of my friends asked him what they do there.

"What's all the hush-hush?" Maisie was sixteen and going through a rebellious stage. She liked to rile up her parents, or mine when she slept over on the weekends. "My father has taken a vow of silence. He won't tell my mother a thing." She leaned against my father's Mercedes. "Do you guys import a bunch of strippers and play strip poker under the redwoods?"

My father looked at her levelly and opened the car door. "Maisie, I think it's time you went home. I'll drive you. And I'd like to have a word with your mother."

A few days later my father received a written apology from Maisie in the mail, and she was not allowed to sleep over again.

When a scandal did occur among their friends, the culprit was ousted from the Pacific-Union Club and the Bohemian

Club, and his social invitations were rescinded. A few of my father's friends were self-made like he was, but most were descendants of the robber barons: Leland Stanford, Charles Crocker, and Mark Hopkins. They had spent the last hundred years making their names respectable; they weren't going to let any blackguard tarnish their circle.

So how had I fallen for Andre, I asked myself, hurling the stones so they fell in the middle of the lake. Was I just taken in by his looks, by his Continental charm, or in the beginning had he been a gentleman?

That first summer Andre treated me like a princess. Whenever he arrived at the house he brought presents for Rosemary, my mother, and me. For Rosemary it was often a tomato from the restaurant's garden, for my mother a small bouquet of lilacs or daisies, and for me a special chocolate dessert. At first I questioned his motives—he knew I was an heiress. But as the summer progressed and we explored the city together, he kept saying he enjoyed my company. And he thought I was beautiful. No one except my parents had ever called me beautiful.

In August my mother seemed more herself. She started going to lunch with friends. She wore her favorite color, pink, and she began accepting some of the invitations that kept pouring in. I thought about the fall and New York. I had mentioned my plans to Andre. He hadn't said anything for or against. He hadn't tried to sleep with me either. I was partially relieved. I was the only twenty-two-year-old virgin I knew and was terrified he would shrug me off as a juvenile if he found out. But each time he left me at the front door with just a long, deep kiss, my whole body quivered.

Sometimes I thought he was just filling his days off. I would leave for New York, and he would kiss me good-bye at the airport and find a new girl to hang out with in Pacific Heights. The week before Labor Day he proved me wrong. It was a Tuesday evening. I had worked all day at the boutique and was in the kitchen nibbling popcorn. My mother was at her book club and Rosemary was upstairs, turning down the beds. I heard a knock at the back door. I went outside and turned the corner toward the front of the house. Andre was sitting on a bench holding three bunches of roses. Beside him were a bottle of champagne and two glasses.

"Pick a bouquet," he said as I approached.

"Why?"

"One of them holds a prize. A prize for me, but I want you to pick." He smiled. His green eyes were like emeralds in the evening light. He wore a crisp white shirt, open at the collar, and navy slacks.

"Okay." I stood uncertainly in front of the roses.

"Pick this one," Andre said.

I took the bunch of roses he offered. "Why this one?"

"Look inside."

I undid the tissue paper and found a small red box sitting at the base of the rose stems.

"Open it," Andre said quietly.

I opened the box. Inside was a white gold ring with a small, square diamond.

"You are my prize, Amanda. Will you marry me?" Andre

took my hand, which was shaking, and put the ring on my finger.

"Why do you want to marry me?"

"You only get to answer 'yes' or 'no.' Not why," Andre told me.

"Before I answer yes or no," I replied, trying to sound like an adult, "I have to know why. I don't have a brilliant career. I'm not sexy."

Andre put his finger on my lips and kept it there till I stopped talking.

"In California I have met a dozen women. They all have breasts out to here"—Andre stuck his hands out in front of him—"and blond hair down to here"—he touched my back—"but they have nothing up here." He put a finger on my forehead. "You have hair like the Mona Lisa, eyes like a tiger, and up here"—he touched my forehead again—"you are an angel."

I studied the small diamond on my finger. I looked at Andre, kneeling in front of me like a medieval knight. I wanted to believe he thought I was beautiful, but when I looked in the mirror I saw brown curly hair that frizzed up in the summer. My eyes were green but they were placed too close together, and though I was tall I had a neck like a giraffe.

"But we're so young. We hardly know each other," I said, trying another avenue. My whole body wanted to say yes, but somewhere inside me I knew a sophisticated Frenchman wanted more than a twenty-two-year-old virgin.

"Getting to know each other will be an adventure. You make me feel happy, Amanda. You give me something to look forward to when I am working."

I sighed. He almost had me convinced. I had to bring up the one subject we had ignored: my money. "You know, I'm not really rich. All my money is in trust and I only get an allowance. I don't see any real money till I'm thirty."

Andre did not take his eyes off my face. He stayed kneeling and he held on to my hand. He chose his words carefully.

"Amanda, I know you were raised like a princess, and I will not be able to support you like that yet. But one day I will have my own restaurant. I promise I will never ask to borrow money from you, and we will never live on your income."

We were both silent. I smelled the scent of three dozen roses. My parents had married after six weeks and they lasted twenty-three years.

"Yes," I said, nodding.

Andre stood up and kissed me. He crushed the roses against my chest and he held my hand so tightly my new ring left an indentation on my finger.

🦋 🦋 🦋

We were married at Thanksgiving in my father's library. It was too soon after my father's death to hold a big wedding, and I didn't want to wait. Since the day Andre proposed, I was a bundle of nerves. Like most girls who stay a virgin into their twenties, I became obsessed with sex. I clung to some romantic notion that we should wait till our honeymoon to really "do it." Maybe I still thought I wouldn't live up to Andre's expectations and he would call off the wedding.

Thanksgiving morning was foggy and drizzly. I wore a simple Jackie O–style wedding dress: white and short with a full skirt. Andre wore a gray suit and a red rose in his lapel. His partner, Eric, was his best man and my best friend from high school, Kate, was my maid of honor. My mother gave me away. She was completely charmed by Andre and pleased that I was starting my own life.

"You and Andre haven't known each other very long, Amanda, but he seems to make you happy," she said in my bedroom on the morning of the wedding.

"I'm deliriously happy," I replied, trying to tame my hair into a bun and slipping small diamond earrings into my ears.

"Deliriously happy doesn't last," she said, stubbing out her cigarette. She still smoked a pack a day, but she tried to stop when she was around me.

"You and Dad acted like life was one big party."

"Your father lived large, but he had a solid backbone."

"Andre is going to be very successful. The restaurant is doing really well. Dad started small." I slipped my feet into ballet flats. Andre was tall, but I wanted to be looking up at him when we said our vows.

"You're right. I'm just playing devil's advocate. Marriage is a long haul." She looked in the mirror and smoothed her pink Chanel skirt. She was over sixty but her face was smooth. Only her neck was wrinkled, hidden under a bright Hermès scarf.

"We'll be great, Mother. I had the best role models." I hugged her.

She snapped open her bag to find another cigarette. "I'll go downstairs and see if the caterers are here."

The ceremony was short, performed by one of my father's old friends, Judge Hansen. Afterward we popped a bottle of champagne and nibbled salmon and rice balls. The wedding-Thanksgiving lunch was served in the long dining room under crystal chandeliers.

Andre sat at the head of the table, my mother at the other end. I was on Andre's left, Kate on his right. Andre kept his hand on mine the entire lunch, so I had to eat one-handed. While we waited for the pumpkin pie that was going to be our wedding cake, Andre stood up to make a toast.

"This is my first Thanksgiving. I am so lucky to be welcomed into this family. And Grace"—he nodded to my mother—"I will treat Amanda like this champagne flute: delicate, perfect, and priceless. Thank you for allowing her to be my wife." He lifted his glass and we all drank.

Later, when I was changing into my going-away outfit, Kate knocked on my door.

"What do you think?" I asked. Kate and I had known each other since grade school.

"A little corny," she said, pulling off her heels and lying down on my bed.

"What do you mean?" I frowned.

"I like Andre," she said carefully, releasing her short blond hair from its ponytail holder. "He's just a little clichéd."

"Well, thanks." I sat down on the bed next to Kate.

"He's just sooo romantic. So French."

"What's wrong with that?"

"Nothing. I hope it lasts."

"You're jealous." I laughed. "You want someone to shower you with rose petals."

"I'm fine being single. Sorry, I wasn't trying to be nasty."

"I forgive you. It is my wedding day," I said. I closed the

overnight bag that held my La Perla negligee. "And tonight is my wedding night."

"Maybe you should have had the wedding night first," Kate giggled.

I threw a silk pillow at her. "Maybe I should have made you catch the bouquet."

We checked in to the Mark Hopkins on top of Nob Hill. I felt electric shocks run up my spine when the concierge welcomed us as Mr. and Mrs. Blick. I wore a taupe Eileen Fisher skirt, a Donna Karan silk bodysuit, and camel-colored Prada flats. I had straightened my hair and it lay in silky layers over my shoulders. I looked like a confident San Francisco twenty-something. But as Andre and I stood in the elevator, climbing to the twenty-third floor, I felt like a little girl going to her first ballet class. Andre placed his hand on the small of my back. I was too nervous to make polite conversation with the bellboy. I pretended to search my Michael Kors clutch for some imaginary item until we arrived on our floor.

While Andre inspected the room I stood by the window, hoping the familiar view of San Francisco Bay would steady my nerves. I watched the ferry leave its wake in the gray water, and I studied the Golden Gate Bridge. I took a deep breath and turned to face Andre.

"So, Mrs. Blick, may I pour you some champagne?" Andre held my shoulders and kissed me slowly.

"I think I had enough champagne at lunch," I replied.

"Then let's get out of these clothes, yes?" he asked. He unzipped my skirt and slipped off my bodysuit without waiting for my response. Then he took my pantyhose and rolled them off my legs. He took my hand and guided me to the bed.

"I am the luckiest man," he said when we were lying naked facing each other. I had never seen Andre completely naked. His skin was olive and completely smooth. His arms had rows of small muscles from years of working in a kitchen. His stomach was flat and he had a smattering of black hair over his chest. Every time he touched me I felt an electric shock.

He moved slowly, touching my hands, my stomach, my breasts. He planted little kisses up and down my spine. He pulled my hair to one side and covered my neck with his mouth. I thought, how did I end up in bed with this Roman god? Me, who had known the same skinny boys all through grade school and high school, who had not been on a real date since senior prom?

Andre's kisses grew deeper. I kissed him back and placed my hands tentatively on his chest. Andre climbed on top of me, covering his body with mine. We began moving together. I tried to give in to just feeling and follow him. He kept moving, stroking my hair and murmuring my name. When he finally shuddered to a stop, groaning softly and rolling off me, I moved to the side of the bed and lay perfectly still. I waited till I was sure he was sleeping and then I turned my head and looked at him. I studied his curly black hair and his long black eyelashes. I followed his long legs wrapped up in the sheets. I closed my eyes, and I thought at that moment nothing else mattered. The world outside the big picture window did not exist. I was complete.

I got up from the bench and stretched my legs. I thought maybe if I did some yoga, looking straight at the mountain, I could ease the pain that was squeezing my chest. I tried standing in a Half Moon and clearing my mind of unwelcome thoughts. Andre and Ursula danced before my eyes like hand puppets at the fair. I conjured up Max's face, his blue eyes that were just like my father's, but that made me start crying again. I relaxed the Half Moon and slumped back on the bench. It was easier just to hate him.

I remembered our first year of marriage when I was Andre's willing sex slave. We rented an apartment in Cow Hollow and my mother decorated it for us as her wedding present. It had a tiny kitchen, a small living room, and a bathroom with a shower and no tub. But the bedroom was large enough for a king-sized bed, and it had a window with a view of the bay. Andre laughed at me and called me his little trollop because I would wait up for him till he closed the restaurant. I met him in bed so we didn't waste time eating or talking about our day. I just wanted him between the sheets, as fast as possible.

"You are not really American. American girls do not like sex like you," Andre said after we had been married a month. We were sitting in bed at noon. I brought him orange juice and croissants and the newspaper.

"How many American girls did you know?" I teased him.

"I have no memory of anyone before you," he said seriously. I didn't press him. If he claimed he had forgotten all his past girlfriends, I wasn't going to argue. I was too busy enjoying the present to worry about the past. I didn't think much about the future either. My days were full. I had everything I wanted.

🦋 🦋 🦋

In our second year of marriage two things happened that changed our delicious routine: Andre had a falling-out with his partner, and I got pregnant. It was just after Christmas and I had a nasty cold that turned into walking pneumonia. I was given a course of antibiotics and told to stay in bed. With nothing else to do, and the restaurant closed for the holidays, we made love three times a day. The antibiotics canceled out the Pill, and by February I realized my period was late.

I panicked. Andre and I never argued because I never voiced an opinion that was different from his. I bought my clothes and books with my allowance so I wasn't even a drain on his income. I confided in Kate that I was pregnant and afraid to tell Andre.

"What are you afraid of? He's the one who knocked you up." It was a Thursday afternoon. Andre was at work and Kate arrived from the spa in her workout clothes.

"We're so young and Andre works so hard. He's at the restaurant almost every night. Now he'll come home to a screaming baby instead of a sexy wife."

"Amanda, you have to stop being scared of your husband. He works hard because he wants to. Having a baby won't cramp his style," Kate said, taking a banana from the fruit bowl.

"What do you mean, what 'style'?"

Kate was silent while she ate her banana. "Nothing. Just I'm sure your mom will help out with the baby. She'll be in stitches over having a grandchild."

"I don't know why you don't like Andre." I was feeling bloated and grumpy.

"I like Andre, but you treat him like a god. He won the jackpot when he married you."

"Andre and I don't talk about money. I don't come into my inheritance till I'm thirty, Kate." I narrowed my eyes.

"Just tell him you're pregnant." She threw the banana skin in the garbage.

🦋 🦋 🦋

I told Andre I was pregnant on Saturday. Andre and Eric got in a huge fight on Sunday. When he came home early on Sunday night, and told me he quit, somehow I thought it was my fault.

"You can't quit, it's your restaurant," I said. We were lying on our bed and I was rubbing his back. He had come home, flung off his clothes, and thrown himself spread-eagled on the bed.

"I can't work with Eric anymore. He is making a bastard of French cuisine."

"But what will you do?" I kept rubbing his back.

"He wants to serve flavored crepes. Cinnamon crepes, mocha crepes. We are not the House of Pancakes."

"Can you buy him out?"

"I can't afford to."

Finally I said, "We could ask my mother. She could help us buy him out."

Andre sat up and held my arms tightly. "I told you I will never ask you for money."

"But what will we do? With the baby, I won't be able to work." I made a tiny salary working at the boutique, but somehow I had to bring up the subject of the baby.

"You think I can't support our child? Do you think you married a boy?" Andre raised his voice.

"I'm just being practical. You love the restaurant," I said evenly.

"I'll find another partner, and another restaurant," Andre replied. He placed his head between my breasts. "I'm sorry, sweetheart." He nuzzled my breasts and pulled me down on the bed next to him.

He caressed my thighs. He turned me toward him and stroked my hair. I closed my eyes and gave in to the luscious release of sex. After we made love and Andre was asleep, I felt a sharp stab of uneasiness about our future. Our bedroom with its wonderful king bed did not have room for a crib. For a guilty moment I wished I were back in my bedroom at my parents' house, looking up at my beautiful ceiling with its gold stars and dark sky.

The next morning I ate a piece of wheat toast to settle my stomach, and walked to my mother's house. I usually loved walking up the hills of San Francisco, turning at the top of every street to look out at the bay. But I was tired and feeling queasy. My stomach did little flips like goldfish trying to escape from their bowl.

My parents' house was set behind a rose garden. The house was three stories, all looking out on the bay. Ivy climbed the walls and the windows were hung with thick gold curtains.

I rang the doorbell. Rosemary opened the door. "Is my mother home?" I gave Rosemary a quick hug.

"She is in the morning room. Would you like a cup of coffee?"

"No thanks, Rosemary. I'll go say hi." I walked through the long hallway with its black-and-white-marble floor and faux-painted walls. My mother was sitting at the breakfast table reading the paper. The table was covered in a gold table-cloth and set with sterling silver. My mother was perfectly dressed in a belted Gucci dress and pumps. She stubbed her cigarette out when she saw me.

"Do you have to smoke at breakfast?" I asked.

"That's not much of a greeting." My mother got up and kissed my cheek.

"I just want you to live a long time." I took a deep breath. "Since you're going to be a grandmother."

"What?"

"I'm pregnant, we're having a baby." My eyes filled with tears.

"That's wonderful. Why are you crying?"

"I'm not crying," I said, but then my voice wobbled and I burst into tears.

My mother held me in her arms while I sobbed. Finally

she pushed me gently away and smiled. "Welcome to pregnancy. I used to cry when I read fortune cookies."

"I know. I can't wait to have a baby." I rubbed my cheeks. "It's just . . ." I started crying again. This time I couldn't stop.

"Okay, tell me what's wrong," my mother said.

I told her Andre and Eric had a falling-out and he quit the restaurant. I told her how I was afraid we couldn't fit the baby's things into our tiny apartment. I told her Andre was determined to pay for everything himself.

"I know I'm being selfish," I finished.

"I understand Andre wants to support you. But I could be a silent partner in a restaurant with him. He would run it, I'd back him financially," she continued.

I shook my head. "He would consider that helping out."

"But I believe in Andre. He is a great chef, and he's charming and charismatic. I would like to be a partner."

"I wish you could, Mom. But he'll be furious with me if you suggest it. I can't risk it." I shook my head.

"I'm sure he'll find another partner then."

She picked up a cigarette from its thin gold case. She lit it, and then quickly put it out. "I'm sorry. I can't smoke around you when you're pregnant. Your father was stubborn and proud, too. Marriage is tough."

"Thanks for telling me," I said glumly.

"Amanda, you're having a baby! We should be so happy. Think of all the fun we'll have shopping! Andre can't fault me for buying the baby presents. We'll get a lovely crib and baby blankets. And lots of newborn outfits, and a stroller so you can go on long walks. What if"—she paused—"what if I buy you an apartment in the baby's name?"

"Let's not push our luck. I'm happy with a crib and a stroller," I replied.

"Well then, let's go shopping. We can run down to Neiman's and get a few newborn outfits." She took one last sip of coffee and picked up her cigarette case.

"Mom, I'm not due for seven months!"

"It'll be fun. And we can buy a couple of maternity outfits, too. Some of the young designers have come out with really pretty things."

"Okay." I gave in and followed her to the garage.

"Good girl. One thing your father taught me is a day's shopping can fix almost anything."

"I'm sure the credit card companies loved him for that," I chuckled, getting into the passenger seat of my mother's silver Mercedes.

"American Express used to send him a bottle of cognac every Christmas." She nodded as we pulled out of the driveway and drove to Union Square.

🦋 🦋 🦋

Andre found his new partner at a dinner party given by one of my prep school friends. I didn't want to go to the dinner. I was still really queasy and the last thing I wanted to do was spend the evening stuck in front of a plate of salmon and rice sauté. I wasn't too keen on the company either. The hostess, Stephanie, had been one of the biggest flirts at school. She had big lips and huge breasts and toyed with all the male teachers, the soccer coach, even the headmaster.

Stephanie and I lost touch after graduation. She went off

to Penn to major in international finance. Now she was back, living in Marin, and somehow heard I had married a French chef.

"You have to bring him over to meet Glenn." Stephanie called out of the blue soon after Andre quit the restaurant.

"Who's Glenn?" I asked.

"My husband, silly. We got married in St. Moritz last Christmas. Glenn loves French food and French wine. When Kate told me you married a French chef, Glenn said I had to have a dinner party in your honor. Friday night, eight o'clock." Stephanie hung up before I could make up an excuse to beg off.

I picked up the phone and called Kate. "When did you see Stephanie and what did you tell her about Andre?" I fumed.

Kate laughed. "Sorry, you know how nosy she is. She came into the spa and somehow your name came up. I didn't know you were hiding Andre."

"I'm not hiding him. But she invited us to dinner. I don't want to go."

"Then don't go," Kate replied.

"Andre will want to go. Her husband wants to meet a French chef." I sighed.

"It's only dinner, Amanda. Are you afraid of Stephanie and her very large breasts?" Kate laughed.

"I have very large breasts of my own right now."

"Then think of it as one night you don't have to cook."

"I don't like food, and food doesn't like me." I hung up the phone.

I casually mentioned the invitation to Andre when he returned from one of his long afternoons spent at Starbucks reading the newspaper. His face brightened and he kissed me on the mouth. "Of course we'll go," he said. I knew what he was thinking. He had had no luck finding a new partner and he was running out of ideas.

W W W

We drove across the Golden Gate Bridge in Andre's old Volkswagen. Andre drove with one hand on the wheel and the other on my thigh. His hair was tied back in a shiny black ponytail; his white shirt was open to the third button.

Stephanie and Glenn lived in Ross, down the hill from our prep school. Ross was a tiny town centered around a patch of green called "the commons." The commons was the home of the Fourth of July barbecue, Family Day in October, even a Winter Festival in December with fake snow. It was always full of kids playing soccer and mothers standing around admiring each other's Gucci shoes.

Andre and I pulled up in front of Glenn and Stephanie's house: It was a big Craftsman style with a three-car garage and a yellow Porsche in the driveway.

"I guess Stephanie married well," I said as we approached the front door. I knew Stephanie hadn't grown up with a lot of money, and real estate in Ross was astronomically expensive.

"Maybe her husband will want to be my partner," Andre said.

W W W

Glenn wasn't interested in investing in Andre, but Stephanie was. From the moment she opened the door, wearing a green

velour Juicy Couture sweat suit, her platinum-blond hair falling over her breasts, I wanted to throw up. She hugged me
and kissed me on the cheek. She pouted prettily at Andre. I
grabbed a glass of champagne from the bar.

"Amanda, should you be drinking?" Stephanie shot me a
quizzical look. She had one hand on Andre's arm and was
guiding him to the bar.

"One drink every now and then is fine," I said, giving
Stephanie a wide smile. If Stephanie didn't let go of Andre's
arm I might strangle her.

"In France most pregnant women drink wine at dinner,"
Andre said supportively. But he didn't remove his arm from
Stephanie's grasp.

"I'll tell Glenn to open one of our best French wines."
Stephanie disappeared into the kitchen.

Andre stood close to me and put his hand on my back.
"Relax, Amanda," he whispered into my ear.

"I forgot what a vulture she is."

"She is an attractive woman," Andre said. "But no one is
as beautiful as you."

I was trying to figure out how to respond when a man
wearing khakis came down the stairs. He must have been at
least six foot three, skinny as a stick. He was almost bald and
wore round brown glasses.

"Hi, I'm Glenn. You must be Amanda and Andre. I'm so
glad you came." He shook our hands.

"Andre, help yourself." Stephanie held the tray in front of
Andre. "I tried some French recipes in your honor. Tell me
what you think of my escargot." She picked up a small round
snail and popped it in Andre's mouth.

I took a swig of champagne. I hadn't eaten anything but a handful of saltines since lunch. The champagne floated straight down to my shoes.

"How did you and Stephanie meet?" I asked Glenn.

"I spent my junior year at the Sorbonne and Glenn was working at Lehman Brothers in Paris. We ran into each other at a café near to his office." Stephanie was beaming.

I took a piece of toast with liver pâté from the tray. It looked and smelled awful, but I had to put something in my stomach that didn't have bubbles.

"We had a lovely time exploring Paris," Glenn agreed.

I knew what Glenn saw in Stephanie: five feet seven inches of perfect bronze flesh. But why had she picked him? Glenn looked like a very thin version of Gumby. I glanced nervously at Andre and wished he'd button up his shirt.

"He just swept me off my feet. Proposed to me at the top of the Eiffel Tower. With this"—she stuck her engagement ring under my nose. It was an emerald-cut diamond, at least five carats. She had a matching diamond wedding band. I noticed the large diamond studs in her ears and the floating diamond hanging on a gold chain around her neck. I was beginning to understand what Stephanie saw in Glenn.

My legs felt wobbly. I sat down on the sofa. I saw Stephanie staring at Andre. Her pink mouth was open in a small *o* and she ran her tongue over her teeth.

"Who else is coming?" I asked.

"Oh, just a couple of guys Glenn knows from Lehman's and their wives. Boring. I thought it would be such fun to have you two here. Maybe Andre can improve my French cooking." Stephanie continued to beam.

Andre was either oblivious to her advances or didn't want to offend her. He smiled at Stephanie and made no move to sit next to me.

"Actually, would you mind if I stole your husband for a moment? I want to show him my entrées." She pulled Andre into the kitchen.

I was left alone with Glenn. He sat down on the sofa and offered me a bowl of pretzels.

"No, thanks." I shook my head, thinking if I put anything in my mouth I would choke.

"So you and Stephanie went to prep school together?" Glenn asked pleasantly.

"Yes. It was a small school so all the kids knew one another pretty well." I smiled weakly. I wanted to tell him that I knew Stephanie too well: She was a cheating hussy after his money and he should get out now, before they had kids.

"Stephanie has very fond memories of school. When I took the position in San Francisco she convinced me to look at houses in Ross. We fell in love with this one."

"It's a beautiful home. But didn't Stephanie want to stay in the city?" I asked.

"She thinks Ross is a perfect place to raise a family. We're hoping to have kids soon."

"Are you talking about me?" Stephanie emerged from the kitchen. Andre came up behind her. His shirt was smooth, his expression bland. They had only been gone a few minutes. Maybe I was making something out of nothing.

I looked at Glenn closely. He seemed so innocent. He must be one of those "numbers" guys who was a fox with figures but a lamb in the real world.

"You're lucky, Amanda." Stephanie refilled Andre's champagne glass. "I want babies so badly." Her face crinkled into a sexy pout. "But it hasn't happened yet."

"We've only been trying for three months," Glenn reminded her.

"I guess we'll have to try harder," Stephanie said. She seemed to be talking directly to Andre.

Before I could get up and strangle her, the doorbell rang. Stephanie dashed to answer the door.

I looked at Andre leaning against the bar. He wore navy wool pants and leather loafers. It was time I stopped being a jealous wife and became Andre's supportive partner. As much as I abhorred Stephanie, I trusted Andre. Stephanie and Glenn could obviously afford to invest in a restaurant, and we had no other prospects. I put down my champagne glass, rubbed my stomach, and went and slipped my hand in Andre's.

Andre turned and gave me his radiant smile. I squeezed his hand tighter. When Stephanie returned with two other couples, Andre and I stood side by side, shoulders touching.

🦋 🦋 🦋

Stephanie seated Andre on her right at the long cherry dining room table. Glenn was on my left, and a man in his mid-forties named Harvey was on my right. Harvey's wife, Jane, sat across from me. Harvey and Jane oohed and aahed over each course Stephanie served. It was as if she invited them to be her own personal cheering section, just in case Andre didn't notice how wonderful she was.

"This bread is too good to be store bought. Did you make it yourself?" Jane dipped a chunk of bread in her soup and made appreciative smacking noises.

"Stephanie has been taking some Cordon Bleu courses," Glenn said proudly.

The other couple were named Tom and Dell. Tom had a face full of acne that made him look like a teenager. Dell had small brown eyes framed by brown hair. Stephanie was like a movie star at her own premiere. She flitted around the table flashing her breasts every time she bent down to serve a dish.

"Stephanie told me Andre has a restaurant called Crepe Suzette on Sacramento Street," Glenn said, sipping his expensive French wine.

"Had a restaurant, unfortunately," Andre replied. "My partner wanted to serve peanut butter crepes. I could not bastardize my beloved French cuisine, so I resigned." He bowed his head as if he should be awarded the Medal of Honor for his sacrifice for France.

"That's terrible." Stephanie's mouth formed its sexy pout. "How could he suggest peanut butter crepes?"

"I don't know." Andre let out a long sigh.

"Andre wants to open a new restaurant," I said.

"I'm sure you'll do well," Glenn said. I glanced at Andre. That wasn't the response we were hoping for.

"I thought of opening my own catering company," Stephanie said, licking her soup spoon. "I'd cater dinner parties in town. Just to keep busy, till we have babies."

"You don't want to cook in other people's houses," Andre said and shook his head. "But if you had your own restaurant people would come to you."

"My own restaurant," Stephanie mused.

"I don't think you have time to run a restaurant, darling," Glenn said nervously.

"Andre could be my partner. We could have a French restaurant right here in Ross. I don't know why I didn't think of it before!" she exclaimed.

Probably because there wasn't a hot French chef sitting at her table before, I thought miserably.

"Stephanie, you would make a wonderful maître d'." Andre gave her a movie star–caliber smile.

"There's a space on the commons that used to be a dress shop. It would be perfect. We could have ten tables, very intimate, and just serve dinner." Stephanie almost bounced out of her chair.

I tried to open my mouth and protest. I didn't want Andre commuting to Marin. I certainly didn't want him to be partners with this overripe viper.

"That would be a long drive for you," I said, touching Andre's hand.

"We could move to Marin," he replied, putting his hand over mine.

"You should buy in Ross," Stephanie piped in. "It's the best place to raise children."

"We can't afford Ross," I said quietly.

"Oh, Amanda, stop. We used to call Amanda's house 'the palace' and Amanda 'the princess.' Her parents were so rich," Stephanie said to the whole table.

"My parents, not me," I mumbled.

"Honey, I'd never be bored if we had a restaurant." Stephanie got up and stood behind Glenn. She nuzzled his neck so her guests had a full view of her breasts. Even I was impressed. Mine were big, but hers were big and perfect: two pale pink peaches pushed up by a Wonderbra.

"Sweetie, we'll have kids soon and then where will that leave Andre?" Glenn looked at Andre for support, but Andre's attention was directed at his soup.

"Oh please. I want to do *something*. You don't want me to get antsy," Stephanie begged.

"I'll clear the table," Jane said brightly.

"I'll help you," Dell offered. Both women obviously wanted to escape to the kitchen. Stephanie was like a girl intent on a new toy.

"If you don't mind I'm going to step out and have a cigarette." Harvey pushed back his chair.

"I'll join you. I always like a breath of fresh air between courses." Tom followed him outside.

"Opening a new restaurant is a huge undertaking." Andre turned toward Glenn. "But it might do very well. You have a wealthy client base over here, and not a lot of dining options."

I realized while Andre was studying his soup he was figuring out the best way to approach the situation. Glenn was a numbers man, so Andre was talking numbers.

"I never thought of it like that," Glenn replied.

Stephanie decided to let the men hash it out. "Amanda, help me get the entrées." She gave Glenn a dazzling smile, brushing against him before dragging me into the kitchen.

Stephanie's kitchen was huge, with a giant butcher-block island and a double Wolf oven.

"Wow, what a gorgeous oven," I said, wanting to talk about anything other than a partnership with Andre.

"I told you, I love to cook. But it gets boring cooking for two people." Stephanie removed a ham from the oven and sliced it onto six plates.

"Where did you get these lovely plates?" I admired the plates lined up on the marble counter. The number of times Stephanie said she was bored was making me nervous.

"Where did you get your divine dish?" Stephanie replied.

"What?" I asked.

"Your husband," she cooed. "He is a cutie. How did you snag him?"

"Um, just love," I said, sounding stupid even to myself.

"I never expected you to catch a sexy Frenchman," Stephanie continued.

"Glenn seems really wonderful." I tried to change the subject.

"Glenn's great," Stephanie agreed, adding asparagus tips to each plate and dribbling a hollandaise sauce. "But you got the hunk. I'm impressed."

"Andre's going to be a great dad," I mumbled. I wanted to get out of the kitchen, out of the house, and back into Andre's old VW.

"Here, take these plates, let's see if our husbands struck a deal." Stephanie pushed two plates into my hands and nudged me into the dining room.

🦋 🦋 🦋

"Stephanie, your tips are cooked to perfection. And this sauce . . . Where did you get the recipe?" Andre asked, cutting his asparagus into ribbons.

"See, Glenn, I do have talent. Can I please have my restaurant?" Stephanie turned her don't-say-no-to-me pout on her husband.

"Andre and I were crunching a few numbers while you girls were in the kitchen," Glenn said, slurring his words. He wasn't as good at holding his liquor as he was at working his figures.

"Glenn is a real whiz with numbers," Andre complimented our host.

"A French restaurant in town might have potential," Glenn said, looking well lubricated.

"Please, please," Stephanie purred. "We could call it La Petite Maison." She turned to her dinner guests. "Glenn lived in a pension in Paris called La Petite Maison. It holds special memories." She turned back to Glenn and gave him a secret smile.

"La Petite Maison," Glenn faltered.

"I'll pull out the Dom Perignon and we'll make a toast!" Stephanie jumped up and flew into the kitchen to grab the champagne. I thought if I saw any more bubbles I'd throw up on their Persian rug. I looked at Andre, who was quietly wiping his plate, and thought I'd be sick anyway. I couldn't fault Andre for encouraging Glenn and Stephanie. He needed a partner. I stood up and excused myself to the bathroom.

When I returned everyone was toasting "La Petite Maison." Stephanie was jabbering about calling the Realtor about the space on the commons. Andre and Glenn were discussing "cash flow" and "reserves."

"Honey, have some champagne." Andre reached for my hand and squeezed it tightly.

I couldn't be in their house another minute. I pushed my chair back and smiled weakly at everyone. "I'm actually not feeling well. I think we better go."

"But I made the most wonderful dessert," Stephanie protested. "It's a Belgian chocolate mousse."

"I'm practically allergic to chocolate at the moment," I insisted. "Pregnancy is playing havoc with my stomach. And I just want to be asleep by eight p.m." I grimaced.

"Oh, you poor baby," Stephanie cooed. "Next time just send Andre over. There's so much to discuss!"

"He doesn't like to leave me home alone," I said.

"It's true." Andre nodded. "We will start looking for a place to live in Marin."

"Ooh, I'll help you! Amanda, call me tomorrow, we can go house hunting." Stephanie kissed me on both cheeks. She turned to Andre and he practically disappeared in her bear hug.

Glenn drained his second glass of champagne. "I'll have my attorney get some numbers to you next week."

Finally we were in the car. At first I was so grateful to have escaped I was silent. But as we neared our apartment, my horror of going into partnership with Stephanie surfaced.

"I can't believe you would consider being partners with that human piranha," I said as we neared our building.

"Amanda, you should be thrilled the evening was a success. We are going to have our restaurant." He put my hand to his mouth and covered it with kisses.

"You are not opening a restaurant with that hussy," I hissed.

Andre pulled up in front of our apartment and turned off the engine.

"Are you telling me what to do?" he asked in a low voice.

"How could you even consider it? She just wants a new boy toy."

"Don't you trust me?" he asked in the same stony voice.

"Of course I trust you," I replied. "I just don't trust her. She was doing half the male faculty when we were in high school. We don't need her."

"Actually, Amanda, we do need her. She is the only potential partner we have."

I took my hand away from him and placed it firmly in my lap.

"Andre, we can't," I said plaintively.

"Why not?"

"She's just too awful," I begged him.

"Amanda, jealousy is an ugly trait. It does not suit you. We need an income."

"But you can't commute to Ross," I said, trying another approach.

"You did all through prep school," he reminded me.

"I had a driver, and I didn't have a wife and baby to come home to. You wouldn't get home till midnight."

Andre was quiet. I thought I had convinced him the new restaurant needed to be in the city.

"We'll move to Marin," he said.

"We can't afford to move to Marin." I shook my head.

"There are apartments in Marin."

"There aren't any apartments in Ross. The only way I'm moving to Marin," I said carefully, "is if we let my mother buy us a house."

"Your mother cannot buy us a house." Andre shook his head.

"For our baby. She wants to do something for us. She wanted to be your partner," I reminded him.

"Darling, I would never be a partner with a family member." His voice softened and he reached for my hand in the dark.

"Then let her buy us a house in Ross, in the baby's name. Then you can have your restaurant." I wanted to go upstairs and climb into bed, but we needed to resolve this first.

"Okay," Andre said finally. "But it must be a very small house, and I will pay her back when the restaurant is on its feet." He leaned over to kiss me on the cheek.

"Amanda, why are you crying?" he asked in the dark, brushing away the tears on my cheek.

I couldn't admit I was terrified of Stephanie stealing him away. "Oh, pregnancy," I lied. "I cry about everything."

"Well, stop crying and kiss me. Let's go upstairs and I'll show you how happy I am."

The next morning I lay in bed while Andre ran to the market to buy croissants and orange juice. We had made love last night and again this morning, as if Andre was convincing me he couldn't get enough of me. I leaned against the pillow and willed myself to be happy. We would find a lovely house. Our child would grow up in Ross, playing soccer on the commons. Life would be good. And life was good, until Black Tuesday when I found Andre with his pants down and his legs wrapped around Ursula and it all fell apart.

Chapter Two

*A*fter I stopped hurling stones into the lake, I decided I needed someone to talk to. I didn't trust myself to drive across the Golden Gate Bridge to see my mother. I thought I would visit Stephanie. She was still a silent partner in La Petite Maison; she should know what was going on in the back room.

One of the most surprising things about the last decade was that Stephanie and I became best friends. She did have extremely good taste and the restaurant was a success from the day it opened. La Petite Maison occupied a small shop on the commons. Inside there were ten tables, two of them pressed up against the bay windows. Candles sat on linen tablecloths and big murals of Provence covered the walls. The menu was simple: soups and fish and fondue. Over the years, the variety of fondues grew and people came from San Francisco to try Andre's chocolate fondue and cream cheese fondue.

In the beginning Stephanie was very involved in the restaurant and I was anxious from morning to night. Andre and

I found a small bungalow on a leafy lane near the commons. My mother was thrilled to buy it for us and insisted on decorating it. It was within walking distance of La Petite Maison and it had a sunny flat garden. When I was still pregnant, I spent most of my time at the restaurant "helping." I was actually spying, making sure Stephanie kept her hands off Andre, and surprisingly she did. She giggled and made suggestive comments, but as far as I could see she kept her hands and her breasts to herself.

Then Stephanie became pregnant and lost interest in the restaurant. She confided in me that she had a bit of a crush on her ob/gyn, who told her standing for long periods in high heels was bad for her pregnancy. Andre hired a new maître d' and Stephanie retired to decorate the nursery.

Max was born in September, and with Stephanie gone from day-to-day operations at the restaurant, I let myself relax and enjoy motherhood. From the moment Max came home from the hospital and I placed him in his crib, he became the center of my universe.

I didn't mind Andre's long hours at the restaurant. Having only one child to follow around, I had plenty of energy to make his meals, rub his feet when he came home late, and to listen to his stories about La Petite Maison. As my mother had predicted, he was talented, charismatic, and charming, and the restaurant established a loyal following.

What my mother had not predicted was that he would screw the chef, and that kind of put a damper on my happiness. As I jogged down the path to Stephanie's, I wondered if he had screwed the waitress, the hostess, the wine stewardess, and all the other women he employed in the last ten years.

Was it the constant parade of young flesh that kept him singing at the restaurant every day? I was so angry I broke into a sprint and arrived at Stephanie's flushed and furious.

I rang the doorbell and waited. Stephanie's house was so big it always took a full three minutes for Gisella, her au pair, to answer the door. I had come to realize Stephanie had gone to Penn and married reliable, wealthy Glenn because she was actually very intelligent. She didn't employ a Swedish au pair with legs longer than a racehorse and white-blond hair that touched her bottom. She hired a short Portuguese woman with a mustache and ankles like boulders.

"Gisella, is Mrs. Chambers at home?" Stephanie liked to keep things formal in her house: to keep the separation between the help and the family evident. I had a lot to learn. When I thought of the welcome dinner I had given Ursula— I had baked bread and tossed a Caesar salad for her—I wanted to throw up.

"Mrs. Chambers is in the garden with the children," Gisella replied. When she talked she displayed a row of gold teeth.

"Thank you, Gisella."

Stephanie had two gorgeous children: Zoe was a few months younger than Max and had a head of blond curls and big blue eyes. She looked and acted like an angel. Graham was a stout two-year-old with permanently red cheeks. He followed his mother and sister around as if they were deities. Stephanie was a very good mother. When she was with her children she shined her light on them as if no one else existed. She didn't boast about their accomplishments like so many other mothers, she just made them feel tremendously loved.

Stephanie was sitting in the sandbox with Graham. Pregnancy and child-rearing had blurred her perfect features. Her breasts were still big, but now they pointed slightly downward. Her thighs were a little wider than when we were teenagers—she complained she couldn't resist finishing the kids' peanut butter sandwiches and chicken tenders.

She wore her hair short, barely touching her shoulders. She did keep it very blond and she still wore bright red lipstick, even at home in the garden, but she didn't scream "sex siren" when you saw her. Today she wore denim shorts, a lace top, and white Keds.

"I thought you did yoga on Tuesdays," Stephanie said.

"I did yoga this morning."

"You don't look very zen."

I glanced down at my clothes. My tights had a rip down the side and my shoes were caked in dirt.

"I went for a run after yoga."

"You gave up running four years ago when you pulled your Achilles tendon."

"I knew I forgot something," I said. I sank into the sandbox next to Graham.

"I'm making Mommy lunch. Want some?" Zoe was in the playhouse making sand pizza.

"How come Zoe isn't at school?" I asked Stephanie.

"Orthodontist appointment."

"A first grader doesn't need braces," I said, shaking my head.

"I agree. But tell that to Zoe. Four girls in her class already have them. She feels left out." Stephanie poured sand into Graham's bucket.

I thought of Andre and his slightly crooked smile. I burst into tears.

"Zoe, take your brother and ask Gisella to make lunch," Stephanie instructed her daughter.

"But I'm making sand pizza," Zoe complained. "You asked for sand pizza."

"I'll have my lunch when you come back. I need to talk to Mrs. Blick for a few minutes."

We waited till Zoe and Graham disappeared into the kitchen. I tried to stop my shoulders heaving until I heard the kitchen door bang shut. Then I collapsed into Stephanie's arms.

"I'm glad I don't take your yoga class," Stephanie said.

"I stopped by the restaurant after class and I found Andre doing Ursula."

"What do you mean, 'doing Ursula'?" Stephanie asked.

"The same thing we meant when we said it in high school: fucking, screwing, giving it to her. Sticking his big long prick inside her Scandinavian thong."

"I get the picture," Stephanie said with a shudder.

"What am I going to do?" I cried.

"What did he say?"

"I didn't give him time to say anything. I slammed the door and backed out of there. I think I broke your beautiful cut-glass door, I'm sorry."

"Oh, Amanda," Stephanie said. Then we were both silent.

"I thought we were happy," I said finally. "We have our beautiful little house. The restaurant is doing really well. Max is an easy child." I added up the things we had to be grateful for, all erased by the picture of Andre and Ursula wrapped around each other like Saran Wrap.

"You need a drink," Stephanie said.

"A drink won't help. Yet . . ." I replied bleakly. A shot of tequila sounded tempting, but it was only noon. I couldn't start down that road.

"Why did he do it? I know he's really handsome, and women fall all over him. But we have a great sex life. We had sex last night!" I threw a plastic shovel at the playhouse. First I was tossing stones at ducks, now I was hurling shovels.

"He's a man," Stephanie said simply.

"I've never seen Glenn look at another woman. I know I'm not a bombshell like you, but I keep myself together." Over the years I found a style that suited me. I wore my hair in thick waves that were perfectly highlighted by my mother's Union Square stylist. I visited her salon to keep my brows shaped, and I learned to apply makeup so I had a natural glow. I still loved fashion, and my mother and I had regular lunch dates at Neiman Marcus, where I scooped up designer sweaters and my favorite Tod's loafers.

"I'm more shelled-out bomb than bombshell," Stephanie laughed. "And you are a young sophisticate. I've always envied how you wear clothes."

"Thanks," I blubbered, and burst into tears again.

"Glenn's different from most men. He's in his head, so he doesn't notice normal things, like women."

"Are you saying most husbands screw their employees in broad daylight at their workplace?"

"Maybe most men don't give in to their urges," Stephanie said hesitantly.

"I just married a world-class jerk," I said. We were both silent again.

"Maybe," I said, wiping my eyes, "maybe it was just a moment of madness. I can confront him and tell him if it ever happens again we're finished." I sat up straight, filled with a ray of hope.

Stephanie kicked the sand with her Keds. "I don't think it was a momentary madness."

"What do you mean?" I looked at her suspiciously.

"Andre has done it before," she replied, not looking at me.

"With you?"

"Of course not with me! I would never cheat on Glenn."

"I remember when the restaurant opened, you were drooling over Andre," I huffed.

"That's the point, Amanda. It's okay to drool, just not to touch. I know I used to be a big talker, but I never did anything about it. I know how great my husband is."

"Then what do you mean?"

"Ummm." Stephanie examined a spot on her shirt.

"Ummm what?" I demanded.

"Remember Bella?" She still didn't look at me.

"The summer waitress from Michigan?"

"I fired her because I found her and Andre in the restaurant garden."

"Picking tomatoes?" I asked hopefully.

"Having sex in the shed."

"I thought she went back to Michigan to take care of her grandmother." My body crumpled like a deflated balloon.

"No," Stephanie said simply.

"Remember Angie the wine sommelier?" she continued after a minute.

"The one with the great credentials and really tight ass?"

"The credentials were real, the ass was surgically enhanced," Stephanie said.

"What about her? She was only there for a few months. Andre said the clientele wasn't responding to a female sommelier."

"I caught him responding to her in the wine cellar."

"The restaurant doesn't have a wine cellar."

"Okay then, in the coat closet where we keep the wine bottles. They were doing it on a customer's fur coat."

"Nobody wears real fur in Ross," I said.

"That's probably not my point, Amanda." She looked at me for the first time. Her eyes were watery.

"I know," I said. My eyes filled with tears that spilled over onto my cheeks and down my shirt.

"Why didn't you tell me?" I asked, suddenly angry at her years of duplicity. Bella had been a waitress the summer after Max was born.

"The first time I thought it was a one-off. I didn't want to rock the boat. I thought Andre was just young, sowing his wild oats. He'd calm down and realize how great he had it. You are great, Amanda, and you have a fantastic son. And you don't hold over his head that you're a millionaire heiress. You live on his income just like you promised. You could buy the biggest house in Ross and you're still living in a two-bedroom bungalow."

Stephanie was right. Two years ago when I turned thirty I gained access to my inheritance. I spent many delicious mornings strolling the shady lanes of Ross, picking out which house I might like to buy. When I broached the subject of moving to Andre, he put on a stony face.

"I am not living in a house my wife bought," he said in his proud, don't-argue-with-me tone.

I should have replied, "We're living in a house my mother bought, just a small one." But I didn't.

"Wouldn't it be lovely to have a pool and a big garden and a real dining room?"

"Everyone would know you bought the house. I couldn't afford it on my income from the restaurant," he insisted. We had the discussion in our kitchen. He was standing under the skylight, his green eyes glinting in the sun. Even after ten years of marriage I grew weak when I looked at him. His stomach was still completely flat; his muscles were those of a teenager's.

"Oh," I said, deflated. I adored our bungalow, its proximity to the restaurant, the short walk to school. But I loved big houses and beautiful furniture. I had promised Max we would get a big dog when we bought a house.

"You are so sexy when you pout." Andre put his arm around my waist. "I have an idea," he said, nuzzling my neck. "Why don't we buy a piece of land in Napa and build a weekend house. You can have your pool and a big garden."

"That's a fantastic idea!" I said, and it was a great idea. We could have friends up for the weekend and even spend summers there. Lots of our friends had houses in Napa, some even made their own wine.

"Good. Call a Realtor and look at some land." Andre kissed the back of my neck.

I contacted a Realtor, but it was hard to look at property when Max had school every day. Two years later I still hadn't found the perfect lot. Now I wondered if Andre had suggested it so he could get rid of me for whole summers. He could keep La Petite Maison his own personal brothel.

"I still don't understand why you didn't tell me." I was desperate to transfer some of the blame.

"When I found him with Angie he said he was going to change. I believed him."

"And you didn't think I'd want to know? I might want the opportunity to see if he was full of crap?" My voice shook.

"I didn't want to hurt you." Stephanie was close to tears. Her face was pale; she looked as wretched as I felt. "And Andre seemed so sincere. I knew he didn't want to lose you. I believed he wouldn't do it again."

Stephanie and I stared at each other. We both had believed Andre. We were both fools.

"Were there others? After Angie?" I asked in a whisper.

Stephanie nodded slowly. "I didn't know what to do, so I just kept firing the women."

I laughed. "A full-time job, apparently."

"What are you going to do?" Stephanie asked.

"What am I going to do about my wonderful husband who has been screwing around for eight years and coming home every night with a smile on his face? What am I going to say to my son who is the light of my life and loves his daddy like I loved mine?" At the thought of my father, who had a backbone like a ruler and had treated my mother like a queen, I fell apart.

"When I was ten, my father had a really good friend named Charlie Ambrose." I blinked away the tears. "They played golf every Sunday and he came over for poker once a month.

Charlie was a lot younger than my father and really handsome, with blue eyes and white-blond hair that flopped across his forehead. He let me sit next to him while they played poker, and I'd point to the card I thought he should put down." I closed my eyes, remembering a time when all men seemed safe. "One month he didn't show up for the poker game, and I sat at the top of the stairs waiting for him to ring the doorbell. The next Sunday, I waited for my father to return from golf, because he usually brought Charlie over for a drink after eighteen holes. But he brought a new friend home, Stewart Pratt, who was bald and had a nose like a beak."

"What happened to Charlie Ambrose?" Stephanie asked.

"I got up the courage to ask my mother and she just said my father and Charlie had a falling-out." I remembered how nervous I had been asking my mother, and how she answered my question curtly, and then turned away and went back to writing place cards.

"A couple of years later, I was at dance school and I was paired up with Charlie's son. I was taller than he was and he had to stand on his tiptoes to dance with me. I mentioned his father hadn't been at our house for a long time, and he looked at me as if someone had died and I forgot to come to the funeral."

"Did Charlie die?" Stephanie leaned forward in the sandbox.

"No." I shook my head. "Charlie had a dalliance with his son's German tutor and was living in a penthouse on Nob Hill. My father was so moral he wouldn't be friends with a guy who screwed around. He never spoke Charlie's name, and Charlie never came to our house again. My father's favorite line was: 'It's not how much money a man has that makes him a success, it's the strength of his character.'" I sighed. "How could I marry a weasel?"

"Andre is a great actor. He pulled one over on all of us." Stephanie shrugged.

"But I'm married to him. I should be able to read him." I dug my fingers into the sand.

"We can sit here all day wallowing in tears or we can think of a plan of action," Stephanie said.

"Such as?" I gulped.

"We could put hemlock in his wine."

"I think hemlock went out as a poison with Romeo and Juliet," I replied.

"Then you think of something."

I tried. I thought of all kinds of revenge. But revenge took energy and planning. I was wiped out. "I guess I'll tell him it's over."

"Just like that?"

"Stephanie, you just gave me a list of girls' names longer than Santa Claus's."

"I don't think you'll get rid of him that easily," Stephanie said slowly.

"What do you mean?"

"In Europe it's more accepted for men to forget to keep their pants on. I don't think he wants out of the marriage. They are all just flings. Work freebies."

"That's disgusting," I said, and shuddered.

"Come on, let's go inside." Stephanie stepped out of the sandbox. "It is officially afternoon and you need a drink."

We went into the library and Stephanie poured me a shot of tequila, and then another. By my fourth shot I was feeling a little better—in a cowboy-about-to-shoot-up-the-bar sort of way. What a morning. I had seen my husband making another woman into a swizzle stick. I used more swear words than I had since high school. I got drunk before afternoon pickup. Then I passed out on Stephanie's leather love seat.

When I came to, Gisella was standing next to me with a jug of water.

"Where's Mrs. Chambers?" I asked groggily.

"Mrs. Chambers took the children to pick Max up from school. She said to tell you she be right back."

"Oh, my head. Do you have any aspirin, Gisella?"

"Yes, Mrs. Blick."

I was armed with aspirin and tonic water when Max and Zoe and Graham piled through the kitchen door. Max ran straight into the library and hugged me. He was getting so tall—the top of his head was in line with my chest. I breathed in the avocado shampoo mingled with sweat and playground dirt.

"You smell funny, Mommy." Max squirmed out of my embrace.

"Mrs. Chambers and I had Mexican food for lunch," I improvised.

"Tacos?" His blue eyes sparkled. Max loved Mexican food.

"Sort of liquid tacos," I mumbled. My vision was still blurry. I was not an experienced noon drinker.

"Can I have some?" Max asked.

"Ask Gisella to make you a snack. And Zoe wants to show

you her new Wii game. She's in the family room," Stephanie instructed, coming into the library.

Max disappeared and I sunk back onto the love seat, my "mommy" strength dissipated.

"How are you doing?" Stephanie asked.

"Thanks for picking him up. I have to practice my tequila shots."

"Practice makes perfect."

"A rule my husband lives by. What am I going to do?" I groaned.

"What do you want to do?" Stephanie perched on the love seat next to me.

"I love Ross and Max loves his school. But it's such a small town. No one stays in Ross when they get divorced." When Ross couples divorced, they moved away. The houses and mortgages were too big for single parents.

"Don't even think about moving. Max has lived here his whole life. You belong here."

"But how can I walk by La Petite Maison every day and think about who Andre is screwing now?"

"Andre can move. He can open another restaurant in San Francisco."

"He loves the restaurant. I think he would rather part with Max than with the restaurant. Obviously he would rather part with me."

"I told you, I don't think Andre will want a divorce. In his way he loves you."

"He has a very odd way of showing it."

"He's French, Amanda. You knew that when you married him. Remember that movie *Le Divorce* with Kate Hudson?

She went to Paris to visit her sister, and ended up having an affair with a sexy married Frenchman."

"That's a movie," I told her. "They do lots of things in France they don't do here. They drink their coffee black and they eat dinner after nine p.m. Andre used to give me all that crap about French marrying for life and Americans divorcing too easily. But I don't believe it." I shook my head. "Any French-woman who is in love with her husband couldn't stand know-ing he is unfaithful."

"They say Paris is the city of love," Stephanie replied.

"Maybe mothers teach their daughters not to marry for love, maybe they arrange marriages to carry on the family name or combine vineyards. The wives take lovers and the husbands keep mistresses and everyone's happy." I was on a roll. "You don't know what it's like, Stephanie, to see your hus-band kissing another woman, screwing another woman. You can't turn your head away from that."

"I'm not condoning it. I'm just saying Andre may have been brought up differently."

"We live in America. For the past ten years Andre's been celebrating July Fourth, not Bastille Day. And Andre knows how I was raised. San Francisco society is very conservative. I went to an all-girls school till eighth grade where we had to wear uniforms. At the boys' school they wore ties and blazers, and if they saw a Hamlin girl walking down the street in uniform, they weren't allowed to talk to us."

"Andre isn't a private-school boy," Stephanie replied quietly.

I looked at her as if she was a traitor. "But he knew how I felt about marriage. If he thought it was okay to mess around he wouldn't have been so secretive. I didn't hear him come out and say: 'Amanda, would it be okay if I fucked the waitress on the side, because that is what we do in France?'" I felt all the rage welling up inside me again.

"I get it." Stephanie put up her hand to stop my diatribe. "I'm just saying if he wanted a divorce he would have asked for one a long time ago. These other women are just foam on his cappuccino. You make him belong, you are the American Dream."

"That is the most disgusting imagery. Our high school English teacher would flunk you." I half-smiled.

"I don't think he's going to give you up without a fight."

"I come from a family of fighters. My father fought off cancer for four years." I couldn't believe I was having this discussion. Twelve hours ago I thought I was happily married and my main worry was if I sold enough tickets to the Garden Party fund-raiser.

"You need to talk to him. Leave Max here for dinner. Glenn or I will run him home later."

"I look like warmed-over death." I studied myself in the gilt antique mirror.

"You're right, you do. Let's go up to my bedroom and fix you up. I'll give you something silk to wear, and douse you with Obsession."

"It's three o'clock on a Tuesday," I protested.

"You can't be overdressed for telling your husband to fuck off. You need the highest heels I have. To kick him right in the balls."

An hour later I left Stephanie's feeling like a new woman. I wore a Carolina Herrera dress that managed to look sexy and sophisticated at the same time.

"You don't want to look like one of his hussies. You want to show him what he's missing," Stephanie said when she picked it out of her closet. It had a floral print and was made of a gauze fabric over an ivory slip. My feet were squeezed into four-inch Manolo heels (Stephanie was one shoe size smaller than me) that made me about the same height as Andre. "You don't want Andre to look down on you in any way. If we can make you taller than him that would be perfect."

Stephanie had applied my makeup. She lavished black mascara on my eyelashes and lent me one of her bright red lipsticks. "I know red lipstick isn't really you. But it makes a statement: 'Read My Lips.' He'll pay attention when you talk."

I looked at myself in the mirror and smiled at Stephanie. "You're pretty good at this."

"I wasn't as smart as you, or as rich as you. I had to use my feminine wiles to get ahead." She laughed.

"I wish I had your feminine wiles."

"You're going to do great. Knock him dead." She gave me a hug, sprayed me with perfume, and pushed me out the door.

I walked back to the post office where I had left my car a lifetime ago. The doors were unlocked; my purse was still under the seat. Ross was the safest place in the world, except for tramps who stole your husband. I climbed into the car and drove the two blocks home.

Andre's car was in the driveway. The restaurant was closed on Tuesdays, so he would have no reason to still be there, unless it was to go another round with Ursula. I took a deep breath, fixed the skirt of my dress, and walked inside.

Andre was standing in the kitchen looking out the window. He had a glass of lemonade in front of him. "You look beautiful." He kissed my cheek. "School committee meeting?"

"I don't have meetings on Tuesdays. I leave Tuesdays free for yoga and breakfast at the Lemon Café. Except today the Lemon Café was out of my favorite strawberry muffins. So I thought I would surprise you and we could get breakfast together. But guess who got the surprise? Me! Because it looked like you and Ursula already had breakfast and were working on dessert. Each other." I got it all out in one breath, before I lost my nerve or took off my shoe and nailed him with the heel.

"Amanda, don't jump to conclusions." Andre shook his head as if I were a child.

"What conclusion would you jump to if you found me half-naked with my legs wrapped around another man? Escaping a rabid rat population?"

"We once had a rat in the storage closet," Andre mused.

"You were fucking her, Andre. You were fucking the chef standing up in broad daylight."

Andre drank his lemonade. He put his hand on my arm. Usually his touch sent an electric shock through my body. I willed myself not to react. I would not give in to his charm.

"Amanda." He circled my waist with both hands.

"Andre, I saw you and you saw me." I pulled away. I was shaking so hard I wanted to sit down, but our kitchen was too narrow for a table and chairs.

"Amanda, I am a fool and I am sorry. Ursula was crying, she was homesick and I was trying to comfort her. She has never been so far from home. We got carried away. It was nothing."

"You were fucking her! That's not nothing, that's everything!" I would have taken off my heel and hit him, but then he would have been taller than me.

"It is nothing. You are everything. It will never happen again." He pulled me to him and nuzzled my neck. I felt the warmth of his breath and his wonderful smell of cologne and fresh bread. On Tuesdays he baked bread, we ate fresh bread every Tuesday night.

"Has it ever happened before?" I asked carefully, not moving out of his embrace.

He stepped back as if I had physically wounded him. "What do you think? Of course not! She was just homesick. I will fire her immediately. We will advertise for a new chef."

"You said it's impossible to find a chef in America who knows how to bake fondue."

"I will cover all the shifts until we find a replacement. Nothing is more important than you. I'll find an old ugly chef, one with a hump on her back and a wart on her nose." He kissed my cheek.

"Andre, I know about all the others; about Bella and Angie, your whole harem. I don't think even a wart on her nose would stop you. You are a serial adulterer and I want a divorce."

"What are you talking about?" Andre asked. He was very calm; his green eyes were wide and innocent.

"I'm talking about you using La Petite Maison as a brothel since the day it opened. It is your restaurant, of course, at least sixty percent of it."

"You are mad, Amanda! Who told you these lies?"

"Stephanie, your silent partner, finally spilled the beans. I am furious with her for not telling me sooner, for letting me be a fool for Max's whole life!" I could feel the tears start again. I pushed them back. I couldn't show any weakness or Andre would be on me like a bear with a honey pot.

"She made it up, Amanda. Who do you believe, Stephanie or me?"

"Why would she make it up?"

"She is jealous of you. She has that boring old husband who thinks a fun night is solving a Rubik's cube."

"I thought you liked Glenn."

"I like Glenn, but I don't have to sleep with him. She's always wanted to get in my pants. She's trying to get back at me for rejecting her." He stroked my hair. For one second I faltered. What if Andre was telling the truth? He started kissing my neck and I closed my eyes. But I flashed on the image of him entwined with Ursula, her tall, lean body pushing against his, his hands on her breasts. I opened my eyes and pulled away.

"This is ridiculous, Andre. I *saw* you. Whether it happened before, dozens of times before, is beside the point. I can't live with an adulterer. I want you to leave."

Andre went into the living room and sat down on the low chocolate brown sofa. He kicked off his shoes and stretched his legs. "I don't want to leave," he said.

"Well, you can't stay." I followed him into the living room feeling like I was an actress on *Days of Our Lives*. I was certainly dressed for the part. Only daytime soap stars wore four-inch Manolos in the afternoon.

"I told you when we got married: In France one stays married for life."

"Well, we're not in France, and in America most wives expect their husbands to be faithful—there are a great number of wealthy divorce lawyers to prove it. I want you out of the house." I sounded much firmer than I felt. My stomach did little flips and my underarms were sweating. But I sounded as calm as General Patton leading his troops.

"I am not leaving our house. Think of what it would do to Max. They are only women, Amanda. You are making too much of this."

I almost fell off my heels. How could I have lived with a man for ten years who thought having serial affairs was unimportant?

"Monogamy is in the marriage vows. I feel terrible for Max, too, but you should have thought of that before Bella."

"You know," Andre said carefully, "this is not your house or my house. Your mother bought this house for Max. Maybe you should ask Max who should leave?"

"Now you're crazy."

"I am trying to keep our family together. Your mother bought this house in Max's name. He owns the house, so I am not leaving, and I hope you don't either. I love you, Amanda. Nothing has changed."

"Everything has changed!" I yelled and I took off my shoe and threw it across the room. It didn't hit him, but it made an indentation in the wood floor where it landed, and it made Andre get up. I stopped with the one shoe—I didn't want to be escorted to the police station and charged with assault.

"I'm going to the restaurant to get the bread for dinner. Give you some time to calm down." He slipped his shoes on and walked out the door.

I sank down on the sofa. It smelled of Andre: cologne and fresh bread. I closed my eyes and cried.

I let myself cry for half an hour and then I walked over to the cabinet that constituted our bar and poured myself a brandy. I didn't know how the brandy would react when it met the tequila still in my stomach, but I figured it would be hard to feel worse than I did. I gulped the brandy down quickly. It burned my throat but cleared my head. The first thing I had to do, I told myself sternly, was to stop crying. I had given Andre ten years of my life; I wasn't going to waste another minute on him. Then I had to make a plan. Andre was right about the house; it was in Max's name. I didn't want to spend another night under the same roof as Andre, but for Max's sake I would have to. I poured myself one more brandy for courage. Then I sat down and waited for Stephanie to bring Max home.

Stephanie and Max pulled up just as the two shots of brandy were beginning to make me feel a little fuzzy. Max ran up the steps and hugged me.

"You smell funny again." He wrinkled his nose. I had to stop drinking or they'd cart me away to Betty Ford.

"Daddy and I were making a new dish," I improvised again.

"Is Daddy here?" Max's face lit up.

"He went to get the bread, he'll be right back."

"Can we go to the restaurant? I want to see him and tell him about the turtle we found in Zoe's yard."

"He'll be home any minute. Go inside and change. I want to talk to Mrs. Chambers for a minute."

Stephanie was standing at the bottom of the steps, probably wondering if I was waiting for Andre with a shotgun or a carving knife.

"You look good, but you do smell a little funny," she said, walking up the steps and sitting down next to me.

"Couple of shots of brandy for Dutch courage. Andre says he's not leaving."

"Told you," Stephanie replied.

"That's helpful."

"What are you going to do? Besides drink?" Stephanie asked.

"I'm going to stop drinking tomorrow. I promise. He's not worth it."

"Now you're talking," Stephanie replied.

"Poor Max." My lips quivered. I felt the tears start.

"And you're going to stop crying," Stephanie said.

"That, too," I said, though my eyes were wet. "Max doesn't deserve such a shit for a dad."

"He doesn't, but life isn't fair, even for the privileged classes." Stephanie grinned. "So, tell me again what you're going to do besides not drink and not cry?"

"I'll go see my mother tomorrow and make an appointment with her attorney," I said with a sigh.

"Good girl."

"And I will not throw anything at Andre tonight."

"Did you throw anything at him today?" Stephanie asked.

"Just your Manolo. But I missed him."

"After you see the attorney we'll get you some target practice."

"No, I don't want to impart bodily harm. Well, I do, but I don't want to go to jail. That wouldn't help Max."

"See, you are still thinking clearly, you're stronger than you think."

"Oh, Stephanie." I turned to her.

"No more crying. I have to go home. Gisella gets off at six and Glenn doesn't know how to use a microwave. He'll put the baked potatoes in for ten minutes and burn the house down."

"No, he won't," I said and laughed.

"Really. He doesn't pay much attention to the outside world. He still thinks I'm twenty-five and hot."

"That's because you look like you're twenty-five. You saved my life today. Thanks." I gave her a hug.

"It was nothing. I'm sorry I didn't tell you sooner. I feel like a complete heel."

"Andre's the heel. I'm the dummy who fell for him."

"No, he's the dummy who didn't deserve you. Call me tomorrow after you see your mother." Stephanie kissed me on the cheek and ran down the stairs.

I sat on the steps. The night was gorgeous, warm and clear. I heard crickets and a frog burping. Max came outside in his pajamas and sat down.

"How was your day?" I asked.

"Great. Nineteen more days of school."

"You love school," I said.

"Sure, but summer's better."

"Summer is good," I agreed. We usually spent summers at home, with weekend trips to Lake Tahoe. Last summer Max went to sleepover camp for the first time. He came home full of stories of giant spiders and the one fish he caught by himself. Andre and I spent most of the week Max was gone in bed, reliving the first year of our marriage. What would Max and I do this summer? I felt the tears start and rubbed my eyes.

"I don't want to go to camp this summer," Max said, linking his arm through mine.

"But you caught that huge fish. And this year you learn archery. Grandma bought you the bow and arrow set for Christmas."

Max considered this. The bow and arrows had been lying at the foot of his bed since December. His little friends tramping through his bedroom on playdates were jealous of the five bows with the real feathers.

"I do want to do archery, but I want to stay with you and Daddy. Maybe he can teach me archery?" Max asked.

"We'll ask him," I said. I held Max's hand and we listened to the crickets. For a moment I wavered. How could I divorce

Andre and deprive Max of having a father around to teach him boy things? But what kind of husband would Max become if he learned from Andre?

"C'mon, let's go to bed. I think we could both use a good night's sleep."

"But Daddy isn't back yet," Max protested.

"I'll make sure we eat his bread for breakfast, with warm butter. How's that?"

"I wanted to say good night."

"I'll lie down on your bed with you, and when Daddy comes he can say good night to both of us," I suggested.

Max smiled. I never slept in his bed with him, so this was a huge treat. I took off my shoes and tucked my body against the wall, leaving Max as much of his bed as I could. I waited till I heard him snoring softly and then I closed my eyes.

Later I heard the front door open. I glanced at the clock; it was almost eleven o'clock. I held my breath, trying not to move and wake Max. I didn't want to talk to Andre; I didn't want to see him. I heard Andre go into our bedroom. I imagined him undressing and climbing into bed. I buried my face in Max's pillow and surrendered to sleep.

Black Tuesday was finally over.

Chapter Three

*W*hen I pulled up at my mother's house the next morning, I was reminded of how wealthy she was. Her attorney made house calls. Dean Birney, senior partner of Birney and Sutton, arrived before me, his black Mercedes with its tinted windows and gold rims parked in the driveway. I parked behind him and opened my door. The wheels of divorce were in motion.

Rosemary threw open the front door before I made it up the steps. I had called my mother after I dropped Max off at school and told her the whole story.

"Drive right over here. I'm calling Dean Birney," she instructed. I could almost hear her fishing for a cigarette.

"Shouldn't we take this slowly?" I asked as I maneuvered onto the Golden Gate Bridge. I hoped she would tell me I was being hasty, all marriages had problems, even she and my father weathered low periods. But she hadn't. Instead she started swearing under her breath, either at Andre or at the cigarette she was trying to light. I hung up and concentrated on my driving.

Now I stood in the foyer and let Rosemary hug me. Rosemary had been hugging me all my life: when I failed a Spanish test in the first grade, when the kids in middle school made fun of me for having a neck like a giraffe, and when she found the crumpled college acceptance letters in my garbage can.

Until yesterday I had a husband to hug me. But he turned out to be a lying, cheating scumbag. I straightened my black Max Azria side-slit skirt and joined my mother and Dean Birney in the morning room.

"Amanda." Dean stood up when I entered. "Grace has been briefing me on the situation." Dean Birney was in his early sixties. He had a thick head of white hair, a long nose, and thin lips. In the thirty years he had been our attorney I had only seen him smile twice: at my father's sixtieth birthday party, and at my parents' silver anniversary. He was Harvard educated and fiercely loyal. Andre Blick was a dead man.

My mother held my face, checking for pain. Her hair was the same white-blond shade it had been all my life, cut in the same sleek pageboy. She wore a two-piece navy Dior suit and an ivory silk blouse. I glanced at my watch: It was ten a.m. and my mother looked as if she was dressed for an evening at Masa's, or for battle with an errant son-in-law.

She sat next to Dean and motioned for me to sit on her other side. She reached for her packet of cigarettes and lit one before I could protest. The year Max was born she tried to give up smoking but failed. Now she insisted she only smoked one pack a day, and Rosemary backed her up, but for all I knew she bribed Rosemary to fib to me. I noticed she wore her Dior belt on its tightest notch and her skin was a translucent shade of gray. I promised myself I would say something when I could think straight.

"You discovered your husband has been having affairs for at least eight years and you want to file for divorce," Dean said matter-of-factly.

I looked from Dean to my mother. I was thankful she had briefed him so I didn't have to repeat the details, but the more people who knew, the more real Andre's infidelities became. I glanced at the sideboard to see if Rosemary had put out any alcohol—a bottle of scotch would have done nicely—but there was only coffee, tea, and lemon. I'd have to survive on caffeine until lunchtime. I got up and poured myself a cup of black coffee, my third for the day.

"Yes," I said.

"He admitted to having affairs?" Dean asked.

"I caught him in the act. He wasn't playing canasta."

"Does he want a divorce?"

"No." I shook my head.

"But he doesn't want to give up the other woman?"

"He said he'd fire her. He said it meant nothing, and I was the only one who was important to him." I swallowed hard.

"You don't want to give him another chance?" Dean asked.

"My friend Stephanie, who is also his silent partner, gave me a list of previous flings. He changes girls more often than he changes menus."

"I just want to be certain you want to make this step. That the marriage can't be saved," Dean said.

"Dean"—my mother stubbed out her cigarette and lit another—"we went over this. Andre has been lying to Amanda for my grandson's whole life. I don't want her to spend another night under the same roof as him."

"I needed to hear it from Amanda," Dean said and smiled at me. "Divorce can be pretty brutal." He squeezed my hand. I felt my eyes fill with tears and took another swig of coffee. Why couldn't I have married a man like Dean: someone with white hair and kind eyes? Why had I fallen for a sexy Frenchman with zero morals?

"All right, I'm going to take some notes." Dean released my hand and snapped open his briefcase.

"Your son is how old?" he asked.

"Eight," I replied.

"And what property do you own?"

"Just the house in Ross."

"Which I bought," my mother interjected.

"That's the problem. My mother bought the house for us when Max was born and put it in Max's name. Andre says it's Max's house and he doesn't have to leave."

"Why did you put the house in Max's name?" Dean turned to my mother.

"Because my bastard son-in-law was too proud to take any charity from me. Amanda would have been living in a one-bedroom apartment with a baby unless I intervened."

"And you want him to leave?" Dean turned back to me.

"I do." I realized it was the only thing I felt strongly about. I loved our little house. I adored pottering around my garden. I loved sitting on the front steps watching Max skateboard up and down the street.

"Can't we kick him out?" my mother demanded.

Dean took his time answering. "No, actually, we can't. Your inheritance is safe. Your father left the bulk of his estate to you and any heirs, but since he died before you were married it is not considered community property. But if the house was bought in Max's name it is Max's house. I'm afraid your husband has as much right to live there as you do."

"Oh." I couldn't think of anything else to say.

"You could move?" Dean suggested.

"I love Ross. Max has so many friends at school." I shook my head.

"I mean move to another house in Ross," Dean said.

I wanted to call Rosemary and ask her to bring in the vodka. But it was not even eleven a.m. "I was hoping Andre would have to move out of Ross. It's such a small town. Everyone would talk, especially with the restaurant."

"Let's talk about the restaurant for a minute." Dean pulled a fresh sheet of paper from his briefcase.

"Who owns the restaurant?" he asked.

"Andre does. And Stephanie and Glenn are silent partners."

"You're not an owner?" Dean asked. I heard the surprise in his voice and I swallowed again.

"No."

"Why not?"

"Andre was so proud he didn't let my mother or me invest in the restaurant. He wanted to make it without our help. He was planning on buying Glenn and Stephanie out soon. We were going to buy some land in Napa and build a weekend house. With a pool and tennis courts." I was over the edge.

"Mother, do you think Rosemary could get me a scotch? My throat is really dry."

"Rosemary!" my mother called. I smiled. My father and mother had never been afraid to turn to alcohol in tough times.

"Amanda, if Andre's restaurant is in Ross and you have no grounds to kick him out of the house, it looks like you may have to make the town big enough for both of you." Dean looked up from his notes.

I waited till Rosemary appeared with a scotch on the rocks. I downed it one gulp. "I thought he'd move back to San Francisco, open a restaurant here," I mumbled.

"I don't see why he would," Dean answered carefully. "He is living mortgage-free and has a successful restaurant. Opening a new restaurant is never easy. I don't think he's going anywhere." Dean shook his head.

"You could buy another house in Ross, Amanda. Buy a big house, make him look like the tiny man he is," my mother said.

I felt a little better after the scotch. I remembered how much my mother had adored Andre, how he had brought her flowers and imported chocolates.

"You could," Dean said with a nod, "but if you buy another house before the divorce is final it might become part of the settlement: community property. I would rent for the next six months."

"I don't want Max to move twice."

"You are a very wealthy young lady, Amanda. You can live anywhere and do anything." Dean was so patient. I was used to Andre and how everything revolved around Andre:

his restaurant, his fondue, even our sex life was dictated by when he wanted me.

"I just want to stay in Ross and go on being Max's mom," I finally answered. "I want to pick Max up from school and take him to chess club. I want to be on the library auction committee and organize the annual garden party. Ross is like Mayberry, and we belong there. I don't want to live anywhere else." As the words came out I realized they were true. I had tossed out my dreams of studying fashion and moving to New York with my prepregnancy jeans. I was completely content being a wife and mother in the small grid of my freeway exit.

Dean glanced at his gold Bulova watch. "Grace, Amanda, I have a lunch date I can't break. Why don't you two talk and we'll discuss filing later this afternoon." He gathered his notes and snapped them into his briefcase.

"Thanks for coming at such short notice." My mother got up and pecked him on the cheek.

"Everything will be fine. You girls have a nice lunch and hash it out. I'll be with my cell phone all afternoon."

"I'll phone just so you can call me a 'girl' again." My mother smiled. She led Dean to the foyer and I took the opportunity to refill my scotch glass.

"I told Rosemary to serve us a proper lunch in the dining room. You look like you haven't eaten," my mother said, coming back into the morning room.

"*You* look like you haven't been eating. Do you have cigarettes for lunch, too, or only breakfast?" I snapped. My mother's ankles looked like they belonged on a bird, and her Cartier watch hung on her wrist like a bangle.

"We're here to talk about you," she replied.

"I know, I'm sorry." The scotch on an empty stomach made me grumpy. And the news Dean had given me made me suicidal.

"Come on, let's go out to the garden while Rosemary prepares something." She took my hand and led me out the French doors.

Looking at the view of the bay was almost as calming as doing yoga. The fog had cleared and it was a beautiful spring day. My parents' garden was lined with rosebushes. The cars on the Golden Gate Bridge sparkled like diamonds, and the boats under the bridge dodged back and forth.

"You could always move back home," my mother offered. "There's plenty of room for you and Max. You could have your own floor, two floors. I'd stay out of your way."

"That's a tremendous gesture, since we know how well Max respects your marble floors," I laughed. On his last visit Max had turned the library into a skateboard park. Rosemary had almost fainted when she found him stacking first editions as obstacles.

"He's a boy," my mother said and shrugged. I noticed how thin her shoulders were: When she lifted them the bones stuck out.

"You're right," I said. "You were lucky I only used the library to host Barbie tea parties."

"This house could use some young energy. Even Rosemary qualifies for senior discounts." My mother sighed.

"Thanks, but the one thing I'm clear on is I want to stay

in Ross. We belong there; I don't want to lose that. Because then Andre's taken everything."

"I know what you mean." My mother picked a rosebud. It was pale pink and when she held it to her nose to breathe its perfume, her cheeks looked even paler. I promised myself I would say something about the cigarettes at lunch.

"When your father died, this house became my best friend. And this view."

"That's how I feel about Ross. I love the school, and the commons, and the lake. I just don't know how I'll feel running into Andre every time I turn around."

"Mrs. Bishop, Amanda, lunch is ready." Rosemary stood on the stone patio.

"Come on, we need some food before we can have a cocktail and decide what to do." My mother steered me to the dining room.

"Absolutely." I nodded. "I wouldn't want to make any major decisions with a clear head."

🦋 🦋 🦋

We sat across from each other at one end of the long dining room table. My mother insisted on eating in the formal room. Perhaps she thought the beauty of the fine chandeliers twinkling above us and the elegance of the emerald velvet chairs would entice me to move home. Instead I wished I were standing in my galley kitchen serving Max a peanut butter sandwich. I also wished Max's father wasn't a cheating pig. I nibbled at my Cobb salad and decided wishing was for little girls who still believed in Santa Claus.

"School is out in three weeks," I said, giving up on the salad and biting into the olive Rosemary had placed in my martini.

"You have to eat something," my mother said, pushing a plate of ham and French bread in front of me.

"I am eating my olive, and I am washing it down with this lovely liquid," I replied, draining my glass.

"Amanda, think of Max."

"I don't see you making a dent in your salad. For once my eating habits match yours. I'm following your example." I smiled sweetly.

"I'm not a good example," my mother muttered, pushing back her plate and reaching for her cigarettes.

"You certainly are not!" I could feel my anger at Andre welling up and being directed at my mother. "Give me one of those cigarettes. If you can kill yourself, I can, too." I reached across the table and grabbed her cigarette case.

"Amanda, stop it." She pulled the case out of my hands. For her birdlike appearance, her grip was strong.

"I mean it! You look like a solitary confinement inmate. Martinis and cigarettes are not a lunch."

"I miss your father," my mother said.

"Mom, Dad has been gone for ten years. That's no excuse for trying to kill yourself. I need you and Max needs you. You have to stop smoking."

"I can't," she said; her face was blank.

"You can do anything you want," I retorted.

"It's too late anyway," she muttered, staring at the table.

"What did you say?" Suddenly my lovely martini haze lifted.

"I said it's too late."

"And what did you mean?" I picked up a sterling silver knife and put it back down.

"This isn't the time. We need to talk about what you and Max are going to do. You could stay with Stephanie till school gets out," my mother said, changing the subject.

"Mom, we are not discussing anything except you and your cigarettes. What have you not told me?"

She sighed and looked at me. Her head looked too heavy for her thin neck. "Dr. Jensen wants me to leave San Francisco for the summer. He says the fog is bad for my lungs."

"What's wrong with your lungs?" I asked.

"They found a little spot on my last X-ray."

"You didn't tell me?" I demanded.

"I was planning on telling you, I was even going to ask if you and Max wanted to come with me. Maybe go somewhere hot and exotic, play on the beach. But your phone call this morning distracted me."

"Mom." My eyes filled with tears.

"But actually," she said brightly, tapping at her cigarette case the way she did when she got excited, "we could solve your problem and mine at the same time."

"You don't 'solve' a spot on your lung, Mom. And you don't keep smoking."

"You and Max can come with me. We'll pick somewhere wonderful. You'll be away from that miserable man and Max will think we're on vacation. Where shall we go?" When she lit her cigarette her hand shook. Her wedding ring was too big for her finger and had been sized down twice since my father died. But her voice was bright, like a sorority sister planning spring break.

"You're not listening." I tried to play the responsible daughter, but the idea of a luxury getaway was tempting: just pack all my problems in a suitcase to be unpacked at the end of the summer. I could lie on white sand, watch Max splash in the waves, and pretend Andre had stayed in Ross to take care of the restaurant instead of to screw his Swedish chef. The image of the two of them entwined together popped uninvited into my head.

"You have to say yes. It's the best thing for all of us. There's a wonderful new St. Regis in Laguna Beach. It has a private beach club with surf butlers. Max would be in heaven. And it's in California so Andre can't make a fuss about you taking Max far away. The service is supposed to be excellent—as good as the St. Regis in New York. You know that was your father's favorite hotel."

I remembered when I was a child, she and my father would fly to New York midweek to catch the latest Broadway show and eat at the Four Seasons. When they returned she would fill my bathroom with St. Regis soaps and scents and tell me about the incredible service: chocolate truffles waiting on their pillows at night, a silver tray with a Chinese proverb and fresh strawberries placed on the coffee table in the late afternoon. Even their underwear and socks, my mother told me, were laundered and returned wrapped in white tissue paper and tied with yellow bows.

"How long were you planning on going for?" I asked.

"We'll leave the day after school ends and come back Labor Day weekend. Three months of five-star service and beautiful sunsets. I'll book the Presidential Suite so we won't get in each other's hair. Say yes, Amanda."

I played with my olive. I closed my eyes and saw cliffs dotted with houses wrapped in walls of glass. I saw an oceanside bar where people gathered to watch the sunset and drink colorful sugary drinks. My vision did not include any handsome Frenchmen or Swedish blondes.

"I guess there's no reason not to," I replied slowly.

"And a million reasons to go! I haven't had you and Max to myself in ages. I'm going to call my travel agent right now."

"Mom, wait." I didn't want to make any decisions. Somewhere deep inside me there was a stubborn hope that the last thirty-six hours were a dream. I would wake up to find my husband had never cheated on me, we were still madly in love, and summer would consist of shooting bows and arrows on Ross commons.

"I'll make you a deal," she said. "If you spend the summer with me, I'll stop smoking."

"You said you can't stop."

"I can for you, and for Max."

"You promise?"

"Scout's honor"—she held up her palm—"the minute we get on the plane."

"Deal," I said. How could I say anything else? I had been trying to get my mother to stop smoking since I was twelve years old.

"Deal." She was beaming. "I'm going to call the travel agent."

I looked at my watch. "Oh my gosh, I have to go or I'll be late to pick up Max."

"Can you drive, Amanda?"

"I'm fine. I'll go outside and take big gulps of fog before I get in the car."

The fog had slid over the Golden Gate Bridge and the air was icy cold. My mother waved from her study on the second floor. She held the phone with one hand and blew me kisses with the other. I slid into the driver's seat, shaking my head. Had it been that easy to convince my mother to stop smoking? Just agree to spend the summer with her in the Presidential Suite of a luxury resort and she'll quit cold turkey? I guess she was prepared to do anything to get me away from Andre. If she could be so mature so could I. I was going to stop feeling sorry for myself . . . and stop wanting to kill Andre. I pictured shivery cold margaritas, and for the first time in almost two days I smiled.

I pulled up in front of the restaurant and checked my watch. I had forty minutes till Max got out of school: enough time to confront Andre. I opened the door of the restaurant, half expecting to see Andre lip locked with Ursula. Instead he was in the back room, sitting at his desk running his hands through his hair. He wore a white shirt, navy silk shorts, and leather sandals. I could see his tan calves stretched out underneath the desk. I had always found his calves sexy. I swallowed.

"Hi," I said. I sounded weak. I cursed myself and tried again. "I'm filing for divorce."

He looked up and smiled. "I don't want a divorce."

"You should have thought of that before you took up extramarital fucking."

"I told you it means nothing. I love you." Andre reached forward and put his hand on mine.

I pulled my hand away. "The only person you love is yourself."

"Amanda, the sex means nothing. You and Max are my life." He actually sounded angry.

"Sorry to be so bourgeois, but the sex means everything to me. If you wanted a cosmopolitan wife, you should have married one. I am a hometown San Francisco girl who believes in family values. In my language, adultery spells divorce."

"I'll never do it again. You have my word." He put his hand over his heart.

"We already had this conversation. I wasn't brought up in a house that condoned adultery. I've seen my mother's attorney and I'm filing."

I saw a flicker of worry pass through Andre's eyes. He had met Dean Birney at family functions. He knew I was serious.

"I'm not moving out. I have as much right to the house as you do."

"I know, Dean told me."

"We can make it work, Amanda. I will fire Ursula." He reached for my hand again.

"You haven't fired her already?" I almost laughed. "I thought you said she was packing her bags the minute you untwined your legs."

"Ursula's an excellent chef and really knows fondue. She and I are over."

"No, we are over. When our divorce is final I'm going to buy another house in Ross. I don't want Max to be uprooted. In the meantime, Max and I are going to Laguna Beach for the summer with my mother."

"You're doing what?"

"They found a spot on my mother's lung. Her doctor wants her to leave San Francisco for the summer and we're going with her. We're going to the St. Regis in Laguna Beach. Max will swim and surf. When we come back we'll look for a new house. Maybe you'll have come to your senses and moved out of town."

"I'm not leaving Ross. My house and my restaurant are here."

"Whatever," I said with a shrug.

"I won't let you take Max away for the whole summer."

"Really?" I spat at him. "Shall I tell him that his father screws other women? He's not stupid and he's not a baby. We're going. You can have your precious house all to yourself."

"I said no, Amanda," Andre replied in a steely voice.

"Well, I say yes. My mother said if I go she'll stop smoking. So I have to go. You can visit Max if you want, it's an hour's flight."

Andre was silent. I hated using my mother's condition as ammunition, but I knew Andre thought the world of her; to him she was the original American princess.

"She really said she'd stop smoking?"

"Yes," I said. We were almost a married couple again, facing my mother's illness. For a moment I remembered the good things about Andre: his compassion, his charm, his intelligence. I shook myself. Why did men have to think with their dicks and screw everything up?

"I guess it will be good for Max to be at the beach, and good for your mother to be with her grandson. Take the summer to think about us, Amanda. We are so good together," he replied in a soft, coaxing tone.

"I'm done thinking. Max and I will stay with Stephanie until school is over." I turned and walked out before he could argue. I got in the car and drove around the block to the school entrance and waited for Max.

The wonderful thing about being a mother is the minute you see your child—his smile smeared across his face, his shoes untied, and his backpack bumping along behind him—everything else disappears. I opened the car door and hugged him.

"Hi, Mom, how was your day?" Max hugged me back.

"Great, I went and saw Grandma and we have a surprise for you."

"A new skateboard?"

"Better." I smiled.

"A motorized car?"

"Even better. Hop in, we have to go see Mrs. Chambers and I'll tell you."

On the short drive to Stephanie's, I described the St. Regis in vivid detail. I told Max he could order milkshakes in the middle of the night. He could swim in five pools, and ride in a tram like they had at Disneyland. I could see Max's eyes grow wide in the rearview mirror.

When we pulled into Stephanie's driveway, Max jumped out to find Zoe and tell her about presidential suites and beach clubs and surf butlers. Stephanie was in the kitchen peeling Fruit Roll-Up from Zoe's lunch box.

"Hi, girl warrior, how goes the battle?" she asked.

"Bad." I sat down at the kitchen island.

"Is it tequila time?"

"My tequila days are over. The morning after is too gruesome."

"How about a double espresso with a sprinkle of nutmeg?"

"Perfect." I slipped out of my heels. While Stephanie attacked her Italian espresso machine, I told her about my meeting with Dean Birney.

"Bitch," Stephanie said, setting a demitasse of dark brown liquid in front of me.

"Who's a bitch?" I sipped it. It was awful, like castor oil. I don't know how Italians could drink espresso and look so happy.

"Life's a bitch. Andre shouldn't get to stay in the house. It's not fair."

"Next time I ask for espresso remind me I like a cup of Nescafé with extra cream. I realized the one thing I want to do is stay in Ross. Max belongs here. When the divorce is final, I'll buy a house here for Max and me."

"And live across Ross commons from Peter Pan?"

"I have to behave like a grown-up and think about what is best for Max. He needs to be close to his father," I said.

"Even if his father is a world-class prick?"

"Even if. But in the meantime, Max and I are going to have a fantastic summer." I told her about the vacation my mother had planned: the St. Regis service, views of Catalina, private beach club.

"Now you're on to something. I wish I were going. We have to visit Glenn's parents in Michigan."

"You and the kids should come for a week."

"No, you don't want an old married woman hanging around. You want to meet fresh, single meat."

"Stephanie, I'm not going to meet a man. I'm going to get away from a man, and to keep my mother company." I shivered.

"You never know. There's nothing wrong with meeting a new man."

"I've had enough of men."

"No, Amanda, you've had enough of Andre. There are plenty of good men out there. Even some who will love and cherish you."

"I'm terrible at picking men." I put the cup on the marble island. "Isn't it funny. You ended up with the big house in Ross, two kids, and a dog. And I'm homeless with a broken heart."

"You're only homeless by choice, and only for a few months. You could buy this whole street if you wanted to." Stephanie stacked lunchboxes in the pantry.

"How were you smart enough to pick Glenn?"

Stephanie sat on the stool next to me. "My father was in advertising. He met my mother on the set of a Clairol commercial. He got her pregnant and promised he was going to marry her. One day he came home from work and said he was offered a job with a big ad agency in London: creative director, worldwide. He told my mother he loved her but it wasn't 'the right time' to get married. He couldn't pass up the opportunity, and he didn't want to be saddled with a wife and child in a new country—"

"I never knew that," I interrupted.

"Everyone at school had fathers who drove into their offices in San Francisco on weekday mornings, and watched their soccer games on the weekend. I told the other kids my father was 'traveling.' For eighteen years," she laughed.

"Do you ever see him?" I remembered the Stephanie I knew in high school. She had a mane of golden hair, and a body like Jessica Rabbit. She used to strut around the student commons with a guy on one arm and another carrying her books behind her. She was the only girl in the freshman class invited to the senior prom, and on Valentine's Day she received so many Love-o-Grams she couldn't fit them in her backpack.

"No." Stephanie shook her head. "He married a Brit a few years later and has three pale children named Daisy and Nigel and Hamish. But he paid for my education, so I can't complain. I guess when I was shopping for a husband my main criteria was one who was home by five p.m."

"Glenn is more than that," I said.

"He's a lot more than that. But when we were first dating I thought he was skinny, and a bit of a geek. He used to read articles from the *Harvard Business Review* out loud, when all I wanted to do was sample chocolate croissants at Parisian bakeries and make out."

"What changed your mind?"

Stephanie thought for a minute. "He told me I was smart, and all the other men I'd been with were just interested in my cup size. I started to listen when he talked, and I realized we wanted the same things: house, kids, and enough money to give kids a great childhood. When he took me to the top of the Eiffel Tower, he pointed down at the streets of Paris and said, 'I want to put the world at your feet.' I knew he'd never walk out on me. There are a lot of different kinds of love."

"And I picked Andre like a teenager choosing pinup posters for her room." I tried to laugh.

"You had the world at your feet. You had your own skating rink for Christ's sake."

"I didn't have my own skating rink." I shook my head. A rumor had started sophomore year that we had a skating rink in our basement. An ambitious party planner had installed fake ice for one of my parent's parties, but it had been removed the morning after the event.

"You had a mansion and two parents who were like royalty. We used to call your family 'the Kennedys.' You couldn't know there were cads out there. They weren't allowed in your house." Stephanie got up and opened the fridge.

Max and Zoe came running into the kitchen.

"Mom, Zoe doesn't believe in surf butlers. She thinks I'm making it up," Max protested.

"She'll just have to come see for herself," I said, pouring the espresso down the sink.

"You did get something special out of the deal." Stephanie nodded toward Max as the kids zoomed out of the kitchen.

"I did," I agreed, trying to keep the tears from my eyes.

Somehow we made it through the next three weeks. Max and I stayed in Stephanie's guest room, sharing the king-sized bed. I told Max our house had a giant ant infestation. Thank goodness he was so thrilled to watch the sixty-inch TV in Stephanie's family room and play their Wii, he didn't ask questions. I took him by the restaurant every evening before it opened so he could see Andre. I waited in my car while they hung out and drank lemonade.

I didn't see Ursula, but I didn't go inside the restaurant either. It wasn't my business whether he fired her. I did notice the new hostess who came out to set up the tables on the sidewalk wore fishnet stockings with seams down the backs. Her heels were ridiculously high for someone who was on her feet all night. But maybe she wasn't on her feet all night. Maybe Andre put her on her back at the end of the night, and helped her out of her stockings. I reminded myself that wasn't my business either. I was finished with Andre. I couldn't wait to get on the airplane so he would be out of sight. I ticked off the days on Stephanie's kitchen calendar, and when the last day of school came I think I was happier than all the third graders tumbling out of their classroom. We were free.

Chapter Four

We landed at John Wayne Airport in Orange County in the late afternoon. On the plane I had sat next to a girl wearing a pink T-shirt dress and rainbow flip-flops. She sported huge white sunglasses and a gold toe ring. Looking at her, I already felt like I was on vacation. After we disembarked, we made our way down to baggage claim and found our bags in the hands of a man in a blue-and-gold uniform.

"Good afternoon, Mrs. Bishop, Mrs. Blick, Max. My name is Michael, I will be your driver to the St. Regis. Allow me to escort you to the car."

"Wow!" Max ran ahead of us. Michael opened the door of an ivory-colored Bentley.

"Mother, what is this?" I asked, sliding into the cream leather seat and admiring the walnut interior.

"This is how we are going to live from now on." My mother settled herself into the front passenger seat.

"Let me know if I can adjust the air for you. Would Max

like to listen to Radio Disney?" Michael asked as we rolled away from the curb.

"Are these Jelly Bellies for me? Look, Mom, strawberry smoothie in a can! Wow, this is awesome!" Max riffled through the contents of a maple box secured in the middle of the backseat.

"All for you." I grinned. Michael raised the windows and I watched the Pacific Ocean fly by. I examined my new Tory Burch sandals, orange with giant gold buckles. I wore a Theory sundress in lime green. Orange and green, Stephanie had said on our predeparture Union Square shopping spree, were *the* spring colors. I felt silly handing over my purchases to the salesgirl at Neiman's. I hadn't kept up with spring colors since Max was born. My wardrobe for the last eight years had many designer pieces, but they were designed for the suburban mom. But Stephanie had threatened to use her own credit card and pack my suitcase herself. Now I was glad I had given in. I felt different, not like Amanda the mom, Amanda the betrayed wife. More like the girl on the plane with the white sunglasses and toe ring.

"Unless of course there might be a daiquiri in here for me. It is cocktail hour," I said to my mother and Michael in the front.

"Side compartment, Mrs. Blick. Or a martini if you like, already stirred, over ice."

"Martini for me," my mother chimed in.

I handed my mother her drink and sipped my ridiculously sweet banana daiquiri.

"Wow, look, Mom, a Nintendo DS." Max found a new treasure.

"Goodness." My mother laughed. "We're not even at the hotel yet!"

We pulled into the St. Regis as I contemplated finishing the jar of gummi bears Max had opened. At this rate I would have to head straight for the spa and hit the elliptical machine. The St. Regis was a giant Tuscan villa with seven floors spilling down to the ocean. We were greeted by an army of bellboys: one to open each car door, one to carry our bags, one to present Max with a yellow sand bucket and spade and shovel.

"Can we go to the beach, right now?" Max asked, waving the spade and shovel in the air like twin swords.

"Let's check in first," I said. Any fear I had of Max missing his father was fast dissipating. His eyes were wide and his mouth set in a permanent *o*. We were treated like royalty; escorted from the Mediterranean lobby with its giant palm trees and mosaic tile to a private elevator that carried us to the Presidential Suite.

"The seventh floor can only be reached by a special key, so you have complete privacy." Our bellboy waited for us to exit the elevator. We walked down a carpeted hall and stopped in front of gold double doors. "You have a butler at your service twenty-four hours a day. We stocked the fridge as per your instructions, and the Kids' Club assembled some books and games for Max, but please don't hesitate to ask for anything." The bellboy swung open the doors and I stepped into paradise.

I stayed in many fine hotels with my parents when I was young, but since I married Andre our vacations had consisted of overnights to check out French restaurants in Napa Valley. Once he had agreed to join my mother in Hawaii, but insisted it was so Max could play in the warm ocean. I sighed, thinking of all the effort I spent during my marriage so that Andre would not feel like a "kept" man, while he spent all his energy screwing other women. I had forgotten the pleasure of perfectly arranged linens, huge white bath sheets, rows of skincare products and beauty oils lining a marble vanity.

The Presidential Suite was bigger than our house in Ross. The living room had matching love seats and a baby grand piano. A separate dining room housed a gleaming mahogany table and twelve chairs upholstered in burgundy velvet. A small kitchen held a full-sized fridge and microwave and a pantry stocked with gourmet coffees, tiny tins of caviar, and boxes of crackers, cereal, oatmeal, peanut butter, jams, and jellies. I thought Andre would have been impressed by the gourmet selection of foods. Then I tried, for the hundredth time, to push all thoughts of Andre out of my head.

The bellboy drew back the curtains and we moved onto the balcony. Below us was a grand lawn with a white rotunda and a circle of palm trees. Waiters crisscrossed the grass, carrying frosty pink drinks down to the pool.

"Look, Mom, the pool has a fountain! Can we go swimming?" Max squeezed his face between the railings.

"Tomorrow; now it's dinnertime," I said.

"I'm not hungry!" Max protested.

"Jelly Bellies and a strawberry smoothie are not dinner. The pool will be there tomorrow." I tried to sound firm, but

I was so tired I just wanted to climb into the giant canopied bed. Suddenly, I couldn't see the pool or the ocean. All I could see was Andre in the green Speedo he wore in Hawaii. I told him men in America didn't wear Speedos. He asked why not, and I remember looking at the distinct outline of his crotch under the spandex and saying it was indecent. He laughed and called me a puritan. Then he kissed me and said, "In France I would be overdressed. Many men walk the beach naked." I closed my eyes, willing the image away.

"Tell you what; I'll order room service." I walked back inside and picked up a leather-bound menu. "How about starfish-shaped chicken nuggets with baby peas and carrots?"

"I'll take room service." My mother came into the living room. She looked tiny next to the piano and the large canvases of art on the wall. "Get me a salmon please, with broccoli."

"How about some bread or mashed potatoes, Mom."

"I think I'll mix a martini, would you like one?" She walked over to the bar and scanned the bottles of alcohol.

"No, I overdid the gummi bears. I'll never fit into a bathing suit. Go easy, Mom. You need fruits, grains, vegetables."

"Nonsense, I need a drink!" She filled her glass and sipped it carefully.

"Delicious. A toast." She turned to Max, who was playing with the TV remote. "To my darling grandson and my beautiful daughter: May we have a summer of fun, and may all our dreams come true!"

I closed my eyes, wishing for my mother to be healthy, my son happy, and for the slide show of my pathetic husband to stop playing in my head.

While we waited for our dinner, I started making the suite feel like home. I insisted my mother take the "presidential" bedroom and its en suite bathroom. The bathroom was a work of art: white marble floor with gold inlay, circular Jacuzzi tub with gold faucets, and an ornate shower with one wall of glass. I felt a little more comfortable in the "guest" bedroom, which had a sitting area, a lacquered desk, and a giant mirror propped up against the wall. Its bathroom was still enormous, but I put Max's no-tangle shampoo in the shower, and his racing car toothbrush and Batman toothpaste on the vanity, and it felt more familiar.

I peeked into the living room and saw Max mesmerized by an episode of *Ben 10* on the plasma screen. I could hear my mother on the other side of the suite humming a Frank Sinatra tune. I snuck out to my private balcony and sat down on the wicker love seat. The cushion was so soft I thought I might never get up. I inhaled the salt air, trying to fill up the dead space that existed between my chest and my stomach. "You stupid bastard," I said aloud. "How dare you ruin this vacation? Get out of my fucking head." When I tried to look at the view, all I saw was Andre.

Room service would be here any minute, and if I didn't eat, my mother wouldn't either. "We're going to have a dinner so succulent it will make your fondue taste like wallpaper paste," I said to the night air. "And if the bellboy is cute I'm going to pinch his ass." But I knew my heart wasn't in it. I still didn't notice other men. I put that on my mental to-do list. "Look at other men like you mean it." I slammed the balcony door shut and went to find Max and my mother.

Max was standing at the dining room table peeking under

giant silver domes. "Mom, our food is here. Five different kinds of mustard! That's more than Dad has in his restaurant. And this bread is awesome, try the hummus; it's made with sun-dried tomatoes." All the years of hanging out with Andre at La Petite Maison had made Max gastronomically wise beyond his years.

"Mom, come join us. Your salmon smells delicious," I called to my mother.

"No one does salmon like the St. Regis." She came in from the hall. "Amanda, the bellboy left an itinerary of tomorrow's events. How about surf lessons for Max and Beach Yoga for you?"

"What about you?" I replied, watching as she toyed with sautéed broccoli.

"I'll think of something. The bellboy was cute, by the way. UCLA student. His name was John."

"Mom." I motioned to Max, who still thought his parents were happily married.

"For me, of course. He's only a few decades younger than me." She laughed. "Anyway, with a steady diet of sun and martinis I expect to get younger every day."

"Go easy on both, Mom. Promise you won't drink before six p.m." I bit into my scallops.

"Don't spoil my fun. That salmon was divine." She pushed away the huge white dish that held her entrée. "Let's see what we have for dessert."

The dessert tray held four chocolate-covered strawberries and six ice cream bonbons. "Amanda, this one has a caramel center. You have to try one." My mother pushed the bonbons toward me. When it came to dessert my mother was like a child: She craved chocolate, and she could eat whipped cream by the spoonful.

"No, absolutely not." I shook my head. "I am wearing my new pink-and-green bathing suit to the beach tomorrow, the one Stephanie insisted I buy."

Max giggled. His chin dripped vanilla ice cream. He was a happy eight-year-old boy who thought he was on a dream vacation with his mom and his grandmother while his father stayed home to work. I wasn't going to spoil it for him, though I wondered how Andre was spending his first night of freedom. Did he have another woman in our bed? Was she the new hostess or one of the regular female customers with pouty collagen-injected lips? Would she drink my organic coffee in the morning? Would Andre make her an egg-white omelet for breakfast?

"Mom, are you crying?" Max asked, puzzled.

"Only because I am so happy to be here, with the people I love best in the world." I hugged him in a way that always embarrassed him.

"You forgot Dad," he said.

"Right. And Dad. Now let's get you in the shower and into bed. The faster you get to sleep, the faster those surf lessons will be here."

While Max was in the shower, I called Stephanie.

"Is it heaven on earth?" she asked.

"I feel like a movie star or a princess," I sighed.

"Then why do you sound so miserable?" she asked. "Zoe, put that down. Glenn, did you give her those marbles? She's too young to play with marbles. She'll swallow one. I am not being paranoid, I am being a mother," Stephanie snapped. I imagined her with the phone pressed to her ear, moving around her kitchen.

"You sound busy, we can talk tomorrow," I said.

"I would much rather hear about the Presidential Suite than deal with a husband who just gave our daughter a lethal weapon."

"A marble is not a lethal weapon." I smiled.

"It depends whose hands it is in. Why do you sound so depressed?"

"Because I miss Andre. When will I stop being in love with the stupid bastard?"

"You don't love him, Amanda. He is completely unlovable. You just lust after him. We are going to find you a new man, even if I have to fly down there and pass your cell phone number out to every man on the beach with a flat stomach and a decent head of hair."

"I don't want a new man, Stephanie," I said for the thousandth time.

"You don't know what you want. Have a shot of brandy, go to bed, and wear your new one-piece tomorrow."

"I'm going to look like a watermelon," I grumbled.

"Pink and green are *the* colors for swimwear this season. Zoe! Do not put the marble in your ear. Amanda, I have to go. I'll call you tomorrow."

I hung up the phone and took the new bathing suit out of my suitcase. I placed it on the chest of drawers and said aloud: "Okay, you and I are going to have fun."

The first two weeks of vacation passed in a blur of activity. Each day started at the beach: surfing for Max, Beach Yoga or Beach Boot Camp for me. Afterward we indulged in breakfast at the beach club: fresh strawberries with brown sugar, oatmeal pancakes, papaya juice. A couple of days we rented bicycles and explored the beach trails. One day Max convinced me to try jet skiing, which was half an hour of terror and five minutes of fun. Max often went to Kids' Club and I headed for the gym. By evening we were exhausted, sunburned, and starving. We usually ordered room service for dinner and ate it with my mother, who spent most of her time in the Presidential Suite listening to classical music in surround sound.

One night we sat on our balcony, observing a party on the Grand Lawn and sipping our cocktails. We were beginning to feel like we belonged: easing into the daily routine of life at the resort. Max drank his favorite St. Regis concoction, a Strawberry Surfrider: strawberry ice cream, milk, and a chocolate wafer shaped like a long board. My mother and I sipped Lemon Drops made exactly the way we liked them, with two olives each and a dash of salt.

"Guess what, Mom, tomorrow is the monarch butterfly release. I get to hold a butterfly."

"What fun. Who told you?" I picked at a plate of celery sticks that curled like flowers.

"Erin at Kids' Club said it's the coolest. You hold a butterfly and make a wish and then let it fly away. I know what I'm going to wish for." Max's cheeks held new freckles and his hair was bleached white by the sun.

"Well, don't tell me or it won't come true." I hoped he wished for something simple like a new surfboard or Frisbee.

"Sure it will. I wish Dad could come down and join us all summer. I want to show him I can surf." Max finished his drink and unwrapped a St. Regis mint.

"How about you, Amanda? What do you wish for?" my mother piped in. For the first time in years she did not resemble a sparrow. Her hands looked pinker without holding their habitual cigarette. She wore her hair loose at her shoulders and she had exchanged her Chanel suits for Michael Kors cotton dresses.

"I'm too old for wishes. Maybe Erin can take you and I'll go to the gym and work off tonight's dessert." Each night my mother and I tried a different dessert. I told myself I did it for her, to fatten her up. But the butterscotch sundae, the chocolate parfait, and the pecan ice cream that we had sampled were little bits of nirvana.

"Please come, Mom. Erin said they have champagne for the grown-ups and those little sandwich things without the crust."

"Max, how do you know so much? You sound like a St. Regis pro," I said with a smile.

"I think you should go," my mother chimed in. "You never know who you'll meet."

I gave my mother a look that said "not in front of Max." "How can I pass up free champagne and those sandwich things without the crusts?" I said aloud. "But afterward you spend the afternoon at Kids' Club, and I'll hide out at the gym."

"Cool. Wait till you see my butterfly. I'm going to name him before I let him go. What do you think of Oscar?"

"Sounds like a goldfish," I replied, glad that we were on to the safe subject of naming animals, always one of Max's favorite games.

"What do you think, Grandma?"

"I'll have to wait till I meet this butterfly." My mother wrapped a St. Regis cashmere blanket around her shoulders.

"You're going to come?" Max beamed.

"No, I think I'll watch from here. Come up after and tell me everything." My mother looked straight at me. Like Stephanie, she thought if I just met a new man, all my problems would disappear. Unlike Stephanie, she thought the hotel was a better place to meet men than the beach.

Each morning while Max slept, she would read the calendar of daily events and remark: "I see Morgan Stanley is in-house today." Or, "They're holding a lunch on the Grand Lawn for regional directors of Chase Manhattan." Every few days, a couple of hundred men employed by Fortune 500 companies would check in, moving in packs of dark suits and white shirts; their cell phones jammed to their ears and their laptop bags slung over their shoulders. I would pass their huddled groups when I crossed the Grand Lawn, and some of the men were cute in a clean-cut, corporate way. But I felt nothing. Even when I overheard a slow southern drawl, or a clipped Boston accent, even when I checked and they weren't wearing a wedding ring, I couldn't get myself to smile flirtatiously or nod hello. I was an asexual clod, a walking wax figure.

Andre called every night at six p.m. He purred my name when I answered the phone. "*Ma cherie,* Amanda, *je t'aime.* May I please speak to our darling Max?" The first few nights I was almost brainwashed. Andre couldn't stand to be away from us. He would appear at the double doors of the suite any minute clutching two dozen roses and a blue Tiffany box with a diamond eternity ring. After the first week, the calls grew shorter. Andre would cut Max off mid-sentence. Andre needed to take the bread out of the oven or put the finishing touch on a dessert. I realized they were "duty" calls. Andre's attorney probably told him to check in with Max every evening. He called at six p.m. so he could have the rest of his night free: to flirt with the Ross housewives who came into the restaurant on a girls' night out; or to go to one of the hip singles bars in Mill Valley and sit at the counter, waiting for the woman next to him to comment on his French accent, which was still unbearably sexy after all these years. At first he said he would be down to visit in a few days, then at the weekend, but he hadn't appeared. "The restaurant is so demanding in the summer" was his excuse to Max. I knew it was the string of women with thick lips and long legs that kept him tied up.

Max went inside to finish the game he had saved on his Wii, and my mother retreated to her bedroom to watch *The Young and the Restless,* which she had TiVo'ed. I sat on the balcony watching the party on the Grand Lawn move into full swing. A band played eighties surf tunes on a specially constructed stage. Stations of food lined each side of the lawn. Guests wearing Hawaiian shirts and Bahama shorts wafted from station to station: filling their plates with steak and shrimp and caviar. I could hear the clink of glasses, clapping, and drunken laughter.

In the morning the stage and the tables would be gone, whisked away by the hotel crew who worked all night like

Santa's elves. I wasn't ready to join the mixers or the sunset cocktail hours. I couldn't imagine strapping on sandals and spraying my wrists with Obsession to go mingle and flirt. But at least I could enjoy the fun from my balcony.

🦋 🦋 🦋

There was an excited buzz in the lobby when I took the elevator downstairs the next day. Little girls in party dresses ran in circles, and boys wearing collared shirts stood awkwardly, sipping lemonade. Gloved waiters dispensed flutes of champagne and rounds of hors d'oeuvres.

"Mom, over here." Max waved to me. He wore a St. Regis Kids' Club T-shirt and green boardshorts.

"The other boys are dressed up," I admonished him.

"They're just here for the butterfly release. We're here all summer."

"You could at least brush your hair." I ran my fingers through his hair, which had grains of sand stuck in it and was sticking straight up from his head.

"Overrated," Max scoffed and headed out to the balcony.

I grabbed a flute of champagne from a passing waiter, trying not to feel that even my son didn't need me anymore.

"Always have a bit of food when you drink champagne during the day."

I turned around, thinking it was a waiter with a plate of sandwiches, but it was a man wearing Bahama shorts and a navy ribbed sweater. He had steel-gray hair, blue eyes, and a thick jaw. His nose had a serious bump in the middle but somehow the overall effect was attractive.

"Then I would have to spend the rest of the day in the gym," I replied.

"The secret is protein. You can eat as much protein as you want and never gain an ounce." He took a steak tartar on toast from a silver tray. He had big, suntanned hands and no wedding ring.

"Eat this." He swallowed the steak in one bite. "You never gain a pound. Go with the cucumber sandwiches, it's off to the stationary bike."

"Cucumber is good for you," I said. This man was at least ten, maybe fifteen years older than me, and his body was stocky, unlike Andre, who was all long legs and slim chest. But over my flute of champagne he looked sexy in a prize-fighter kind of a way.

"Cucumber is fine, it's the slab of butter they put under it that's not. Also the white bread, nutritional value of cardboard."

"You sound like a diet book."

"I own a restaurant. I know a little about food."

"Oh, God." I choked on a strip of steak.

"Did I say something wrong?"

"You own a restaurant."

"It's not a crime. We sell seafood, not heroin." He smiled, which made his nose look more crooked.

"My husband, well, soon to be ex-husband, owns a restaurant." I wanted to bite my tongue as the words slipped out. Couldn't I have my first conversation with an attractive man without mentioning Andre?

"Is it a breakfast place that serves greasy bacon? Did you leave him because of too much fat in the diet?" We were standing in the lounge beside the twelve-foot doors that opened onto the balcony. I glanced at Max stuffing his mouth with popcorn.

"No, it was the too many women in his diet."

"Ah, sorry. Edward Jonas." He held out his hand.

"Amanda Blick." We shook hands. I remember the first night I met Andre and he kissed me on the cheek. I felt so special and sexy. I'm sure these days his first-nighters get a wet kiss on the lips. Followed by an invitation to lie down and open their legs.

"Here for the weekend?"

"For the summer."

"You picked a nice place to lick your wounds. I went through my own divorce five years ago. It seems like a rite of passage these days, like getting your first bout of acne. No one escapes it."

I relaxed and took another sip of champagne. "It hurts," I said honestly.

"It turns your life upside down and rips your heart out. I was an entertainment lawyer in Los Angeles with a home in Pasadena, a swimming pool, two great kids, and a Porsche 911."

"And?"

"All gone. The wife got the house. The kids wanted to stay with her, and who can blame them? Their first dog is buried in the garden. Their Nancy Drew and Hardy Boys mysteries are in the attic. They're both in college now but they spend their summers at home. A swimming pool is a big draw for parties."

"I take it you got the Porsche." Maybe he was another Andre in a different shape. Maybe his wife found lace panties in the passenger seat of the Porsche and kicked him out.

"I sold the Porsche to pay their tuition. Divorce destroys your wallet faster than a tsunami. Twenty years of financial planning decimated by a year of unplanned extramarital fucking." He stopped. "Sorry, not very polite of me."

"I'd love to hear someone else's war story."

"Julie and I took a trip with another partner in the firm and his wife. German guy named Jorge. Had the best manners you ever met. It was always: 'You choose the wine. Please have my seat, it has a better view.' He wore perfectly tailored suits and shirts with stiff collars. How could my wife screw someone who wore stiff collars? He was the opposite of me. Foreign, polite, and well dressed. What does that say about our whole marriage?" He stopped and swallowed a caviar ball. His face broke into a wide smile, his eyes crinkled at the corners.

"I haven't let loose like this in years. You must want to run through those doors." He nodded toward the balcony.

"No, I'm just watching my son, Max. He's waiting for a butterfly. Keep going."

"We took one of those package tours. 'Explore Down Under in Fourteen Days. See Ayer's Rock,' etc. The four of us were on a train in the middle of Australia, miles of nothing out there. I was sitting in the observation lounge reading a Dick Francis paperback when I realized I hadn't seen Julie in hours. I went back to our cabin and she wasn't there. It was a really skinny train. You were either in your cabin, the dining car, the observation lounge, or . . . it finally dawned on me, someone else's cabin. I knocked on the door of Jorge's cabin and I heard giggling, then moaning. I thought it was Jorge and his wife, Emma, but I realized I had passed her in the dining car. I knocked again, dead silence. Did they think they could jump out the window? The windows didn't even open on that train." Edward stopped and sipped a glass of water. I liked that he wasn't embarrassed.

"I waited until finally they came out of the cabin. They had all sorts of excuses. But I'd heard them."

"I saw my husband wrapped around another woman and he tried to make up a story." For the first time the image of Andre and Ursula didn't make me crumple inside.

"Adulterers live in their own fantasy world. The minute we touched ground at LAX, I filed for divorce. Apparently Jorge had been doing Julie for almost a year. I was like an emu. That's an Australian bird, like an ostrich, head in the sand."

"You can't blame yourself," I said.

"I just wonder if marriage is an outdated idea. It seems someone is always looking for a new sex partner. Sorry, I should shut up. You're young and beautiful. You'll meet a stand-up guy and get married again." He smiled.

I felt a flicker of disappointment. If I was beautiful why wasn't he interested in me? Did I have a big "damaged goods" sign on my forehead? I took a deep breath and decided to take a leap.

"I haven't even been on a date. What's the name of your restaurant? Maybe I'll take my son there."

"It's called Laguna Beach Tackle. Kind of corny, my part-ner used to be in advertising, he likes the glib stuff. Come as my guest. I'll have the chef make octopus. That will give your son something to talk about."

"We'd love to."

"Mom!" Max raced inside and thrust his hand under my nose. "Look, I've got a butterfly. What shall I name him?"

"Did you make a wish?" Edward asked him.

"How did you know about wishes?" Max asked.

"The monarch butterflies are pretty famous around here for their magical capabilities. Because of the monarchs, I just met your beautiful mother."

"Um, this is Mr. Jonas. He owns a restaurant like Dad. I thought we could eat there."

"It can't be as good." Max looked squarely at Edward, reminding me too much of Andre. "My dad makes the best fondue anywhere."

"I wouldn't want to compete. But you could try eel and octopus. When my son was your age he loved eel soaked in butter."

Max was a sucker for disgusting-sounding foods. "Okay. When will we go, Mom?"

"Tonight?" I looked at Edward. I had never set up a date in front of my son, who thought his parents were still happily married before.

"Tonight sounds great. Here's the address." Edward handed me a card. "I'm going to leave you two with your butterflies. Why don't you come around eight?"

Max dragged me onto the balcony to release his butterfly. "He flew away, Mom. So cool! I'm going to get another one."

I sat on one of the sand-colored sofas and pulled out my cell phone. "What do you wear on an almost date at a seafood restaurant?"

"What is an almost date?" Stephanie asked. Thank god Stephanie always answered her phone.

I explained about Edward.

"I can't believe your first date is with a guy who owns a restaurant."

"It's not a date. I'm going with Max, and Edward's going to be there. Though he sort of invited us. He said the chef would prepare us something special." I realized I wanted it to be a date.

"Couldn't you meet a banker or a doctor or a horse wrangler? Don't you think you've played the restaurant card?"

"He is completely different from Andre. He was married for almost twenty years and his wife cheated on him."

"Great, you can be pity partners. You need some romance. Find a Venezuelan polo player who seduces you in Spanish and leaves rose petals on your pillow."

"You haven't even seen him. He's pretty hunky," I protested. It felt nice to be interested in someone.

"Okay, go on your almost date. Wear your Stella McCartney print dress. Is he tall?"

"No, he's stocky, and for some reason I find it really sexy."

"It's probably reaction-attraction."

"What?"

"You're attracted to him because he's the opposite of Andre. It won't last."

"Since when did you become Dr. Phil? I just want to know what shoes to wear."

"Flats, obviously."

"Thanks, I'll call you tomorrow."

"Have fun, but keep your eyes open for a polo player. Or a

professional volleyball player. I bet you could find one of those on the beach."

"Bye, Stephanie." I hung up.

"Mom, I caught a butterfly for you." Max placed a butterfly on my hand. I stroked its wings. They were black and gold and smooth as velvet.

"Make a wish," Max insisted.

I held the butterfly up high and closed my eyes. I blinked and looked down at the golf course that spilled into the Pacific Ocean. The greens and blues blended together like a Monet painting. I didn't know what to wish for.

🦋 🦋 🦋

"Mom, Max and I are going out for dinner tonight." We were sitting on the deck of the suite sipping cocktails. One of my mother's biggest thrills was when the butler tapped on our door every evening at six p.m. to mix us drinks.

"How can I say no? I don't want to offend him," she demanded when I commented nightly cocktails were not going to improve her health.

"He's not going to be hurt, it's his job," I countered. The glasses he set on the sideboard—tall, frosty mimosas—accompanied by cut pineapple pieces and cantaloupe wedges, looked delicious.

"Of course he'll be offended. Rosemary has worked for me for thirty-five years and I have never sent back anything she made. You have to know how to treat staff." My mother sipped her mimosa. "Perfect. I will compliment him tomorrow."

I stopped arguing. It was lovely sitting together, watching the sun turn pink and melt into the horizon. Sinatra sang "Fly Me to the Moon" on the outdoor speakers. Max built a Lego scene of a surfer being bitten by a shark.

"Where are you going?" my mother asked.

"I met a man who owns a restaurant."

"It won't be as good as Dad's," Max piped in. "But I get to eat eel and octopus."

"You met a man who owns a restaurant?"

"Don't sound like Stephanie. Max, go put on some decent clothes and brush your hair."

"I'm building the part where the shark bites the guy's leg."

"Max, now, please."

"You met a man who owns a restaurant?" my mother repeated when Max sulked off to get dressed.

"He was very nice, he invited Max and me to come for dinner. He was an attorney for twenty years. He's only had the restaurant since his divorce."

"Sounds complicated." My mother shook her head.

"I'm not marrying him, it's not even a date. Max and I are just going out for dinner, like you want me to do."

My mother finished her drink. "I guess dating at your age isn't easy."

"Thanks. I can't win with you or Stephanie."

"Sorry, sweetheart. I'm glad you're going out. I just don't want you to get your heart broken again."

"It's not written into the creed of restaurant owners, 'Break a Woman's Heart.' He was kind of funny and sweet. I think you'd like him."

"Children?" my mother asked.

"Two in college."

"Sounds a little old for you," she said.

"It's not even a date!" I jumped up. "I have to get ready."

"I'm being nosy. Maybe run down to the salon and get a blow-dry?"

"It's not a date," I repeated, slamming the door to my room.

I kept saying it over and over as I slipped into a Stella McCartney dress and brushed my hair with a St. Regis wood hairbrush. If I didn't consider it a date I wouldn't be hurt if Edward ignored me, or worse, didn't even remember inviting us.

I looked in the mirror. The dress was deep brown, like an overripe plum. It was some weird fabric you would only find on a Stella McCartney dress, a mix of linen, silk, and a touch of spandex, so it fit snugly against my hips. I hadn't dressed to impress a man in ten years, and though I kept telling myself I was dressing for me, I wanted Edward to think I looked attractive.

I slid three gold bangles on my wrist and slipped into my favorite Coach sandals. I rubbed Bobbi Brown lip gloss on my lips and gave my hair a final brush. If I let it grow below my shoulders it became a nest of frizz, but tonight it sat smoothly on the nape of my neck.

"I can do this." I picked up the Burberry clutch, which was the closest thing I had to an evening bag, and called Max before I chickened out.

"Wow, you look nice, Mom." Max was wearing khaki pants and a white polo shirt. He had on loafers and no socks.

"You're pretty fancy yourself."

"Grandma made me wear this stuff." He shrugged. "She said I had to make a good impression."

"Anytime my beautiful daughter and her son go out to dinner they should look their best. That's just good etiquette." My mother fixed Max's collar.

"We're not going to the symphony opening."

"Max isn't even wearing socks, strictly casual. You look lovely," my mother appraised.

"Thanks, Mom. Let's go." I pushed Max out the door, feeling like I was on a prom date. Riding in the elevator, sitting in the house car that drove us to Laguna, I tried to put myself in Mother Mode: "How was Kids' Club? Are you really going to eat octopus? Get your hair out of your eyes." But I wasn't seeing Max sitting next to me in the Bentley. I wasn't even remembering the way Andre drove with one hand on the steering wheel and one hand on my thigh. I could only see the shy, nerdy twenty-two-year-old I was before I met Andre. Is that what Edward would see? Could I be someone interesting besides Andre's wife and Max's mother?

"Let us off here, please. We'll walk the rest of the way," I said to the driver when we reached the village. I didn't want to pull up in front of the restaurant in a gleaming white Bentley.

"Certainly, Mrs. Blick. I'll wait with the car. Call me when you are ready to return to the hotel." He hopped out and opened our doors. Tourists wearing souvenir T-shirts and Crocs stopped to see if we were celebrities.

"I feel like Jay-Z." Max grinned.

"I don't look like Beyoncé," I replied. The driver handed me my clutch, and I heard a woman mumble, "Who drives around in a white Bentley?" I smiled. Maybe I was a little in-teresting after all.

❦ ❦ ❦

Laguna Beach Tackle was on a street across from Main Beach, wedged between an art gallery and a cigar shop. It was a narrow space with fishing nets hanging from the ceiling. A large fish tank sat at the entrance, and a few children pressed their faces against the glass, waiting to be seated.

"Look at the fish, Mom. Do you think they scoop them out of the tank and serve them for dinner?"

I didn't answer. I nervously scanned the room for Edward. It was after eight, so he should be here. I kicked myself for not calling to confirm. What if he was in the kitchen? What if he had forgotten and was home taking a bath? I told myself to slow down. I would not be able to handle the next forty years of my single life if I could not handle one dinner out with my son.

"Party of two?" the hostess asked me. She was a pretty, blond twenty-something wearing a low-cut white blouse and a black miniskirt.

"I'm waiting for someone," I mumbled.

"Okay, let me know when you're ready." She had a sweet Southern California drawl. I resisted the urge to hate her for having perfect cheekbones and working in a restaurant.

I saw Edward leaning over a booth near the back of the restaurant. He wore a striped red polo shirt and tan pants. He said something to the guests and walked toward the front of the room. He seemed to look straight through me. I grabbed

Max and turned to the door, but then I felt his hand on my back.

"Amanda, I'm glad you came." He smiled.

"You have some cool fish." Max's nose was pressed against the tank. "Do you eat these, because if you do I want the neon purple one."

"These are just for looking, but I've asked the chef to cook you our biggest eel, extra slimy."

I exhaled. He had remembered we were coming. I tried to relax as he led us to a booth.

"I can sit with you for a few minutes, but then I'll have to work the room for a bit." Edward slid in next me. He smelled liked garlic and butter.

"Want to arm wrestle?" Max asked.

I laughed. "Max, we're at dinner."

"I arm wrestle at Dad's restaurant. Zoe and I sit in the back, I take her every time."

"You arm wrestle a girl?" Edward asked.

"She's pretty good. She does tae kwon do, too. She's an orange belt."

I exhaled again. Should I let Max keep talking? Should I try to say something funny and intelligent? No one had told me the rules of postdivorce dating because no one in Ross was divorced. I started to panic.

"I wrestled in college, so you don't want to arm wrestle me," Edward was saying to Max.

"Cool!" Edward now had two points in his favor. He knew how to cook octopus and he could wrestle. I started feeling uninteresting again.

"That's how I broke my nose." He pointed to the bump in the middle of his nose.

"Did the other guy kick you in the face?" Max asked.

"Actually he did. I didn't let my son wrestle in college. He's playing cricket."

"What college plays cricket?" I managed to get my first words into the conversation.

"He's at Wake Forest on a cricket scholarship. It's a growing sport. And the bats are made of wood, safer than baseball." He grinned.

"What's your son's name?" I asked.

"Edward, and I have a daughter named Jessica. She's a freshman at Tulane."

"But your name is Edward," Max piped in.

"I know, pretty boring, huh. It's a family name."

"Wouldn't it be funny if I was named Andre, Mom? That's my dad's name."

"I think one Andre is enough," I mumbled, picking up the menu.

"You are a credit to your mom." Edward got up. "Let me get your special order in with the chef, and if you like your eel you can go thank him yourself."

"Do you have live lobster in the kitchen? Can I throw it in a pot?"

I shook my head but Edward was laughing. He touched my arm before he walked to the front of the room to greet new diners. I practiced inhaling and exhaling. I was glad he and Max hit it off. Maybe I didn't have to be a twenty-something supermodel. Maybe I was fine just being a mom.

I was usually terrified of ordering fish, having been poked by too many tiny bones. I scanned the menu, momentarily wishing for the menu at La Petite Maison with its familiar fondues and delicious fresh breads. But then I remembered that the fondues had proven more dangerous than any fish bone, and I said firmly to the waitress: "I'll have the halibut, please, grilled with lemon and butter."

"And you, sir?" The waitress turned to Max.

"I'm having the eel," Max said proudly, like he was an explorer discovering the New World.

"That's right, Mr. Jonas already put your order in. Oh, and he wanted to give you this, compliments of the house." She placed a bottle of champagne on the table.

"For both of us?" Max asked.

"That's up to your mom." The waitress smiled.

"It's for you." Edward appeared at the table with a champagne flute. "I thought we could continue where we left off at lunchtime."

"Where was that?" Max was suddenly suspicious. No man other than Andre had ever paid me much attention.

"While you were catching butterflies I was giving your mom some nutrition tips."

"As long as she doesn't use them on me. I don't want to eat celery all day."

"That was once. I was on a celery and cabbage diet," I explained to Edward.

"Moms eat weird things." Max shook his head.

"Tell your mother she looks perfect," Edward said, pouring me a glass of champagne.

Edward didn't come back to our table, but I watched him greet other guests. I realized, sipping my champagne, that Andre's work mode at La Petite Maison had always been flirtatious, briefly touching a woman's hand, smiling at her a minute too long, seeming too interested in what she was saying. Edward's approach was neutral, businesslike. He didn't linger at any table; he spoke to the husbands in the party as much as the wives.

The waitress served Max and me our entrées and we ate them companionably. After Max ordered and polished off a bowl of vanilla ice cream, I wondered if this was the end of our evening. Edward hadn't returned to drink a glass of champagne with me or even to ask how Max liked the eel. I felt deflated. My beautiful Stella McCartney dress had not even been admired in the dim light of the restaurant. I would have to save it for another night, and probably another man.

"Would you like to meet the chef? Tell him what you think of the eel?" Edward appeared as I was paying the check.

"Sure, it was a bit lemony." Max wiped chocolate sauce from his mouth.

"Straight back through those doors." Edward touched my arm as he directed Max to the kitchen. "I wanted to get a few moments alone together to thank you for coming." He turned to me, and his face broke into the crinkly smile I remembered.

"It was delicious," I said.

"You have a great son. He's smart, and he says what he thinks." He picked up my hand, held it for a second, and then placed it back on the table.

"I'd like to see you again," he said. "Maybe we could go for a walk on the beach?"

I felt like I had passed some giant first-almost-date test. "Sure."

"Do you have your phone?"

I handed him my cell phone, an old flip phone in a purple plastic case. He punched in a phone number and pressed save. He pulled out his phone and entered my number into his contacts.

"You have an iPhone!" Max picked that moment to climb back in the booth. "Can I check out your apps?"

"Max, Edward has to work." I put my phone back in my clutch, feeling it now held special, secret information.

"I wish Mom had an iPhone, they're so cool."

"I'm an old-fashioned mom with a boring phone." I shrugged.

"I'll show you the apps next time. I have one that sounds like a dog barking. And one that shows you how to build a robot." Edward slipped his phone into his pocket.

"Told you, Mom; you should get one," Max persisted.

"You have enough gadgets, and I use my phone for talking." I got up, tugging at my dress so it didn't show my upper thighs.

"Thank you for inviting us." Max stuck out his hand.

"Thank you for coming. Next time you'll have to try the octopus." Edward shook his hand.

Edward held my arm as we maneuvered through the room.

When we reached the front door he moved his hand to the small of my back.

"Can I walk you to your car?" Edward opened the door. The outside air smelled like sand and suntan lotion.

"It's okay, we got a driver waiting in a Bentley," Max piped in.

"A Bentley." Edward laughed. "I can't compete with that."

❦ ❦ ❦

We walked around the corner and I called the driver.

"Thanking Edward was very polite. I'm proud of you," I complimented Max, as we waited for the Bentley.

"Grandma said she'd pay me five dollars if I used good manners," Max replied.

"That's a good way to get rich." I shook my head.

"I think you should get an iPhone. Erin at Kids' Club has one. I can play 'Chopsticks' on it." Max climbed into the leather seat of the Bentley.

"Erin should be taking you to the beach to look at tide pools," I said, but I sounded stodgy even to myself. I would put "get an iPhone" on my list. I had already accomplished the first thing on my list—notice attractive men—so who knew what I could do next?

❦ ❦ ❦

After Max had gone to bed and my mother had grilled me about our evening, I went into my room and put on a fluffy white St. Regis robe. I stood at the mirror and coated my face with age-defying night cream. The maids had turned down the bed and there was a tray on the comforter with a jug of springwater and a wrapped chocolate shaped like a butterfly. I climbed into bed and closed my eyes. I didn't call Stephanie to discuss the nuances of Edward placing his hand on my back but not kissing me on the cheek good night. For the first time since Black Tuesday, I just wanted to savor the feeling of being alone but not lonely.

The next morning I did Beach Boot Camp. I ran a mile alongside a small army of Botoxed women and did extra lunges to compensate for last night's champagne. I tried to keep alive the feeling of well-being I had gone to bed with. But Andre intruded on my thoughts. I remembered how he would stroke my naked breasts when I climbed into bed and purr, "I am so lucky, *ma belle cherie.*" Had he used the same line on Ursula and Bella? I made myself do one hundred sit-ups and fifty crunches. I figured eventually physical pain would blur the images that filled my brain.

After class I sat at the counter in the Beach Club and read the menu. Max was out surfing and I contemplated ordering eggs Benedict or Belgian waffles. It was Sunday. I deserved one day off from grapefruit and granola. My phone buzzed. I had two unread texts. The first was from Stephanie, demanding to know all the details of my date with "the old divorced guy who owns a restaurant." I pressed delete. She would think it was a "nonevent." "A guy his age makes a move on the first date, at least a kiss on the cheek. He just asked for your number to be polite. Forget him, find some young hunk." I could hear her voice in my head. The second text was from an unfamiliar number. I read, "Beach walk tonight? Don't have Bentley but can pick you up in Mini. E."

I looked at the phone. When I dated Andre, texting didn't exist. Shouldn't Edward call to ask me out? I took a breath and texted him back. "No Bentley needed. Would love beach walk. What time?"

The phone beeped in my hand. "Six pm so we can see sunset. Meet you in lobby."

"Lobby great. See you then." I hit send and picked up the menu. I ordered an egg-white omelet and waited for Max.

"Mom, I stood up for five minutes." Max ran into the club, covered in sand and grinning from ear to ear.

"Fantastic." I smiled. "Have a seat, I just ordered."

"I'm starving. Can I get Belgian waffles?" Max asked. He shook the sand out of his hair and sat on the stool next to me.

"Sure. If I can't have them, I can watch you enjoy yours," I said.

"That was the longest I ever stood up, I can't wait to tell Dad." Max shook the last of the sand onto the counter. "Can I have your phone?"

"Sure, hold on." I erased the texts. I never kept secrets from Max. This new world of being single was full of minefields.

"I want to call Dad and tell him." He pressed the speed dial. "He didn't pick up," Max said eventually.

"Try him again. Sometimes Dad doesn't hear it when he's at the restaurant."

Max tried again but it went to voice mail. I could see the hurt in his eyes that he couldn't tell his dad his big accomplishment. I wanted to grab him and run for the plane and back to Andre so we could be a family. I wanted to stop not knowing where my husband was, stop texting new men, stop worrying about how I looked in a one-piece. I wanted to put our life back the way it was before Max discovered it was different.

"Hey, can I go to Kids' Night Out tonight? We get to watch a movie on the lawn and then make s'mores." Max doused his waffles in syrup.

"Sounds great." I took small bites of my omelet. It tasted like paper, but it wouldn't make my stomach stick out in my bathing suit. I listened as Max babbled on about waxing his surfboard. I realized I couldn't get on a plane because the Andre I knew wouldn't be waiting for me at SFO. It would be the Andre who screwed other women, the Andre who was too busy doing God knows what to answer the phone when his son called mid-morning. At least if Max was at Kids' Night Out, he wouldn't wonder what I was doing. I was going to wear my new Theory tunic dress and watch the sunset with Edward.

My mother, of course, wanted to know exactly where I was going, why my date wasn't coming up to our suite to collect me, and why he was taking me for a walk on the beach instead of out to dinner.

"Mom, I'm a soon-to-be-divorced woman. Edward doesn't

have to get my mother's approval." I stood at the bathroom mirror, fiddling with my earrings. Erin had picked up Max at five p.m., and I had spent the last hour deciding what accessories worked with my dress. I was determined not to call Stephanie for advice. I had to start making my own wardrobe decisions. My mother stood behind me, sipping her dry martini.

"You can't wear pearls for a walk on the beach. If he had invited you to the theater or to a restaurant, you could wear pearls. The only earrings you can wear for the beach are coral," she muttered. My mother disapproved of a date that didn't include cocktails and dinner.

"There's not a lot of theater in Laguna Beach. And honestly, I'm sick of restaurants. Please don't judge Edward without meeting him."

"That's the point." She finished her martini and set the glass down on the marble counter. "You won't let me meet him." She took a brush and brushed my hair with long strokes. I had spent a lot of time on my makeup. My cheeks were bronze and my eyelashes were fat with ultra-thick mascara I had discovered at the spa. The woman in the spa boutique showed me how a smudge of pale pink eye shadow made my eyes looked greener. If I could tame my hair, which frizzed like a halo around my head, I would like my own reflection.

"I don't want him to be intimidated by the Presidential Suite. You should have seen his face when Max told him we had a driver and a Bentley." I rubbed lip gloss on my lips.

"You have to stop being embarrassed by your money. You don't want another Andre situation."

"My 'Andre situation' was caused by his ridiculous sense of entitlement. As in 'this is my restaurant and I am entitled to fuck every woman who works for me.'" I saw her flinch. "Sorry, Mom. But you'd be surprised how swearing can clear my head."

"Swear all you want, honey. I just don't think you should hide your wealth. It's part of who you are. I don't want you to get hurt again."

"Money isn't a coat of armor, Mom. And Edward was an attorney for twenty years. He lived in Pasadena and is putting two kids through college. He's nothing like Andre."

"You'll have to bring him up here so I can see for myself." She blotted my lip gloss with a tissue and hugged me. "You deserve someone who treats you like a princess."

"I will, I promise." I slipped on the flip-flops with two-inch heels I had bought at the gift shop.

"Your father always treated me like a queen." My mother went to the bar and poured herself another martini.

"I'll see if I can find a dragon for Edward to slay."

"Funny. Do you want me to have room service send up a boxed dinner?"

"I'm not even hungry." I kissed her cheek. "I'll see you in a few hours."

I admired my dress in the elevator mirror. It was navy with a crisp white collar and a wide white belt. I looked everything I didn't feel: tall, tan, confident. My phone buzzed. I flipped it open; it was Andre with his six p.m. duty call. I pressed ignore and put it back in my purse. For once, he could see what it felt like when his wife and son didn't answer.

A three-piece band played in the lobby. Guests sat at candlelit tables nibbling pistachios. I didn't see Edward, and I stood at the bar wondering if I should calm my nerves with a drink.

He tapped my shoulder. "It seems I'm always sneaking up behind you." He was wearing a short-sleeved shirt with a sea-shell pattern, brown linen pants, and deck shoes. His gray hair was slicked to one side with gel.

"Hopefully not with more nutrition tips. I did Beach Boot Camp this morning and had an egg-white omelet for break-fast." I was an inch taller than him in my new flip-flops.

"Then you will be suitably hungry for this." He held up a large wicker picnic basket. Purple grapes were wedged be-tween a bottle of wine and a loaf of bread. I could see a round of cheese, a jar of olives, and a small tin of caviar.

"I thought we were just going to watch the sunset."

"Sunsets can last awhile. The moon rising is going to be pretty special tonight, too. But maybe you can use your influ-ence here and score us a couple of glasses and a knife. I forgot utensils."

I leaned over the bar and asked the bartender for glasses. I was touched by his gift, and by the fact he admitted to for-getting silverware. During our entire marriage, Andre had never admitted to making a mistake. He even believed screwing other women wasn't his fault. He was just being "French."

Edward lugged the picnic basket outside and we waited for the tram to take us to the beach. I couldn't help noticing how defined his muscles were on his upper arms. I never dated an athlete, except for one stringy long jumper in high school. Andre possessed a beautiful body but he didn't play sports.

"Tram's here; after you." Edward broke into my thoughts.

We squeezed next to another couple on the tram, our thighs and arms smashed against each other. Suddenly I felt trapped by the closeness of his body. I wasn't ready for this, I didn't want this. The driver prattled on about the tides and I leaned out of the tram, sucking in big gulps of salt air. By the time the tram pulled up at the beach I felt like a wilted lettuce leaf that had been in the salad spinner too long. I wanted to go home.

But then Edward got up and held out his hand to help me out. He kept my hand lightly in his as we walked onto the sand. He joked that last time he was on a surfboard it was ten feet long and made of wood. It was nice standing together, watching the sun peel over the horizon. There was something about his solid body, his slightly crooked nose, his gray hair and blue eyes that made me feel safe.

"You're tricky to shop for." He set the picnic basket down and produced a striped beach towel. "I had to stay away from French cheese and French wine. You'll have to settle for a Napa Valley chardonnay and a Dutch camembert."

"I'm not allergic to all French things, just French husbands." I watched him put the ingredients of our feast on the towel. He laid out sliced peaches, chocolate truffles, and a can of whipped cream.

"Remember, I've been through the big D. Every time I heard an ad to 'put a shrimp on the barbie' I wanted to stab someone with barbecue tongs. Anything that reminded me of our trip to Australia made me crazy."

"Well, I love Dutch cheese. But what is the whipped cream for?"

"Food fight. If we run out of conversation we can turn it on each other and spray." He grinned.

"You have very refined dating habits." I laughed. I took my flip-flops off because they were digging in between my toes.

"I learned them from my son. That's the beauty of having children. They grow up and teach you all sorts of things: how to create PDF files and use Zip drives and manage five hundred apps on my iPhone."

"I got a lot of heat for not having an iPhone." I pulled my hair into a ponytail and plopped down on the towel. I took off my belt, rolled it up, and put it in my purse. Suddenly I felt overdressed. At least I hadn't worn pearls.

"Sometimes I think we're all too plugged in. If I can see the ocean, I'm pretty happy." He handed me a glass of chardonnay.

"Thanks." I took a sip. "My parents and I used to spend every July in Hawaii. I was the Royal Hawaiian sand castle champion."

"A woman who enjoyed her childhood. Pretty rare these days." He sat opposite me and cut thick slices of bread.

"I adored my parents and they worshipped each other. Max is not going to have that."

"It's not your fault. My kids knew it was over between Julie and me when we opened the front door. The air changes, you can't hide it."

"I feel like I'm half of something that doesn't exist anymore." I sifted sand through my toes. I hadn't wanted to talk about divorce, I wanted to impress him with my knowledge of literature or art or travel. But he was so easy to talk to. Being with Edward was like rubbing a magic bottle and having a middle-aged genie pop out.

"You'll become a new something. Look at me; forty-eight years old, living in an artsy beach town, part owner of a tacky tourist restaurant. Ten years ago I sweated every day trying to reach my goals by age forty: make a half mil a year, represent the biggest stars in Hollywood, guarantee my kids a golden future, and kill at tennis at the country club."

"It's not a tacky restaurant."

"It's not Wolfgang Puck's. Divorce makes you look at the now: What am I doing every day that makes me feel good?"

"Life isn't just about feeling good," I said. I felt a little prickly. Andre's life was about squeezing big breasts and tight asses; things that made him feel good and made me feel like shit.

"Of course it isn't. It's about taking care of your kids and separating bottles and cans in the recycling bin and giving jobs to the people who don't have any. But it's also about creating your own happiness. You have to be your own best friend."

"I guess I don't want me as a best friend at the moment. I'm a bit of a loser." I stuffed a piece of bread in my mouth and hoped the soft cheese would glue it shut. I hadn't meant to say that.

Edward put down his wineglass and sat next to me. He waited till I swallowed and then he took my head in his hands and kissed me on the lips. He tasted dry and sweet like the wine. He kissed me for a long time, as if he was trying to discover something or erase something. Then he put his hand under my chin and tipped my face up to him.

"You are a gorgeous woman with a fantastic kid and a Bentley that waits at street corners. I don't see loser written anywhere. What did you want to do before you married the dickhead?"

"I wanted to go to Parsons and be a fashion designer. But then my dad got cancer and I went to Berkeley instead. I met Andre right after I graduated and my dad died. I liked being Andre's wife and Max's mother. I love the town we live in. I love the school, and the lake, and the post office where everyone picks up their mail every day."

"It's all still there. Minus the dickhead."

"Ross is a family place: two parents, two-point-two kids, one big dog, and a couple of bikes per household. I don't think I'd fit in."

"Then try somewhere new. Go to New York and be a fashion designer."

"I'm too old."

"How old are you? Thirty? You look like the kids I see on campus when I visit my son. I'm old enough to be a grandfather and I started over."

I played miserably with the sand. Tears formed in my eyes and I stared at the blanket, willing them to go away. It had felt good when Edward kissed me; it had felt like the tenuous start of something new. But now I felt like an infant.

Edward put his arms around me. He held me quietly until I stopped shaking. After a while he turned me toward him and kissed me again. This time I summoned all my dormant sexuality and kissed him back. I tasted his mouth and his tongue, I stroked his hair. I let his hands travel down my back and rest on my waist.

"I'm sorry," he said finally.

"For what?"

"Life postdivorce is a roller coaster. You don't have to be ready for new things or new places."

"I'm ready to eat cheese and drink wine. And I might even be ready for a food fight." I picked up the can of whipped cream and squeezed it into my mouth. Then I leaned forward and kissed him wetly on the lips. I could see the surprise in his eyes. I was surprised, too. Maybe I could do this. Maybe I could learn to enjoy being a woman.

The rest of the night went better. Edward told me funny stories of tourists who came into the restaurant. I wrote out my favorite pumpkin cheesecake recipe on a napkin and he promised to give it to his chef. We discovered we both liked reading Dean Koontz, listening to Jay-Z, and watching Austin Powers movies. I even made a mini sand castle with the empty caviar tin and olive jar. When we finally folded the blanket, and I slipped on my flip-flops and shook my hair out of its ponytail, it was past ten p.m.

"I enjoy being with you," Edward said, putting his arm around me as we waited for the tram.

I snuggled next to him and wondered what happened next. Should I invite him to the suite for a nightcap? Should I kiss him good-bye in the lobby? What if someone saw me? I was *Mrs.* Blick to all the employees.

The tram picked us up and drove back up the hill to the hotel. As we climbed I felt less the wanton woman on the beach and more the awkward almost-single mother. By the time we reached the lobby, I regretted kissing him. What if Edward thought I was a cheap hussy? I certainly wasn't ready to have sex with him. The thought of seeing a new man naked made me want to crawl into my old princess bed and pull the covers over my eyes.

"My son and daughter are staying next week. Would you and Max like to come over for a barbecue?"

"Yes, sure," I replied quickly before I got nervous and backed out.

"How about Thursday night? I'll meet you guys in the lobby around five p.m. If you're comfortable driving in the Mini." He grinned.

"Max thinks they are the coolest thing since Matchbox cars. There's only one problem."

"I promise my house is perfectly safe. No drugs, no Great Danes, no restaurant mafia. I actually have a view of the ocean and a Jacuzzi."

"It's my mother. I promised I would introduce you to her."

"So I have to meet the San Francisco society queen before I can have her daughter and grandson over for dinner?" He was smiling. "I could invite her, too."

"No." I shook my head vigorously. All I needed was my mother critiquing Edward for a full evening. "She doesn't really like to leave the resort. How about if you pick us up from the suite. We can have a drink before we go."

"A cocktail in the Presidential Suite of the St. Regis. I think

I can handle that." He put his hands on my shoulders and kissed me lightly on the mouth.

"I'll see you on Thursday."

🦋 🦋 🦋

I snuck into the hotel lobby, wishing I were invisible. Would the concierge wonder why my hair was messed up? Could the elevator boy smell the blend of alcohol and aftershave on my skin? If I was worried about what the hotel employees would think, I shrank from what my mother would say. She wanted me to find a new man, but she was old-fashioned enough to expect at least a monthlong courtship before I pecked him a kiss good night.

I slipped into the lobby powder room to smooth my hair. What had come over me? Did I just want to prove to Andre I was still desirable? I took my phone out of my purse and checked for missed calls. Three calls from Stephanie and none from Andre. He had made his six p.m. duty call and was offline for the evening. I called Stephanie. I felt like a fourteen-year-old who had just finished her first petting session with the school quarterback. I needed her advice, or I'd sit in the powder room and write "Amanda Loves Andre, Amanda Loves Edward" on the St. Regis notepads.

"Finally," Stephanie answered the phone. "I thought you'd sailed off to Fiji."

"I went out with Edward and we made out. Am I a tramp?" I blurted out.

"Calm down. It would take a lot more than one make-out

session to turn you into a tramp. Start from the beginning and tell me everything."

"Edward asked me to go for a walk on the beach tonight. He brought a picnic basket and we laid down a blanket and watched the sunset. But then we started talking about divorce and my nonexistent future and I started crying and he kissed me, and I kissed him back."

"That's it?" Stephanie asked.

"I wanted to be sophisticated and sexy and I acted like a teenager."

"Is he a good kisser?"

"Yes." I remembered how nice it felt when he held my head in his hands.

"And do you like talking to him?"

"Yes."

"So you spent the evening with a man you find attractive, though I don't know why, who's nice to be with and a good kisser. I don't see the problem."

"Oh." Stephanie made me feel like a child, but in a good way. It was like she wrote my problems down in big letters on a chalkboard and if I studied them one by one they weren't that bad.

"I'm assuming while you were locking lips with your middle-aged divorcé you weren't thinking about Andre. That's progress. But are you sure you don't want to take that pent-up sexual energy and use it on a hard-body surfer? Get the *I Am Woman* sex out of your system. It's the only way to move forward."

"Who says?"

"Oprah, Dr. Phil. You've been royally screwed over. I think

dating someone who's been damaged is going to be a summer-long pity party."

"He's not like that. Edward was a wrestler in college. I'm attracted to him, but it's not painful like it was with Andre. My body doesn't collapse with longing when I see him. He's funny, and he has two kids in college so he's pretty hip. He invited Max and me to his house next week to meet his kids."

"Take a picture of him with your phone. I'm glad you're getting out there but don't beat yourself up."

"How's Ross?" I changed the subject.

"Hasn't changed a leaf. The town is getting ready for its blowout July Fourth parade. Zoe is excited because she gets to ride her bike this year. All the way from Woodlands Market to the commons."

"I wish Max was riding next to her." All of a sudden, the tears started. "I want to come home, Stephanie. I miss it all so much."

"Oh, honey. I wish I could be there to give you a hug. I mean, I really wish I could be there. I spent the day washing supposedly erasable crayon from the breakfast room wall. Followed by a family evening of watching *Dancing with the Stars*. Glenn fell asleep before the first commercial, and Zoe insisted I tuck her into bed during my favorite part. Where are you again? At the St. Regis drinking Lemon Drops and frolicking on the sand."

"I want Andre and my life back." I couldn't stop crying.

"I know you do, sweetie. Hang in there. Glenn just woke up from his coma and wants me to go upstairs. Maybe I'll get lucky tonight, God knows it's been a while. I'll talk to you in the morning."

I hung up and looked at myself in the powder room mirror. For a minute I didn't recognize the blotchy face with smeared mascara. I tried washing my face and brushing my hair, but I decided to curl up on the lounge and cry some more.

Chapter Five

I woke the next morning with a throbbing headache. The mix of chardonnay and caviar had left a jackhammer in my head. I couldn't tell how late it was because the shutters in the suite were closed. I fumbled for my phone to check the time. I had two missed texts from Edward. The first read: "Good morning, sunshine." The second: "Tell Max barbecuing ostrich meat, Thursday night." I texted him back: "Had fun. Max will be thrilled." I put the phone down, pulled the goose-down comforter up to my chin, and went back to sleep.

Max was already at Kids' Club when I opened the door to the living room. I had showered and put on my most conservative Ella Moss sundress. It was yellow with puffy little-girl sleeves. I tied my hair in a bun and wore my Tiffany heart necklace. I wanted to prove to my mother, and maybe to myself, that I was still a respectable married matron.

"How was your evening? You got back so late I didn't wait up," my mother said in a deceptively neutral tone.

"I sat in the lobby talking to Stephanie on the phone. She keeps calling and I haven't returned her calls."

"Really," my mother said.

"Really," I replied.

"How is Edward?" my mother tried again.

I poured myself a cup of coffee from the silver coffeepot. I put some grapes, kiwi, and cantaloupe on a plate, and took two bites of a blueberry muffin while I decided how to answer my mother.

"We had a lovely time. He brought a picnic basket with caviar and camembert and a delicious chardonnay." I knew she would be impressed. My mother loved caviar almost as much as chocolate.

"It's hard to enjoy a good chardonnay unless it is adequately chilled," she replied.

I put down my coffee cup and laughed. "Mom, I know this is hard for you, but it's hard for me, too. I haven't dated since senior year in high school, and that was with Jerome Baskin. You forced me to go to the prom with him because his mother was on the board at the Asian Art Museum."

"I didn't force you, Amanda. I thought he would be a suitable date. You had an interest in Japanese design and so did he. Plus he had that head of beautiful curly blond hair. You looked so cute together."

"Yes, well, 'looking cute together' hasn't done very well for me. I'm going to try to stay away from 'cute' and look for 'mature' and 'faithful.'"

My mother hugged me. She was wearing a vintage Diane von Furstenberg wrap dress and her "daytime" pearls. Even though she never ventured farther than the Grand Lobby, she was always perfectly dressed and coiffed.

"You can have both. The first time I saw your father I thought I was looking at Cary Grant." She smiled. "He breezed into the Opera House wearing white tie and tails, like he just stepped off the set of *Philadelphia Story*."

My parents had been huge movie buffs. They were regulars at the Presidio Theater and often watched a double feature: *Vertigo* and *North by Northwest*, *Rebecca* and *How to Catch a Thief*. For special occasions, they would take me to Ernie's Restaurant for dinner, and point to the autographed photos of Cary Grant, Grace Kelly, and Alfred Hitchcock that lined the walls. Gary Cooper and Gregory Peck were my mother's idols, and she made me watch *Breakfast at Tiffany's* three times to learn how to accessorize a little black dress.

"Well, I didn't do so well going that route." I sipped the black coffee. It was very strong, like a shot of petroleum. "Do you think I should have waited to get married?" I felt my heart beat faster. I didn't want to ask the question out loud, because I wasn't sure I wanted to hear the answer. But it had been spinning around in my head for days. Had I been too impetuous? Should I have gone to New York and had a career? Would Andre have respected me more and remained faithful?

"I have plenty of friends who waited and then married the first man they met at the Valentine's Ball, when they thought their eggs were getting old. Some of them made happy marriages, others didn't. Waiting doesn't guarantee you'll find the right man."

"But maybe I would have figured out who was the wrong man." I nibbled a wedge of ripe cantaloupe.

"You married for the same reason I did: for love." My mother stood by the door to the balcony, breathing in the ocean air. "I married your father after six weeks. We didn't know each other at all."

"Then how come it worked for you?"

"Sometimes you meet the man you can't not marry. When your father asked me to marry him, I tried to picture life without him. I didn't know his favorite dessert, or the name of his first dog, but I couldn't imagine not talking to him every evening, not seeing the way he smiled when I dropped by his office with an éclair. I had to marry him."

"That's the way I felt," I said with a sigh.

"I know, I saw it when you and Andre were together," my mother agreed.

"But Dad worshipped you. I never saw him dance with another woman at any of your parties!" I could feel the powder on my cheeks cracking.

"Honey, the most gorgeous women in Hollywood have been cheated on. It has nothing to do with you. Andre had a lot of strong points. He is charming and he is a very good father. You couldn't know he'd be unfaithful. In some ways, I blame myself."

"What do you mean?" I asked.

"Your father believed you didn't have to be born into society to act like a gentleman, so I didn't worry about you picking your husband from our social circle."

I rolled my eyes, remembering the debutante balls and winter formals I had been subjected to as a teenager. My parents may not have insisted I marry within our circle, but I didn't have much opportunity to meet anyone else till I got to college. Every boy I knew growing up wore Brooks Brothers shirts on the weekend and was a member of the yacht club or the golf club.

"But maybe after your father died, I didn't pay close enough attention. I didn't dig too deep to see what Andre was about," she said slowly.

"I think Andre is pretty much surface," I replied miserably. "He lets a certain body part do his thinking."

"From now on I'm going to be more vigilant."

"Edward invited Max and me to his house for dinner, Thursday night." Thinking about Andre made me nauseous.

"How are you going to explain that to Max?" my mother asked, turning back into the living room.

"Edward's kids are home from college. I'll say it will be nice for him to meet other kids."

"Max is eight. He's hardly ready to hang out with college freshmen." My mother shook her head.

"Edward is barbecuing ostrich meat. You know how Max likes eating strange animals." I smiled. "And I invited Edward up for a cocktail when he picks us up."

"So I can meet him." My mother nodded.

"Yes, though I don't know why. We're only here for the summer and I'm not even divorced yet. I don't think you have to ask him what his intentions are."

"I wasn't planning on it. I just don't want you to get hurt again. So soon."

"I love you for caring. At least someone cares about me." I put my plate on the sideboard and checked my makeup in the full-length mirror that rested against the wall.

"Andre called last night," my mother said.

"Called where?"

"Called the suite. He said he tried your cell phone but you didn't answer."

"What did he want?"

"Said how much he misses Max, asked about my health, cooed he couldn't wait for his *petite* family to return home."

"He could fly down and tell us himself except he's probably got a new bird on his arm, and in his bed."

"He isn't worth thinking about." My mother poured herself a glass of orange juice.

"No, he's not. Can I interest in you in a ladies' lunch at the Pool Grille?"

"Thanks, honey. I'm going to stay here and have room service deliver a Cobb salad."

"I know you, Mom. You just want to turn on last night's *American Idol* after I leave."

"If I do, you'll never know." She kissed me on the cheek.

My phone rang as I stepped off the elevator.

"Good morning, sunshine. How did you sleep?" It was Edward.

"Like someone who drank too much wine. But I had a lovely time last night, thank you."

"I went to the butcher this morning and ordered ostrich meat. I think Max will be impressed."

"He'll be thrilled," I agreed.

"What are your plans today?"

"A tough day of dining by the pool and working out at the gym," I said.

"Well, I just wanted to tell you it was a fun evening."

"It was," I replied.

"I have to get to work. I'll see you on Thursday."

I hung up and headed to the pool patio. My plan had been to read *The Wall Street Journal* and *The New York Times*. I wanted to take my mind off men and see what was happening in the world. After lunch, I would pick Max up from Kids' Club and have a mother/son afternoon doing whatever he wanted. But after I collected the papers and took a seat at the patio I thought about Edward. He sounded so mature and confident on the phone. And there was Andre, asking my mother in his super-sexy voice when were we coming home. The waiter approached to take my order, and I realized I hadn't opened the paper but had scribbled "Amanda and Edward, Amanda and Andre" in the margin on the front page. I ordered a spinach salad, opened *The Wall Street Journal,* and studied the economic crisis in Dubai until my eyes hurt.

The week passed in a pleasant resort cycle of pool, spa, gym, cocktails, dinner. Max was obsessed with surfing and at dinner recounted how many minutes he had stood up that day. It was always three or four amazing minutes more than the day before. My mother had discovered *The Amazing Race* and *American Idol,* and for someone who had never turned on the television except for CNN's six o'clock news and her lifelong *Young and the Restless* addiction, showed no shame in watching them.

"Your father would have liked Simon Cowell. He has passion, and that gorgeous accent." She huffed when I asked her to turn it off. I'd go onto the deck and look down at the Grand Lawn, cursing our fatal attraction to men with sexy foreign accents.

Edward called or texted me several times a day. It was wonderful to flip open my phone and read his funny texts: "250-pound tourist just ordered cheesecake. Thankfully not wearing swimsuit." Our phone calls were brief and mildly flirtatious. I impressed myself with my own playful comments. I bought a copy of *Cosmopolitan* at the gift shop and read articles on "Kissing for the Modern Woman" and "Make Your Man Happy Without Making Yourself Miserable." I giggled when I flipped the pages. Edward was almost fifty and I looked nothing like the models displayed in lacy underwear in the magazine. But it felt good to have a little fun, and when Andre made his six p.m. duty calls sometimes I answered and sometimes I didn't. That little bit of power was thrilling.

Thursday afternoon I panicked. What was I thinking introducing Edward to my mother? What if Edward put his arm around me or kissed me in front of Max? And the realization that tied my stomach in knots: My marriage was really over. I'm dating another man.

I closed the door to my bathroom, turned on the Jacuzzi jets, and sunk into the bath. After a half hour under the jets, I emerged with my best imitation of a *Cosmopolitan*-reading woman. I had no one and nothing to fall back on. I didn't have a career; I didn't own my own house. And I certainly didn't have a loyal husband I was leaving in my wake. I had to move forward, and that included meeting new people and having new experiences. I wrapped myself in a king-sized bath towel, put on a Jason Mraz CD, and inspected the collection of lotions and perfumes.

When I was sufficiently lathered in seaweed skin moisturizer, goat's milk and honey face cream, and almond foot soother, I approached my closet. Inspired by the women who roamed the hotel wearing colorful silk dresses and delicate gold sandals, I was regaining my love of fashion. I flicked through my Theory burnt-orange minidress, my Juicy velour jumper, and my wildly patterned Pucci wrap, which I had purchased in the lobby boutique, and wondered what was best suited to a home barbecue. Edward's daughter was probably madly fashionable growing up in Pasadena. I chose the Pucci—its silk pattern was so beautiful I could spend hours staring at it—and added a turquoise bangle and a chunky necklace.

When I appeared in the living room, I could tell by Max's expression I had erased the "Ross Mom" for the evening.

"Wow, Mom. Are we going to the circus?" Max looked up from his Nintendo DS.

"Excuse me?" I smiled.

"Your dress has so many colors," he explained.

"That dress is Pucci, young man. And your mother

looks gorgeous. Like a young Sophia Loren," my mother chimed in.

"Who?" Max asked.

"Hardly Sophia Loren, Mom. I have a stick figure and she was an hourglass goddess. Though my stomach does have a bit of a paunch and I guess my skin is fairly brown."

"You look wonderful. And I love the jewelry. The turquoise brings out the blues and greens in the dress." My mother appraised me the way she used to when I went to junior deb parties.

"The dress is pretty," Max conceded.

"And you look dashing." I kissed his cheek. "Ready to try ostrich meat?"

"I hope they have a Wii," Max said.

"Edward said he does. He said his son has ExtremeSport and Rock Band 2."

"Awesome." Max's face lit up.

The doorbell rang and my mother opened the door. Edward handed a bouquet of white lilies to my mother.

"Amanda told me you won't be joining us, so these are for you," he said as he stepped inside. Tonight he wore long pants and a button-up silk shirt. On his arm he wore a gold watch I hadn't seen before.

"How very kind, I love lilies," my mother said and beamed. As she passed me to put the flowers in water, I could smell Chanel No. 5. I remembered how Andre always used to bring her presents: Belgian chocolate and colorful organic vegetables.

"Hey, Max. My kids can't wait to meet you." Edward shook Max's hand.

"I'm going to rule at ExtremeSport." Max grinned.

"Are you going to help me marinate some ostrich?" Edward asked.

"Why ostrich exactly?" my mother asked.

"Amanda said Max is a connoisseur of exotic foods. I'm trying to impress him." Edward smiled.

My mother handed him a drink and I went to my room to get my purse. Edward looked older, closer to my mother's age, than he seemed before. I fumbled to put my phone in my purse and tried to shake off my confusion. *Cosmopolitan* said older men were sexy because they "treated women with more respect than their younger counterparts." That could only be a good thing.

"Edward used to play at Trump National Golf Course when he lived in Pasadena. We had friends who belonged there. Your father loved that course," my mother said when I walked back to the living room.

"Golf is boring. Do you ski?" Max asked.

"Max," I admonished him.

"'Fraid not. My knees can't take skiing anymore. My daughter's an ace skier."

"I'm hungry," Max announced.

I waited for Edward and my mother to finish their drinks. I was used to my mother and Andre chatting over a cocktail, and Andre and Max lounging about together. How did people get divorced? Could you really just slide Andre out of the picture and stick a new man in his place? But then I remembered how Andre had lived in his own parallel universe, where he chased everything in a skirt. Edward caught my eye and winked at me.

"We better go. I don't want Max to fill up on pretzels."
I removed the plate of pretzels and nuts that lived on the coffee table.

"But I'm hungry," Max complained.

Edward put his drink down and shook my mother's hand.
"Pleasure meeting you, Mrs. Bishop."

"Grace, please."

"I hope you will join us for dinner next time."

"Maybe in the St. Regis Grille," my mother said with a
nod.

Edward, Max, and I took the elevator downstairs. Max
and Edward chatted about Wii games. I looked at myself in the
elevator mirror. My mother was right. The turquoise necklace
and bangle did bring out the colors in my dress. I resolved I
was going to enjoy myself.

"Man, this car is cool!" Max beamed when he saw Edward's
yellow Mini parked outside the hotel.

"It's not a Porsche, but I'm pretty fond of it," Edward said.

"How fast can it go? Can it do a loop-de-loop?" Max
asked as he climbed into the backseat.

"I don't think so, but I haven't tried." Edward got behind
the wheel.

"It does resemble Max's matchbox cars," I said as I slid into
the passenger seat.

"I'm sure the manufacturers considered that." Edward
put the car in first gear. "For all the little boys who never
grew up. Or for the ones who grew up, had the Jeep, then the

sports car, and lost them in the divorce. That would be me."
He laughed.

"I like it," I said. I was reminded how I liked that Edward
could joke about divorce.

"Sometimes I feel like I'm twelve when I'm driving it. But
I don't need a big car. It's just me most of the time. I'm happy
you're in it." He placed his hand on my thigh.

"Max, would you like to play with my phone?" Edward
took his hand off my thigh and reached into his pocket.

"Cool." Max grabbed the iPhone in its green plastic case.

"Careful with it," I said.

"That thing is pretty indestructible with the case on. Maybe
you can show me some new apps," Edward said.

With Max enraptured by the iPhone, Edward put his
hand back on my thigh and we gunned down Pacific Coast
Highway. The ocean on our left was the palest blue, calm like
a giant bath. Edward and I chatted about his kids and the
restaurant. My earlier awkwardness dissolved and I felt sexy
sailing along PCH in a cute car with a man who was obviously interested in me.

I wondered if there was any way we could sneak away
tonight. I wanted to feel Edward's hands behind my head.
Stephanie would laugh that I was behaving like a sex-starved
teenager. But I had always liked sex. Andre and I spent many
afternoons in bed while Max was at school, and I often waited
up for him so we could make love before we went to sleep.
I pretended to look in my purse for something so Edward
could not see me blush. I reminded myself I was not ready for
sex with someone new, and then for one long minute I missed
Andre all over again.

We drove through the village of Laguna Beach and up a few windy streets. The road peaked and we pulled into the driveway of a house with a big wooden deck. I got out and turned to look at the ocean. I could see the whole coastline from Long Beach all the way to San Clemente.

"Oh my gosh," I said.

"I know, I'm speechless every time I come home."

"It's so beautiful," I said. It felt like we were on top of the world. We were surrounded by green hills dotted with houses, and bursting with bushes and flowers. Far below us the ocean looked like a sheet of tinfoil. I could see the faint outline of Catalina Island, hovering in a pink mist.

"I often feel like it's the biggest Impressionist painting," Edward said, nodding at the view.

"It's amazing," I agreed.

"I'm glad you like it. Let's go inside." Edward led me up a short flight of stairs to the front door. Max was still attached to Edward's phone, playing with some app that made grunting noises.

We entered a big living room with floor-to-ceiling glass doors that opened onto the deck. The room was barely furnished—just two caramel-colored leather sofas facing the view and two glass side tables. The floor was dark wood with no rugs.

"My wife kept the furniture. It was specially made for the Pasadena house. Louis XVI chairs would have been out of place here."

"You don't need anything with that view," I said.

"I agree, come outside." He took my hand and led me out on the deck. "I pretty much live out here." The deck had a

Jacuzzi, and on the far side a barbecue and a table and chairs. Edward stood close to me and put his hand over mine. I turned quickly to see what Max was doing.

"Max, put the phone down and come out here," I said.

Max reluctantly put the phone on a side table and came outside. I moved an inch away from Edward and took Max's hand.

"Isn't the view fantastic?"

"Sure," Max agreed. "I'm hungry."

"You've probably seen enough of the ocean," Edward said.

"I like the ocean when I'm surfing. You should see how long I stood up today. Like ten minutes," Max replied.

"I want to hear all about it. Why don't you help me fire up the barbecue?"

I stood on the deck, breathing in the crisp air that drifted up from the ocean.

"Hi, I'm Edward," a deep voice said behind me.

Edward's son was very tall, at least six foot one, with a thick chest like his father. He wore a denim shirt with the sleeves rolled up, and Quiksilver boardshorts. He looked like a cross between a surfer and a lumberjack.

"I'm Amanda, nice to meet you." I shook his hand, which was huge. I wondered how Edward, who was shorter than me if I wore anything but flats, had fathered such a giant.

"Edward tells me you're at Wake Forest." We looked out at the view together. He had dark curly hair and lovely blue eyes like Edward's. His chest strained against his shirt and his stomach was washboard flat. *The girls must go crazy over him.*

"I'm studying public policy. It's a great school, and the

Greek system is awesome. Some frat is usually having a party every night."

"That must make it hard to study," I said. I tried not to stare at his chest. I realized I was closer in age to him than to his father. I trained my eyes on the ocean and kept them there.

We chatted about rush week and fraternity parties. He told me how the girls in North Carolina were light years behind Southern California girls. I relaxed. Edward Jr. might be only twelve years younger than me, but our experiences were worlds apart. He was a boy, a giant boy popping out of his clothes and with a man's deep voice, but still a child. I was much more comfortable with my Edward, who had raised children, held a mortgage, owned a business.

The glass door slid open and a slight, pretty girl joined us on the deck. She had blond hair that she wore in a short bob, and almond-shaped brown eyes. She wore a white minidress with a four-inch belt that accentuated her tiny waist, and with platform sandals she came up to my shoulder.

"I'm Jessica." She stuck out a small hand. "I like your dress."

"Thanks. I feel a little overdressed actually. With a view like this, I wish I had worn something simpler. I feel like I'm competing."

"You get used to it, but it's cool. Dad loves it."

The three of us silently admired the view. I wondered what was running through Jessica's head. Did she hate her parents for splitting up? Did she know it was her mom's fault, or did she think Edward was responsible? What was it like to be a visitor in her dad's home, while her own bedroom was in

Pasadena? I shuddered. One day Max would have to deal with these things.

"Hey, I see you've all met." Edward joined us on the deck. "Why don't we go into the kitchen and have a drink? I'm a terrible father letting my kids drink, but when I was young the drinking age was eighteen, at least in a few states."

"I'll be twenty-one in August," Edward Jr. said.

"Does that mean I won't have to support you anymore?" Edward grinned.

"Sure Dad, I'll quit Wake Forest and be a busboy at your restaurant. No problem."

"Touché. But it wouldn't hurt you to get a summer job."

"I work so hard at school, I need the summer to catch up on sleep."

"Yeah, that's why you got home at two a.m. last night."

"There was a sweet band at the Yellow Submarine. To-night I'm staying in."

"You bet you're staying in. We're barbecuing ostrich and lamb. You're going to help entertain Amanda and Max."

I watched Jessica as Edward and his son bantered. She stood in the corner of the kitchen, shelling peas. Her wrists and ankles were no bigger than my mother's. Her forehead was set in a permanent frown. She seemed to be concentrating very hard on popping the peas out of their pods and into the bowl.

"I bet Tulane is a big change from California," I said as I walked up to her.

"New Orleans is a cool city. And my mom went to Tulane, so it's pretty familiar." She didn't look up from her peas.

"I went to Berkeley and so did my dad. It definitely helps," I replied.

I had exhausted conversation with Jessica. I didn't know anything about the music eighteen-year-old girls listened to, the clothes they wore, or the movie stars they were in love with. We had already summed up Tulane with the fact her mother had gone there. I looked for Max, the only person in the kitchen I could talk to easily, but he had disappeared into the living room.

"Amanda, would you like to toss a salad?" Edward put his hand on my shoulder.

"Yes, I'd love to." I moved away from Jessica and watched Edward take lettuce, tomatoes, asparagus, and olive oil out of the fridge. I felt like there was a magnetic field around Edward. As long as I stayed in that field I was safe, but if I strayed outside I landed in unknown territory.

Edward assembled the salad ingredients on the center island and pulled a knife out of a chipped drawer.

"I'll apologize in advance. None of my tableware match. My wife got the carving set, the pepper grinder, the salad spinner, and the silver serving tongs in the divorce. When we separated I was still an attorney; I thought all I needed was chopsticks to eat takeout Chinese."

"Hey, Dad, don't complain. Mom's always going on about how you took the Beach Boys CDs, the backgammon set, and the ocean canoe," Edward Jr. said, trimming fat off a thick piece of lamb.

"Your mother never went near the ocean, let alone in a canoe," Edward countered.

I focused on rinsing tomatoes and trimming asparagus. It was nice to see what an easy relationship Edward had with his son, but it didn't seem to extend to Jessica. She hadn't said a word to either of them since we walked into the kitchen. I pictured the four of them like bowling pins: Jessica and her mother lined up on one side and Edward and his son on the other.

"I bet your kitchen has every gizmo." Edward grinned at me. "Amanda's soon-to-be-ex is a chef," he said to Edward and Jessica. "Owns a restaurant actually. I had to twist her arm to go out with me; she thought all restaurants owners were terrorists."

I blushed and Jessica blushed, too.

"I know; I shouldn't discuss the Big D. Jessica thinks it's like talking about cancer. But it's part of life, and life goes on. I get my two beautiful children to myself four times a year, and when they feel sorry for old pops living in a hillside shack and eating off Pier 1 plates, they're *nice* to me. If I was still married to their mom I'd probably only see them when they wanted cash."

"Dad," Jessica and Edward said at the same time.

"Okay, let's change the subject. Edward, shall we throw these slabs on the barbecue?"

Edward and Edward Jr. carried big plates of meat and seasoning onto the deck. Jessica mumbled something about needing to check her cell phone and disappeared through the swinging doors. I was left with a stack of washed lettuce leaves, which I dried between paper towels.

"Mom, look at this cool new app. See all these hippos are jumping through rings and you try to shoot them with a stun gun." Max came into the kitchen, waving an iPhone in front of my nose.

"Max, I told you to put the phone down. Please go wash your hands, and you can help me toss the salad."

Max put the phone on the island and moved to the sink. The phone buzzed in front of me. I wiped my hands and saw one new text. I quickly turned away; I didn't want to snoop with Edward's phone, but Max had put it next to the olive oil. I picked up the oil to drizzle it over the salad, and black letters appeared on Edward's phone. They said "To Edward Honey Pot" "from Legsuptohere."

I froze. Edward and his son were chatting on the deck. Max was noisily lathering his hands with soap. It was just Edward's iPhone and me staring at each other. I wanted to walk away from it. This was only our second date, it shouldn't matter if Edward got texts from someone who called him "Honey Pot." I closed my eyes and tried to imagine what kind of a woman would sign herself "Legsuptohere."

"Okay, Mom, what should I do?" Max asked.

"Why don't you go help Edward with the barbecue," I said quickly.

Max went out onto the deck. I could ignore the text and finish tossing the salad or I could press read. I still held the bottle of olive oil in my hand. I wanted to slam it down on the phone and watch them both break into a million pieces. I couldn't help myself, I pressed read. The text said: "Had a sexational time last night. I know you have company but sext me later. Ha ha. Love L."

I closed the text and looked up to see if anyone had seen me. Spying was as bad as cheating. I stood by the sink and ran the water to clear my head. Edward told me he had worked last night, obviously not all night. I watched Edward outside, turning the meat and laughing with his son and Max.

"Amanda, dinner is served," Edward announced, poking his head into the kitchen. "Want me to carry the salad bowl?"

"No, I have it." I gave him my most confident smile.

We sat at the table, and Edward passed around plates heaped with ostrich meat, glazed carrots, and grilled onions.

"Okay, whoever is brave enough, try the ostrich. If you don't like it, I have some tame lamb here," Edward said when everyone had their plates.

I didn't feel brave. I felt scared of being with this family, of getting my heart broken, of sitting next to a man who got texts from Legsuptohere. I also knew I couldn't taste the meat, no matter what animal it came from.

"It's awesome," Max announced, eating two large bites.

Normally I would say how proud I was of him for trying it. Most eight-year-olds kept to a strict diet of hot dogs and mac 'n' cheese. But it took all my energy to chew my carrots.

"I want to raise my glass to our guests. I hope Amanda and Max find everything they're looking for in Southern California. They are a welcome addition to the landscape." He winked at me, and I could feel his hand briefly rest on my thigh under the table.

"I like it," Edward Jr. said. "Looks like your chef has taught you a few things."

Jessica pushed a few pieces of carrot around the plate and took a mouthful of salad. Women and girls, I thought bleakly, were victims. Men sailed through life, eating and drinking and screwing whomever they pleased. I tried to remember it was Edward's wife who fooled around, but my brain was frozen around the name "Legsuptohere." I put my fork down. I couldn't even pretend to eat.

Edward and his son chatted about cricket, surfing, and Wimbledon. Max started getting restless, and banged his fork against his plate.

"Max, please stop," I said.

"We'll have dessert soon. Why don't you get my iPhone? Play some games," Edward said.

I almost stood up to stop him, but Edward's hand was back on my thigh. I sat motionless. My throat was so dry I could barely swallow. I took a swig of wine and felt my cheeks flush.

Max brought out Edward's phone and sat down, mesmerized by a new game.

"I'm getting another beer." Edward Jr. got up. "Anyone want anything?"

"I have everything I need," Edward replied. I felt his hand press harder on my thigh. He leaned close to me, his breath smelled of wine and onions. "You look beautiful," he whispered.

I smiled back. My eyes suddenly filled with tears. Is that what men said when they fooled around? That "you look beautiful"? I blinked. I wanted to go home but I was too miserable to move.

"Hey, Dad." Edward Jr. came out of the kitchen, carrying a beer, and an iPhone in a green case. "You think I could cut out after dessert? I kind of have plans."

I looked from the phone Edward Jr. was holding, to the phone Max was playing with.

"You both have the same phone," I said.

"Apple had a special, so my son suckered me into buying him an iPhone, too. Buy one get the second half price. We even have the same cases," Edward said.

"It was a great promotion. And the only other cases were purple or leopard print. What do you say? Do you mind?" Edward Jr. turned to me.

I couldn't answer. All I could think was: *They have the same phone.*

"You were out late last night," Edward said.

"I met this cute girl from Montana. She's only here for a week," Edward Jr. begged.

I could hear my own breathing: inhaling, exhaling. I imagined a college coed from Montana; tall and fit like Edward Jr. *Legsuptohere,* I repeated to myself. It wasn't Edward's phone.

"It's up to Amanda," Edward said. "I promised her a family evening."

"It's fine." The words came out in a giant rush of air.

"Cool. I'll help get the dessert." Edward Jr. beamed at me.

"I think I'll catch a ride down the hill." Jessica had moved all the carrots to one side of her plate and the meat to the other.

"See what I mean." Edward shook his head. "I can't keep these kids around unless I'm handing out twenty-dollar bills."

"It's fine," I said again, this time my voice sounded normal.

We ate dessert: kiwi, pomegranate, and raspberries, topped with vanilla ice cream.

"The ice cream is homemade at the restaurant," Edward said proudly.

Edward Jr. cleaned his plate. "I don't know, Dad, you're getting kind of girly. You should take up poker or something."

"The restaurant is how I pay your mother's alimony. Which hopefully filters down to your child support and puts clothes on your back," Edward replied.

"Yeah, well. Just don't start making doilies." Edward Jr. pushed his chair back, grabbed his bowl and beer glass, and went into the kitchen.

"I think I'm going to go, Dad." Jessica had eaten the fruit, and left the ice cream in a small blob on her plate.

I ate every bite, slowly. My taste buds were functioning again, and the pomegranate and ice cream tasted heavenly.

"We lost them," Edward said as he sat back. "How about you, Max, do you like my ice cream?"

"It's great. Can I play some more games?" He put his spoon on his plate and picked up Edward's phone.

"Sure, why don't you take it into the living room."

When Max left, Edward put his arm around my shoulder and pulled me close to him.

"The iPhone is the greatest babysitter," Edward remarked.

I didn't want to talk about iPhones, or apps or texts. I just wanted to sit with my head on Edward's shoulder.

"My kids like you," Edward said as he rubbed my palm with his hand.

"Jessica didn't say two words to me," I told him.

"She's not big on conversation. Hasn't really talked to me in five years."

"Have you ever told her your wife cheated on you?"

"I can't think of anything worse than a girl knowing that about her mother. We said it was 'irreconcilable differences.' Whoever invented that term has a lot to answer for. Historically, you had to have a reason to divorce: 'she screwed the milk-man,' or 'he fucked the Scandinavian nanny.' People thought twice before they were branded with the scarlet *A*. Now it's 'irreconcilable differences,' like you couldn't agree on what flavor oatmeal to have for breakfast."

"Jessica might be nicer to you if she knew," I told him. I hoped I could be that circumspect with Max.

"She's eighteen. She has to be mad at me about something. It's a teenager's creed."

"She's very pretty," I said. I reluctantly moved my head from Edward's shoulder, in case Max came out on the deck.

"Too thin. That's how she communicates, by not eating anything I cook." He shook his head.

"Is it a real problem?" I asked.

"It was the first year after the divorce. She looked like a toothpick. At first we thought it was just a thirteen-year-old trying to fit into micro minis, but then we noticed at her mom's house she ate fine, but when she stayed with me she drank lemon tea and ate celery sticks."

"What happened?"

"Her mom and I and Jessica saw a therapist once a week. I'd take her to her favorite restaurants on the nights she stayed with me. I figured she wouldn't be able to hide her food in public and she wouldn't want to make a scene. She's a bright girl though. Eventually I think she figured she wasn't solving anything. We were still divorced."

"Wow." I wondered what minefields lay ahead for Andre and Max and me.

"Here I am again telling you the terrors of divorce. There

are plusses. Like meeting you." He turned my face to him and gently kissed me on the lips. I kissed him back. We both tasted like kiwi and pomegranate.

"I think I better get Max home," I said.

"Okay, I'll grab my keys. But our next date is going to be adults only. No kids of any age. Deal?"

"Deal." I waited on the deck while Edward went into the house. I was still shaken by the iPhone incident, but I felt a new sensation creep over me: I liked Edward and he liked me.

Chapter Six

I want to sleep with him," I said to Stephanie on the phone the next day.

"Wow, Sleeping Beauty is waking up. I though all men besides Andre had cooties," Stephanie replied.

"I find Edward really sexy." I sat in a lounge chair by the pool. Max was splashing around with an inflatable palm tree, and I had a stack of magazines and newspapers I hadn't read.

"I knew you'd get your mojo back," Stephanie replied.

"Be serious! Is it too early to sleep with him? What if Max finds out?"

"Sorry, Zoe and I just finished a Disney movie marathon. You might be living in the lap of luxury with a Kids' Club and five pools at your fingertips, but I have a sandbox and one sixty-inch TV with which to entertain my children."

"Don't forget the faithful husband, the gorgeous house, and the devoted housekeeper. I'll trade with you any day," I said.

"Not if you saw my house. Glenn is out of town and Gisella is visiting her mother in Lisbon. Zoe and Graham have turned the living room into an Indian fort."

The thrill of Edward started to wane. I squeezed my eyes shut and remembered the long afternoons spent in Stephanie's sandbox, when my only decision was chicken nuggets or fish sticks for dinner.

"Have you seen Andre around?" I asked.

"Now you're switching gears. Let's focus on Edward. While I disapprove of his age, at least he's not married. I'm beginning to long-distance like him."

I hadn't told Stephanie about the iPhone mix-up and the texts from "Legsuptohere." I didn't want to sound like a hyper-paranoid teenager.

"We had a great time last night," I said. "He has this quiet strength, and he's funny. About everything: his kids, his divorce, his restaurant."

"I can't believe you sit around talking about divorce and restaurants. I would think those are two subjects to be avoided at all costs. Maybe you should sleep with him, so you both shut up."

"You're not getting it, Stephanie," I complained.

"Sorry, I know it's not all champagne and roses, even with a new guy. But try to keep it romantic. You don't want to start doing his laundry and buying his shaving cream. You've been there."

"I'm not doing his laundry! We've been on two and a half dates. He wants to see me tonight after the restaurant closes. I am only asking when is the appropriate time to sleep with him." I couldn't help laughing.

"Well, that's obvious. After he has brought you flowers, taken you out for several dinners, and given you one slightly significant piece of jewelry."

"Jewelry? Just for sex?" I shook my head.

"How do you think I got Glenn?" Stephanie replied. "I have to go, Zoe is trying to make my curtains into a teepee. Don't do anything hasty. Make him wait."

I had a similar conversation in the evening with my mother. We sat on the deck, drinking our six p.m. cocktails. Every night room service brought us something new to try along with the old standbys of martinis and vodka gimlets. Tonight I was sipping a Slippery Slope: rum, tequila, orange juice, and a squeeze of lemon.

"Any plans for the evening?" my mother asked. She had grilled me about my date when Max and I arrived home. After telling her about Edward's spectacular view, and how bright and attractive his kids were, she seemed to be softening. She had even commented that she noticed he wore a Rolex Oyster like my father—a definite sign of good taste.

"Edward has to work, but he wants to take me out for a drink after the restaurant closes."

"Isn't that late?" she asked. My mother had changed in the three weeks we had been at the St. Regis. Her cheeks were almost pink, and her mouth and fingernails were no longer nicotine yellow. She carried herself with more confidence, which meant she treated me like a schoolgirl.

"Mom, I can stay out all night if I want."

"You most certainly cannot. You've only known Edward for a week. And what would Max say if he woke up and you weren't in your own bed. Don't forget your first priority is to be Max's mother." She put down her martini. My mother never sampled the new cocktails. She thought all the alliterated names were gauche.

"I wasn't planning on staying out all night," I mumbled, though I had been considering it. It wasn't about erasing Andre anymore. It was about feeling Edward on top of me, having him kiss my nose, stroke my hair. For some reason, I had been thinking about going to bed with him all day, and I had to stop. As Stephanie said, I had to make him wait.

"I like Edward, but take it slow. You're not even divorced yet. And you're young, beautiful, and wealthy."

"Edward isn't a gold digger!" I snapped.

"From the looks of him he isn't, but you have to be careful." My mother cut a sliver of brie and put it on a water cracker. I noticed she was eating things other than chocolate without being prompted.

"You mean I have to make sure his Rolex isn't a fake?"

"Just get to know him." She took a careful bite and wiped her mouth with a napkin.

"You and Stephanie are such killjoys," I grumbled.

"You've got all summer. You've got the rest of your life. You just shook off one wolf in sheep's clothing; you don't want to be landed with another."

"Edward is not a wolf." I switched from the Slippery Slope to a diet 7UP. Maybe it was the alcohol that was making me horny.

I gazed down at the Grand Lawn where another party was in full swing. I watched people mingle like figures in a

Seurat painting. A band was starting up, and men pulled women onto the dance floor under bright, tinted lights. I realized I didn't envy those people as I had a couple of weeks ago. I didn't want to dance and flirt and drink endless champagne. But I did want to be with Edward. I wanted to see his crinkly smile. I wanted to sit close to him and feel his arm around me.

"I'll meet him for one drink, in the lobby. I'll warn him on the stroke of midnight I turn into a pumpkin," I said.

"Don't get smart. I'm just trying to protect you." My mother smiled.

"Between you and Stephanie, I feel like Rapunzel. But honestly, Mom, I'm making progress. I haven't thought about Andre, I mean really thought about Andre in a while." I got up and went inside to unglue Max from the television.

"I was right about bringing you here"—my mother had to have the last word—"and I'm right about this, too. Please take it slow."

🦋 🦋 🦋

We ate room service dinner together. It was lovely, sitting at the polished table in the suite's dining room with Max and my mother. Max had another great day of surfing and stood on his chair to illustrate "hanging five." He ate spaghetti and meatballs, green beans, and a wedge of chocolate cake, and then plopped himself on the couch to read a surfing magazine. He hadn't mentioned Andre in a couple of days. It seemed all he wanted to do was surf and eat, and lie in front of the TV and play Wii Surf before bed.

My mother ate a chocolate-pistachio mousse and disappeared

into her bedroom. I could hear Ryan Seacrest's voice introducing "America's next American Idol" through the closed door. I gave Max a "thirty minutes before bed" warning, and went into my room to flip through *Vogue*.

I loved the stack of magazines the housekeepers put on my bedside table each day: *Vogue, Bazaar, Elle, W.* I admired new fashions from Zac Posen, Stella McCartney, Ella Moss; even Burberry had some wild styles inspired by Kate Moss. *W* was my favorite because it had page after page of clothes you would never see on the street. I found myself tearing out pages of runway shows like I did when I was at prep school, and would paste them on my dresser. I then critiqued the strengths and flaws of each designer, thinking what I would add—a thicker belt, a shorter skirt—to enhance the outfit. I smiled because it had been so long since I thought about anything besides what Andre wanted and what Max needed.

The phone buzzed and I was so enraptured by a fashion spread of Miu Miu caftans, I answered without checking the caller ID.

"Amanda, where have you been? You haven't returned my calls. I am frantic with missing you and Max." It was Andre.

"Just busy. Max has been surfing all day." I could feel my stomach tighten. I remembered all the nights I had called the restaurant to see when Andre was coming home and his phone was off. I always thought he was busy taking care of lingering clients, I didn't realize he was servicing the staff. I blinked away the image of Andre and Ursula wrapped around each other like two pieces of licorice.

"*Ma petite cherie.* This madness has gone on long enough. When are you coming home?"

"I'm not coming 'home,' Andre. I filed for divorce. We will be back to Ross at the end of the summer," I said, sitting up straight in my bed.

"There are no other women, only you. I want you in our bed, I want to cover you with roses and kisses," Andre said.

"You should have thought of that when you were fucking Ursula."

"Such unladylike language from my princess. I told you it is over, all I want is you."

"Andre, you were cheating for ten years. Why on earth should I believe you?" I tore pages out of the magazine, crumpled them up, and threw them on the floor.

"We can buy the land in Napa and build a summer house. We'll buy a bigger house in Ross if you want. I will do anything to have my *petite* family back."

I pictured Andre sitting on the edge of our bed the way he used to when he came home from the restaurant. He always wore a white shirt, open to the third button, black slacks, and dress shoes without socks. He would tell me about the night and massage my feet, and I found it so sexy I wanted him to undress and make love to me right then. I always wanted him. We had some crazy chemistry that made me want to have sex every time I saw him.

"It's gone, Andre. We're over." I closed my eyes and conjured up images of Andre and Ursula, Andre and Yvette, Andre and all the other women. I wanted to feel the pain now, get it out of my system, so I could be done with it.

"You are just being emotional, my sweet. You are *mon couer*. And I need to see Max, I need to speak to my son."

"He's asleep," I said. I didn't want to go into the living

room with tears in my eyes. Andre could live without speaking to Max.

"You cannot imagine how much I miss Max."

"I'll tell him to call you tomorrow."

"I am going to come down and see you both. I will make my *petite* princess see my love."

"I've seen your love, Andre. But you can visit Max whenever you like. I really have to go. I'll have Max call you tomorrow."

I flipped shut my phone. The room felt horribly silent. I got up and searched my closet for the perfect thing to wear for my drink with Edward. But my body started trembling, first my hands, then my legs, and the tears came in giant hiccups. I climbed onto the bed and let myself cry. I wished I could just forget Andre. Nothing, not even childbirth, was as painful as a broken heart.

🦋 🦋 🦋

I waited for Edward at the lobby bar. I had finally decided on jeans, and a white T-shirt over my Victoria Secret's Miraculous Bra. I hadn't worn tight jeans in years, but my butt was flat thanks to my Beach Boot Camp regime. I wore just a little makeup: bronzer on my cheeks and pale pink lip gloss. I felt very Southern California.

Edward came up behind me and put his hands over my eyes.

"It's your old and faithful admirer," he said.

"Not old but hopefully faithful," I joked.

"You are looking extra beautiful and about as old as my daughter." Edward pulled up the stool beside me.

"Thank you. All the women in Southern California look like they're nineteen. It must be something in the water."

"Or the Botox. But you're naturally gorgeous. I've been looking forward to this all night." Edward ordered two Bacardi and Cokes and a tray of sliders.

"I'm always starving when I finish work," he said.

"It must be very different from a corporate law office."

"Different and not different. The key is to make the client feel like he or she is the most important person in the world, no matter what kind of business you are in." Edward wolfed down a handful of macadamia nuts.

"So how was life at the St. Regis today?" He brushed the hair away from my face and kissed me quickly on the cheek.

"Max surfed all day. I think he's going to wake up one morning with a surfboard glued to his feet. He's totally addicted."

"Southern California hazard. Edward had flippers for hands by the time he was thirteen. There is something about conquering the waves that is Narnia for boys. One day I'll show Max the surfboard I rode when I was a kid. It was about twenty feet long and weighed thirty pounds."

"He is really happy," I conceded.

"And how did you spend your day?" He took a bite of a slider and kept his other hand on my knee.

"Beach, pool, gym. I had an unpleasant conversation with Andre this evening."

"Those will go on for the next few years. The only good thing about my kids being at college is I don't have to talk to Julie. We're down to who they will spend Christmas and Thanksgiving with."

"He wanted to know when Max and I were coming home. He's such a hypocrite." I knew Stephanie would shoot me for talking about Andre. But I didn't want to keep anything from Edward.

"A friend at the law firm gave me the best advice. Tell him: 'I hope the fucking you were getting was worth the fucking you will be getting.' Pardon my language."

"I like that. I find I've actually made 'fuck' one of my favorite words. It says everything you need to say." The Bacardi was strong and I was a little light-headed. Edward's hand on my knee made me feel sexy and dangerous.

Edward leaned close to my ear and whispered: "Fuck, fuck, fuck." Then he sat back and laughed.

I giggled and took another swig of my drink. One more Bacardi and Coke and I would try to have him against the wall in the phone booth. I don't know what had come over me. I was like a call girl–pole dancer version of myself. Reluctantly, I remembered Stephanie's words: "Make him wait." I pushed my drink away and swallowed a handful of pistachios.

"We're really busy at the restaurant. My partner put together a new ad campaign: 'You buy a shrimp cocktail; we'll buy your entrée. Restrictions will apply.'"

"That's pretty clever," I said. I could feel Edward's eyes on my breasts. I looked down, and noticed my Michael Stars T was almost see-through. Even I could see the curve of my bra and the swell of my breasts beneath it.

"Sam is really bright. The entrée you get is either tuna salad or fish and chips. Both cost less than a shrimp cocktail. You should come down to the restaurant and keep me company."

"You don't need me, I'd get in the way." I shook my head. Andre had never asked me to hang out at the restaurant.

"I'm serious. I have to work almost every night, I'd love to have you near me." Edward's hand kneaded the small of my back.

"What would I do?" I asked. In all the years Andre and I were married, I was welcome at La Petite Maison weekend mornings when I brought Max to help Andre bake bread, but it was strictly off-limits during operating hours. Andre said it wouldn't be professional to have his wife around. I had agreed with him. My place was home with Max. I didn't know his place was on the desk with Ursula.

"You could be my secret spy, just kind of linger beside each booth and see if the clients are happy. You know, do they like the soup, are they complaining the bread is stale. You could dress in a miniskirt and fishnet stockings like a Bond Girl."

"I can't quite see myself as a Bond Girl," I laughed.

"Have the Bentley drop you off tomorrow night. I can give you a ride home after we close." He leaned forward and kissed me on the lips. I kissed him back, blocking out the other people at the bar.

"Okay," I agreed. I promised myself I would wear my most conservative outfit. I would make him bring me home, to the St. Regis, without any stops. And I would not drink any alcohol. Somehow I had to quench the raging sex fiend that welled up inside me.

I flipped open my phone and checked the time. "It's almost twelve, I better go."

"Are you Cinderella?" Edward asked.

"According to my mother. She doesn't think it's 'appropriate' to stay out past midnight."

"Well, leave me your slipper so I can keep it close to my heart." He kissed me again.

"No way, these are Manolos. I guard them with my life."

"Let me pay and I'll walk you to the elevator. I'd escort you to the suite but I have a feeling your mother might be breathing fire."

"She likes you. She just wants me to take it slow." I got up from the stool and waited for Edward to pay the check.

"Parents, can't argue with them when we are them. I'd say the same thing to Jessica." He left the tip and took my hand.

We walked hand in hand through the lobby. We stopped in front of the clothes boutique and looked through the glass. "You should wear that to the restaurant," Edward said as he pointed to a slit dress with a plunging neckline.

"I don't think so," I laughed.

He put his arm around me and we moved to the jewelry boutique. We admired the Rolex and Cartier and Patek Philippe watches.

"Good evening, Mr. Jonas." A saleswoman came to greet us.

"Good evening, Louise. This is my friend Amanda Blick," Edward introduced me. "I come here to get the battery replaced in my Rolex. It was my going-away present from the law firm."

"Come inside and see our new displays. We have some lovely jewelry commissioned specially for the hotel." The saleswoman smiled. The hotel never slept. The lounges, the restaurants, and the shops stayed open till the early hours of the morning.

I had been in the boutique with my mother. We had admired the diamond tennis bracelets, the cocktail rings set with semiprecious stones, and the rows of delicate gold chains. I felt a little awkward standing there with Edward, a few minutes before midnight, his hand resting on mine.

"I love those ads for Patek Philippe," he said. "'You're not buying a watch, you're just keeping it for the next generation.' If you're not buying it, why do you have to pay thirty thou?"

"Look at these, Mr. Jonas. They just came in." The saleswoman put a tray of earrings in front of us. They were tiny gold butterflies, dusted with colored gems.

"Oh, those are pretty." I picked one up.

"They're monarch butterflies," the saleswoman said. "Isn't that clever. A local jeweler made them. They're very popular."

"My daughter is mad about earrings. On her fifteenth birthday she got double piercings. Her mother had to take her to the pediatrician who explained if she put any more holes in her ears they'd start leaking," Edward chuckled.

"These are sweet." I put it back on the tray.

"How about you, pierced ears?" Edward pushed back my hair so he could see my ears. His hand felt warm and sexy.

"Of course. My parents gave me pearls when I was sixteen, diamonds when I was twenty-one. My mother is very traditional." I smoothed my hair.

"You have cute ears." He leaned close to me; I could smell the rum on his breath.

I looked at a Cartier under the glass. "Oh my gosh, it's twelve. I have to go. Thank you for inviting us in," I said to the saleswoman.

"Anytime. Good night, Mr. Jonas." Louise gave Edward a wide smile. I'm sure she was used to drunken couples pawing each other over her cases late at night. She probably thought we would sweep in and buy a handful of necklaces and bracelets.

"Good night, Amanda," Edward said when we reached the elevator.

"Good night," I replied. The elevator opened and I stepped inside, but Edward grabbed my hand and pulled me back. He gently pushed me against the wall and put his arms around me. He lifted my hair with his hands and kissed my ears, then he moved his hands down and held my breasts, stroking them through the thin fabric. He kissed my neck and my throat; he bit my lips and finally kissed my mouth. He tasted delicious, like salty beef coated with rum. I was so turned on I thought I would come through my True Religions.

"That's a proper good night," he said, releasing me.

"Very proper," I said, smoothing my hair and straightening my shirt.

"You better go upstairs, Cinderella. I'll see you tomorrow night."

He kissed me on the nose and I got into the elevator. I opened the door to the suite quietly, praying my mother was asleep. I knew all she had to do was see me and smell the scent of sex on me to know I wasn't taking it slow.

Chapter Seven

I spent the next morning watching Max surf, lunchtime listening to him talk about surfing, and the afternoon playing Scrabble Jr. and Clue with him at the pool. I wanted to prove to my mother and myself that my first priority was Max, but flashes of Edward pressing me against the wall kept appearing before my eyes.

My mother didn't ask me any questions about last night's date, but she looked at me quizzically when I declined a drink at cocktail hour.

"Why am I drinking alone tonight?" she asked when I brought a diet 7UP onto the deck at six p.m. Max was worn out from surfing, and was napping on the sofa in the living room.

"Edward asked me to help at the restaurant tonight," I explained. I sat on the lounge chair in my St. Regis robe. I had spent the last hour showering and lathering myself with creams and lotion. I felt decadently relaxed and excited about the evening.

"Help out at the restaurant?" My mother eyed me suspiciously. "We know how Andre handled his female employees."

"Edward is not remotely like Andre. He thought it would be fun for me to come and be sort of a hostess. He has to work every night and we wouldn't see each other if I didn't."

"Is he paying you?" My mother refilled her martini glass.

"Of course not! I'm doing it for fun. I think it's sweet that he asked me. Andre never wanted me near the restaurant."

"What are you going to tell Max?" She smeared pâté on a piece of pumpernickel bread.

"That Edward needs an extra hand at the restaurant. I can even ask him to come with me if you want," I said defiantly. But I didn't want Max to come with me. I wanted Edward to have the chance to hold me and kiss me like he had last night.

"Max and I will watch television together, don't worry about us. How are you getting there?"

"I'm going to have the Bentley drop me off and Edward said he'd bring me home," I mumbled. I knew this would get a reaction.

"I guess you can't get into too much trouble in a Mini." She finished her pâté and swept the crumbs from her skirt.

"Ha, ha," I answered. It was a switch to see my mother eat, while I was too nervous to swallow anything.

"I'm glad you're enjoying yourself and getting your mind off Andre. You can just be impulsive, Amanda. Remember how quickly you fell for Andre."

"You fell for him, too!" I replied. "Remember the chocolates and gifts he brought you. You thought he was a cross between Clark Gable and Cary Grant. You were thrilled when he asked me to marry him."

"That's my point, we were both wrong." She gave me that quiet, stern look she used to give me when I was a teenager and she wanted me to think about what I was doing.

"Point taken. Again," I said grudgingly. "I'll take it slow."

❦ ❦ ❦

I promised Edward I'd be there by eight p.m., which gave me an hour to throw half my closet onto the bed and put together an outfit that was conservative and comfortable, but could become sexy. I finally picked a simple Kate Spade dress, white and green stripes, with its own short green jacket. I paired it with a pair of Gucci pumps and tied my hair in a high ponytail with a green ribbon. My reflection in the mirror was professional and sophisticated. I imagined Edward taking off the jacket on the way home, unbuttoning the tiny green buttons of the dress's bodice, and slipping his hand over my breast. I sprayed myself with Obsession, added extra mascara to my lashes, and grabbed my purse.

"I'll be back later." I kissed Max good-bye. "Go to bed when Grandma tells you."

"She says I get to stay up and watch *Amazing Race* and *American Idol* with her," Max said happily.

"What's next, Mom?" I kissed her cheek. "*Dancing with the Stars*?"

"I'm on vacation," my mother replied, "and I'm doing it for Max. If it was just me I'd be watching *Sixty Minutes*."

"Sure, Mom. Have fun, you two."

I sat in the Bentley, feeling like I was on an adventure. How did I, a Ross mom who was usually trying to get grass stains out of Max's shirts at this time of night, end up sailing down PCH in a grand car, on my way to meet my almost-lover? The driver let me off at the corner; I didn't think it would be a good idea to emerge from a Bentley in front of Laguna Beach Tackle. I opened the door to the restaurant as a crowd was moving inside. The front of the house was chaotic. People were squashed against one another waiting for a table.

Edward saw me and grabbed my hand. "You're here in the nick of time. Sam's promotion is working better than we expected. We've just sold our sixty-fifth shrimp cocktail and we're out of tables. Maybe you can entertain these folks while they wait."

"Entertain them how?" I looked around. The hostess from the other night gave me a cheery wave, and moved through the restaurant with a stack of menus and a party of large tourists.

"Striptease?" Edward winked at me. "Kidding. You could hand them menus while they wait. Would that be okay?"

"I'd love to." I put my purse behind the counter and grabbed a pile of menus. I passed them out and stopped to answer questions. Gradually the hostess, who introduced herself as Gemma, led the diners back to tables and the crowd dispersed.

After half an hour, we finally found ourselves alone at the podium.

"Thank you so much for helping. They would have eaten me alive if you weren't here." Gemma smiled. Her hair was peroxide blond, the kind you only see in hair color commercials, and her eyes were blue with long lashes. She looked like a sexy version of Marcia from *The Brady Bunch*.

"It was fun. My almost-ex-husband owns a restaurant, so I'm pretty familiar. Have you worked here long?"

"Just for the summer. I go to USC, and my boyfriend is a summer lifeguard at Main Beach." Gemma folded napkins as we talked.

"I see you two met." Edward came up behind me and put his hand on my back. "Aren't I lucky to have this beautiful woman helping us?" He smiled at me.

"It's fun. I haven't been doing anything but yoga for three weeks," I said, and blushed.

"Gemma, maybe you could tell Amanda the specials so she has more ammo for the next rush of diners. I have to go shell some shrimp." He rubbed my back and headed to the kitchen.

For the next hour I worked beside Gemma, keeping the flow moving. I liked the low buzz of excitement in the air, the clatter of forks and knives, the sound of corks popping, and the thud of plates heaped with seafood landing on tables. Every now and then Edward would catch my eye and wink, or give me one of his broad, crinkly smiles. When Gemma flipped the closed sign on the front door at ten p.m., my feet hurt but I felt pleasantly energized.

"I'm going to grab some fish and chips and go home." Gemma neatly stacked the menus behind the counter. "Edward is really nice and lets me take leftovers for my boyfriend. He's always starving."

"That's because he's a linebacker at SMU," Edward said

as he came up next to me and draped his arm over my shoulder.

"He is, during the school year," Gemma blushed, "but he's hungry *all* the time."

"My son is eight and he just took up surfing. He eats for an hour straight at night: grilled cheese sandwiches, burgers, pasta. Last night he ordered three entrées from the kids' menu and ate them all," I said, laughter in my voice.

"Again, thank you for helping out tonight. I really appreciated it," Gemma said.

"See, she doesn't bite," Edward murmured, after Gemma had gathered several servings of fish, chips, tartar sauce, and French bread and gone home.

"What do you mean?" I colored. Edward stood at the cash register and I sat in the hostess chair, rubbing my feet.

"I mean," he said as he pulled me out of the chair and kissed me slowly on the lips, "not all restaurant owners want to bonk their hostesses, or their waitresses, or their chefs." He kissed me again, slow, soft kisses like raindrops.

"I can see that." I kissed him back. He put his arms around me and pulled my face close to his.

"Let's close up and get out of here."

We left the waitresses and the busboys to finish wiping down the tables. Edward took me to the kitchen to introduce me to his chef, a young man with oily hair and giant hands, and to his partner, Sam, who was moaning about how much shrimp he'd have to buy at the market in the morning.

"Sam was the best creative director Ogilvy ever had." Edward punched Sam's shoulder lightly.

"Thanks." Sam wore owl-shaped glasses and a brown bow tie. "It seems we're out of shrimp. Not a very clever campaign when you run out of product." He shook his head.

"Sam is always worrying," Edward said to me. "That's why we're so successful."

"We're like Laurel and Hardy," Sam agreed. "Edward's out front making it look easy, while I'm in the back sweating the details."

"Yes, but remember you get sixty percent of the take, and you go home to a beachfront house in Emerald Bay with a community tennis court. You're paid more to worry more."

"He's right," Sam said and smiled at me. "But Edward's the grease of the operation. People wouldn't come through the doors if it wasn't for him."

"Thanks for buttering up my date; we have to go. Amanda turns into a pumpkin at midnight, and her mother will come after me with a pitchfork." Edward grabbed his keys from a ring on the wall and opened the back door for me.

We climbed into the Mini, and I took off my pumps and slid my feet under me.

"You have a really nice group of people there," I said.

"It's not family, but it's like the theme song from *Cheers*. It's nice to be somewhere where everyone knows my name," Edward said.

"I really enjoyed myself. At La Petite Maison I always thought I'd flatten a fondue by accident, and the whole restaurant would deflate." I slid my hair out of its ponytail.

"I can't see you sticking those manicured fingers in a

fondue." He eased out of the back lane and turned the car onto PCH.

"Figuratively speaking. Andre never made me feel welcome. There was always a crisis in the kitchen he had to take care of, or a reservation dilemma he had to solve. If I ever stopped by during business hours he shooed me out the door."

"That's because he didn't want to be caught with the hen in the hen house. Even if he was a clever criminal, one of his sex partners might have given him away."

"I never realized that," I replied.

"Generally restaurants are fun places to be, that's why I agreed to go in with Sam after I quit the law firm. Not a lot of people sue you if they don't like the scampi. You serve them a good dinner, pair it with a nice wine, and send them home happy."

"You do make it look easy." I smiled at him.

"Well, thank you. I really liked having you there. You're a ray of sunshine."

We turned into the gates of the St. Regis, but instead of swinging up to the front entrance, Edward drove the Mini down to the golf course and pulled into the parking lot.

"What are we doing?" I asked.

"I promise I'll get you home by midnight, but if I pull up to the lobby, four valets will swoop down on the car and I won't get to say good night." He pulled me to him and kissed my neck. "Like this."

He took my hand and held it in his, and with his other hand he stroked my cheeks and my lips. He moved his hand down the front of my dress and opened my jacket with three soft snaps of its buttons. The jacket fell off and he put his hands under my breasts and gently squeezed them out of the dress.

"Edward," I said uncertainly.

"Every part of you is gorgeous." He took his fingers and rubbed my nipples, and then he bent down and kissed them so they stood up pink and erect. I sat, pushed back in the seat, like a schoolgirl. I didn't want him to stop, it was so erotic not knowing what he was going to do next, but I didn't want to fuck in a car either.

"Edward, we shouldn't," I whispered.

"I know." He let go of my breasts, and then he gently hiked up my dress, grabbed the edge of my panties, and slipped two fingers warmly inside me.

"Oh God, Edward." I gripped the side of the seat. I could feel his fingers deep inside me. My body strained to reach something I couldn't define. His fingers thrust deeper, stroking me, guiding me. My legs fell open, trembling. I was so incredibly, deliciously wet; I felt I was going to burst.

"I'm going to be a good boy and stop." He pulled his fingers out, and sat back in the driver's seat. "I know your mother wouldn't approve of me making love to her daughter in the front seat of a Mini. But you're so beautiful, Amanda."

Neither of us said anything. I knew if I opened my mouth it would be to say "Please, fuck me, now," so I stayed silent while he started the car and drove to the lobby entrance.

"I'll call you in the morning," he said.

"Good night." I got out of the car, smoothed my dress, and pulled the jacket tight around my chest.

I took off my shoes in the hallway and crept into the suite. My mother's door was closed. I peeked in on Max. He was sprawled across his bed, as if he had fallen asleep before he hit the mattress. I went into my room, shut the door, and started the bath. I waited till the bath was full of hot water. Then I unsnapped my dress, stepped out of my underwear, and submerged myself under water. Only when the bath was full of bubbles did I finally let myself think.

My first thought was that I was a tramp. I was a married woman, still wearing a wedding ring (for Max's sake), and I had let another man finger me. What would Stephanie say? I blew out a batch of bubbles and tried to stay calm. I hadn't had sex; it was only heavy petting. But then I remembered the way Edward's fingers felt inside me, the deep, mysterious sensation of exploration, and I felt the warm, sweet wetness come over me again.

I took a deep breath and tried to think. Was I really ready for a new relationship? What if there was any remote, completely unrealistic chance of putting my family back together? What if Andre promised to take a monk's vow of celibacy or be cursed by God? Had I blown it? What was I doing almost sleeping with a man I had known for two weeks?

I sat in the bath till the digital bathroom clock read one a.m. Then I drained the bath, wrapped myself in a St. Regis bath sheet, and got into bed. I closed my eyes, without having come to a single conclusion, except that the whole night had felt so good.

The next morning I was awake before my mother. I seemed to have a frenetic energy, and instead of being exhausted from only sleeping six hours, I attacked the gym and did forty minutes on the treadmill. Then I joined a nine a.m. yoga class, and afterward went to the breakfast buffet and ate melon, strawberries, and a poached egg on toast. I checked my phone and saw I had a missed text. It was from Edward; it said, "Scouring the markets for more shrimp. Sam in panic. Call you soon. Love E."

I was happy I didn't have to talk to Edward yet. My thoughts were still a mess. I had to bring myself down to earth. I left the gym and walked up to the lobby and out onto the balcony. I tucked myself into a corner chair and called Stephanie.

"Hi," I said.

"That sounds like a guilty 'hi,'" Stephanie replied.

"What do you mean?"

"Usually you call me and launch into what Andre's done, or what should you do about Edward, today it's just 'hi.' What's up?"

"Are you clairvoyant? Maybe I'm just calling to see what you're doing."

"We're doing the same exciting things we were doing last time you called. Graham is making me sand French fries and Zoe is serving them to me. Gisella is back so the Indian fort is gone, but Glenn is still out of town, so Graham and Zoe are sleeping in our bed. With me. What have you been up to?"

"Um . . ." I said.

"Cough it up, Amanda. Remember, your husband fucked his chef, standing up, in front of your eyes. Nothing you've done can be as bad as that."

"Okay," I exhaled. "Edward drove me home from the restaurant last night and we did some really heavy petting in his car."

"What does 'really heavy petting' mean? We're fifteen years out of high school, I'm not up on the lingo."

"I let him finger me," I whispered into the phone.

"Amanda, naughty!" She whistled.

"You're not helping. I feel so guilty."

"That's the only thing you shouldn't be feeling. Like Clinton said, if you didn't inhale you weren't smoking. You're still a virgin."

"Ha, ha," I said. "I feel like a bad mother, I'm still married. Max doesn't know anything that's going on."

"Max doesn't need to know anything, he's eight years old. As long as he's fed and bathed and entertained, you're a great mom."

"He is having a good time," I conceded. "He's surfing every day with the girl from Kids' Club. He's a fanatic."

"See, no need to worry there. What do you want?"

"That's what I don't know! I really like Edward. He's funny and sweet and he tells me I'm beautiful."

"You are beautiful, that's not enough. What do you see in him?" Stephanie asked.

I thought about it. "I see someone who has it all figured out. He's been through a divorce and has made himself a new life. And I don't know if I'm just horny, but he really turns me on."

"Probably just horny, not that there is anything wrong with that," Stephanie said.

"Seriously, I never thought I would want to go to bed with another man, but I do."

"Has he brought you flowers?" Stephanie asked.

"He brought my mother flowers," I replied.

"Has he taken you out to dinner? Bought you jewelry?"

"We can't go out to dinner, what would Max say?"

"You're making excuses. No sex until you have been suf-ficiently wined and dined. I stand by my earlier advice: Make him wait," Stephanie said.

"But I'm not making him wait, I'm making *me* wait," I protested.

"It's good for you, builds character. I'm proud of you. You're making great strides in erasing Andre from your mental landscape. Just ease up on the gas pedal."

"Fine," I mumbled.

"You sound like Zoe when I tell her she can't get her ears pierced yet. I miss you, Amanda. I have no one to gripe with."

"I'll be home soon, three more weeks," I said. I hung up and gazed at the ocean. Summer would be over in three weeks, and I had no idea what would happen next.

🦋 🦋 🦋

I changed into a bathing suit and took the tram to the beach to watch Max surf. I put my phone, a *Vogue,* and some sun-screen in a bag and slung it over my shoulder. I promised myself a peaceful afternoon, but the fact that Edward hadn't called weighed on me.

Max came running when he saw me and covered me with sand. "Hey, Mom. You have to see me stand up. Erin timed me, twelve minutes!" Max beamed.

"That's fantastic," I said. Max was almost completely blond

now, and new freckles appeared through his layers of sunscreen. "Let me put my towel down, and then I'll watch." I laid the towel on the sand, took my phone out of my bag, and sat down. Suddenly, I felt very tired. The late night, the morning workout, and the conversation with Stephanie had drained me. All I wanted was to curl up and sleep.

I was just drifting off when my phone rang.

"Good afternoon, sunshine." It was Edward.

"Hi," I said, and sat up.

"I'm sorry I didn't call earlier. But I found twenty dozen shrimp at a dirt-cheap price. I am the hero of the hour."

"That's great," I said.

"Listen, I have to work a long day, and tomorrow I promised I'd help Edward buy a new truck to take back to school. He's turning into a North Carolina hillbilly."

"Sure," I replied. Maybe Edward was trying to back off. Maybe a finger fuck was all he wanted.

"But I thought we could have lunch at my house on Saturday," he continued.

"Max is supposed to go ocean kayaking on Saturday, but I guess I could change it." I didn't look forward to an afternoon of trying to get two words out of Jessica.

"My kids are going to be in Pasadena for the weekend. I was hoping it could be just you and me."

I could feel the wetness creep back between my legs. "That would be lovely," I mumbled.

"Great, I'll pick you up at noon. We'll have the whole afternoon," he said.

"See you." I hung up. I was going to spend the whole afternoon alone with Edward in his house. I was not going to tell Stephanie or my mother, because I had no idea what I was doing.

Saturday morning Max and I had breakfast at the Pool Grille. He ate pancakes, cereal, yogurt, a banana, and three slices of bacon. I managed half a piece of toast and two bites of grapefruit. My stomach was in knots of anticipation. I had spent the last few days either in the gym or at the beach with Max, so I wouldn't have time to think. At least I was fit and tan. After breakfast, I dropped Max off at Kids' Club. He was so excited about sea kayaking he barely registered a good-bye.

"We'll probably be back by five," Erin said.

"Great, have fun, guys." I took the elevator up to the suite. My mother was flipping through *Architectural Digest*.

"Max is off on his great adventure," I said.

"And what you are up to?" she asked. She was wearing a Lilly Pulitzer pink-and-green linen dress, and she had had her hair done at the salon.

"Edward is taking me to lunch," I replied.

"It's a beautiful day. Where is he taking you?" Her makeup was perfectly applied, pale pink blush on her cheeks and deep red lipstick on her mouth. Every day she looked more like the mother I knew growing up, and less like the stick she had become since my father died.

"He didn't say." I gave her an innocent smile. "I better get ready."

I walked into my closet, irritated at myself for lying to her. I could have said, "I'm going to Edward's for lunch." She

Monarch Beach / 199

didn't know I had almost come in the front seat of his car, or that all I could think about for the last few days was "Was he inviting me to lunch or to bed?" I picked out a strapless Juicy sundress and Gucci sandals. I brushed my hair straight over my shoulders and slipped a couple of silver bangles on my arm.

"You're not wearing much," my mother appraised me when I walked back into the living room.

"It's ninety degrees outside! You have to stop treating me like I'm twelve, Mom. Do you want to measure the length of my skirt?"

"No, but I can tell what color underwear you're wearing. It's yellow." She frowned.

"You cannot see my underwear." I examined myself in the hall mirror. "I told Edward I'd meet him downstairs. I'll be back to pick up Max from Kids' Club." I kissed her on the cheek.

"What time is Max done?" she asked.

"Erin said they'd be back by five," I replied.

"That's a very long lunch." She gave me one of her pointed looks.

"I'm very hungry." I smiled, and closed the door.

Edward's car was waiting outside. I climbed in and he kissed me on the cheek. He let out a low whistle. "You are becoming quite the Southern California beauty queen."

"My mother complained my skirt is too short," I laughed.

He gently brushed his fingers over my thighs. "Not from where I'm sitting."

It was one of those breathtakingly beautiful summer days, when I couldn't imagine being anywhere but right next to the Pacific Ocean. We had the windows down in the Mini and the salt air was intoxicating.

"Sometimes the ocean is so stunning, it's too much," he said.

"I know what you mean. You want to acknowledge its beauty somehow. Fill yourself up with it," I agreed.

"I feel lucky to live here. Especially right now." He put his hand on my knee.

The car climbed the hill to his house and we pulled into the driveway.

"It's so quiet." I faced the ocean. It was completely calm, a deep, still blue like an inkwell.

"No one here but us." Edward took my hand and led me up the steps. "You sit on the deck, while I get lunch." Edward took me outside.

"Can I help?"

"No. I have something special planned." Edward grinned, and disappeared into the kitchen.

The table was already set with straw place mats and white paper napkins. Edward had put a vase of daisies on the table, and a bowl of grapes.

"This is pretty fancy," I said when he appeared from the kitchen carrying two glasses of orange juice.

"I don't have a beautiful lady here for lunch often, make that never." He put the glasses down and kissed the top of my head.

"Virgin orange juice or would you like it hit with champagne?" he asked.

"Virgin." I sipped it. "I'm trying to live by my parents' rule: No alcohol before six p.m. I've become a bit of a lush."

"Luscious but not a lush. I agree. It's too beautiful a day to blur our senses. I'll be right back."

I toyed with a bunch of purple grapes and tried to relax. It was the middle of the day and we were having lunch. Drinking *virgin* orange juice. Nothing was going to happen.

Edward came back on the deck and put two small-lidded pots on the table. He had a loaf of bread wedged under his arm, which he dropped on a plate.

"Take off the lid," he instructed.

I took off the lid. It smelled of the most wonderful cheese and herbs.

"It's broccoli fondue. I made it," he said proudly.

"You made a fondue?"

"I figured it was time to exorcise your demons. Try it."

I dunked a slice of French bread into the fondue. The cheese melted in my mouth and dribbled down my chin.

"What do you think?" he asked.

"It's fantastic. Where did you learn to make fondue?" I asked.

"In my college fraternity. Then it was basically throw everything into a pot and soak it in cheese and beer. The chef at the restaurant gave me a recipe for a more sophisticated fondue," Edward explained.

"You'll have to make it for Max, he'll be impressed." I wiped my mouth with the napkin.

"I don't want to compete with Andre. I'm just trying to help you overcome your fears."

"I'm not afraid of fondue," I laughed.

"Not anymore. We're conquering one phobia at a time:

restaurants, hostesses, fondue. Maybe next we'll tackle para-sailing." He grinned.

"I've never tried parasailing," I said.

"There's plenty of time," he replied.

🦋 🦋 🦋

"Can I help you clean up?" I asked, after we had scraped the pots clean of fondue.

"No, I'll do it. Why don't we have dessert in the living room?" Edward stacked plates and dishes and went into the kitchen.

I wandered into the living room and sat on a low leather sofa. There was one bookshelf crammed with framed photos of Edward Jr. and Jessica. The younger photos showed them in Hawaii, riding bicycles, and clowning around with assorted pets.

"There aren't any photos of Julie, in case you're looking," Edward said as he set down two bowls of vanilla ice cream and a jug of chocolate sauce.

"I wasn't looking, but now that you mention it, there aren't. God, does that mean I'm going to have to go through all my photos of Max and get rid of the ones with Andre in them?"

"At least you're divorcing while Max is young. I had to sift through fifteen years of photographs for Edward, and thirteen for Jessica. I didn't want my ex-wife looking at me every day," Edward said.

"Minefield after minefield," I mumbled.

"But you're getting through them. You're a star," he said.

"The ice cream is delicious." I poured chocolate sauce over it.

"I made the chocolate sauce, too, but don't tell my son. He thinks I'm getting too domesticated."

"I remember. I don't see any homemade doilies lying around, so you're safe," I giggled.

"The first year after my divorce I had the typical bachelor pad: a fridge that held one bottle of vodka, one lemon, and an onion; a loaf of bread in the pantry and a never-ending supply of salami, because it was the only meat that didn't spoil when I was too drunk to put it back in the fridge. One day I looked around and thought: I've never lived like this before, why would I want to live like this now? That's when I met Sam and he convinced me to pick up and move here. He was an advertising exec refugee. His ex-wife was getting seventy percent of his paycheck and he couldn't afford to go to work anymore." He paused and licked his spoon. "Laguna's great, close enough to the kids but far enough from Julie for the wounds to heal."

"That's one thing I'm afraid of. Ross is such a small town." I put my bowl on the table.

"One fear at a time." He leaned close and kissed me on the lips.

"I haven't shown you the rest of the house." He got up and took my hand.

I swallowed. This was the moment when I should say I have to go. I needed to get back to the hotel for Max. My mother was waiting for me. Any excuse to hop back in the Mini, thank him for an amazing lunch, and return, a virgin, to the St. Regis. I knew if I followed him, we would end up in his bedroom, with all my defenses down.

"It's not a very big house." Edward grinned as he poked his head into the study, guest bedroom, and adjoining bath. "The best part is up here." He led me up a steep flight of stairs. At the top was an open space with floor-to-ceiling windows looking at the ocean, and a king-sized bed with a white wooden bed frame. The bed was covered in a pale blue comforter and heaped with pillows.

"Oh, my gosh." I stood at the window, as far from the bed as possible, drinking in the view.

"I splurged up here. I bought a new bed, sheets, pillows, the works. It's even more beautiful at night, when you can see all the lights twinkling up and down the coast."

"It's heaven," I said.

Edward sat on the bed and took my hand. "Come here," he said.

I sat next to him. He kissed me for a long time, rubbing his hand up and down my spine. Then he stood me up and pulled my dress over my head. He turned me around and unsnapped my bra so I was standing in my panties and bare feet. He reached forward and sucked my nipples, gently cupping my breasts in his hands. Then he took one hand and edged my panties down my legs until they lay in a heap at my ankles.

My legs trembled, but he held me up, and slowly he moved his mouth down to my stomach, nudged my legs open, and thrust his fingers inside me, reaching deeper than he had before.

This time he didn't stop, but pressed his mouth firmly against my stomach, and kept pressing his fingers further, until I could feel myself gasping and shuddering and coming.

"Oh God," I whispered, when the waves started to recede.

"I thought you'd like that." He smiled. "Come here." He pulled me onto the bed and lay down beside me.

He took off his clothes; his chest was thick and covered with light gray hair. He kissed my neck and my throat, and ran his fingers through my hair. Then he climbed on top of me, and when he entered me I felt like I was opening up to a place that could not possibly exist. I couldn't wait. I clung to his back, and came again and again.

"Well, wow," I said finally.

"Wow, yourself." He turned to me and traced the tip of my nose with his finger. "I'd say there are a lot of new things we can try together." He grinned.

"It seems that way." My body was still reeling.

"Stay here, I have something for you." He threw on his shorts and walked into a narrow walk-in closet.

"This is for you." He placed a small box wrapped in plain gold paper on the bed.

"For me?" I asked.

"Open it."

I sat up, still naked, and unwrapped the box. Inside was a black velvet jewelry box. I snapped it open.

"Edward!" Inside the box were the monarch butterfly earrings we had seen at the hotel gift shop.

"Do you like them?" he asked.

"I love them, but why?" I examined the tiny pieces of colored gems encrusted in the butterflies' wings.

"Remember when we met, at the monarch butterfly release?"

"Of course. You gave me nutrition tips," I laughed.

"And Max came up and asked you to make a wish?"

"Yes," I said, and nodded.

"I made a wish, too: that I would get to know you better."

"Oh," I said.

"And that wish is starting to come true." He kissed me slowly, on the lips.

"I really don't know what to say." I kissed him back.

"You'll keep them?"

"Of course I'll keep them, they're gorgeous. I might not wear them in front of my mother just yet." I grinned.

"We'll work on her," he said. He kissed me again, and pushed me back onto the bed.

Eventually we got dressed, and I tucked the jewelry box into my bag. We climbed into the Mini and sped down the hill. We kept the windows down so it was hard to hear each other, but I was in a state of sexual bliss and didn't feel the need to talk.

"It was a wonderful afternoon," I said when we pulled up to the St. Regis.

"The best." He grinned. "Be a good girl tonight; I'll call you in the morning."

I headed straight to Kids' Club to get Max. If we went upstairs together my mother could ask Max questions about his day, and I could steal into the shower until my body regained its equilibrium.

"Hey, Max, how was sea kayaking?" I opened the doors to Kids' Club and found Max engrossed in the Wii.

"Awesome! Let me tell you all about it," he replied.

"Why don't you wait till we get to the suite, so you can tell Grandma and me at the same time." I took his hand.

We rode the elevator up to the suite and opened the door. My mother was out on the balcony with a glass in her hand. I stopped at the wet bar and poured myself a gin and tonic. It wasn't six o'clock yet, but I needed a shot of Dutch courage. I remembered my prep school days. My mother had a nose like a hound dog for smelling mischief. If I stood next to someone who was smoking at a party, or dipped my finger in a friend's rum and Coke, she could tell. I sprayed myself with cologne in the guest bathroom.

"Well, hi, you two." My mother came inside. "How was your day?" She looked at me.

"Mine was great," I said, beaming. "Max, tell us about sea kayaking."

Max launched into a description of the amazing fish he saw. I realized even with the gin and tonic inside me, I was a ball of nerves.

"I think I'm going to shower and change for dinner." I put my drink down.

"I'll order," my mother said. "I'm sure Max is starving. Amanda, there's something I want to talk to you about after Max goes to bed. You're not going out, are you?"

"Nope, home for the night." I gave her my sweetest smile and escaped to my room.

Half an hour later, I emerged wearing a long-sleeved Diane von Furstenberg caftan and Chanel ballet slippers. I knew my mother was a sucker for anything with a Diane von Furstenberg label. I hoped the Chanel slippers would remind her of when I was a sweet and innocent ten-year-old who wanted desperately to become a ballerina. As a finishing touch, I tucked my hair into a prim bun. I left the butterfly earrings, snug in their box, on my bedside table.

My mother and Max were already seated at the table. Max was on his third slice of bread and hummus, and my mother sipped a cold gazpacho.

"I ordered you the shrimp risotto. I had it the other night, the sauce is delicious." My mother smiled. She was wearing a yellow Polo dress and pastel flip-flops.

I took a spoonful of rice and shrimp and realized I was starving. One of the things I had missed about sex was the wonderful way it enhanced my appetite. Tonight was the first time I had really tasted food since I had seen Andre and Ursula swallowing each other's tongues.

My mother seemed to have an appetite as well. I watched her nervously as she ate salmon and mashed potatoes, but if she was about to give me a morals lecture she didn't let on. She and Max held an animated discussion on the chances of various *American Idol* contestants, and she ate all the mashed potatoes without any prompting. When we examined the dessert cart she almost fought Max for the chocolate raspberry cheesecake. I nibbled the butterscotch parfait; I had to control myself if I wanted to look good stripped down to my underwear.

Max was tired out from his day of kayaking and needed no encouragement to go to bed. My mother and I took coffee out on the deck, and I steeled myself for what was coming.

"School starts in less than three weeks. Have you decided what you are going to do?" she asked.

It wasn't the question I had anticipated. I expected her to ask: "Why did you come home with that 'I've spent all afternoon in bed and I'm still in a sexual haze' look on your face?" Maybe she was leading up to her inquisition.

"It doesn't seem like Andre is going to budge, so I'll have to look for a house to rent in Ross. Dean said that legally Andre could stay in the house if Andre paid Max rent, and the money would be put in a trust for Max."

"When are you going to tell Max about the divorce?" my mother asked.

"I was hoping Andre would come down here and we could do it together. It seems his dance card has been full all summer. He keeps saying he's coming but he never shows up."

"A man of his word," my mother murmured.

"I guess I'll tell Max when we go back to Ross," I replied.

"Amanda . . ." My mother paused. I sucked in my breath. She was going to tell me I was a terrible mother for jumping into bed with Edward so quickly. I didn't know him at all, I wasn't even divorced, and I should be ashamed of myself.

"I have decided to stay at the St. Regis till spring, possibly longer," she said.

"What?" I was stunned.

"I love it here. I love the weather, I love the beauty, and I love the way the staff takes care of me."

"But you've been in your house for thirty-five years! It's where you and Dad lived your whole marriage."

"And I miss him every day, but that's the problem. In that house he was everywhere, I saw him when I walked into every room. Being here, I realize there are things I still enjoy: eating good food, being around people, even watching trashy television. I miss your father terribly, but I'm not quite ready to join him yet."

Tears sprung to my eyes. I knew I was being selfish, but I couldn't imagine not being able to cross the Golden Gate Bridge and see my mother whenever I needed her.

"You and Max could live in the house, or you could both stay here with me," she offered tentatively.

"We can't stay here, Max's whole life is in Ross. And we can't live in the city either," I replied glumly.

"I'm sorry, honey. I don't want to go back to living in a tomb."

I didn't answer. I admired her for being able to change her life. I was having a hard time imagining living on a different street in Ross.

I watched her sip a decaf espresso, and I remembered when I was a child I would hear her and my father come home from a party late at night. Sometimes they would turn on the record player and dance in the foyer. I even spied them a few times gliding around the ballroom. My father always had a drink in his hand, and my mother would be wearing some glorious gown, her shoes tossed against the wall.

"I think that's wonderful," I said, beaming.

"You do?" She put down her espresso.

"You belong here. You have a five-star staff at your beck and call. It's perfect."

"Are you sure you and Max won't stay? I've heard there are some good schools close by."

"I'm sure. But we'll be down all the time. Max will be thrilled to come and surf." I was exhausting myself with my own enthusiasm.

"I'm so relieved. I was dreading bringing it up to you." My mother patted her hair. Her feet were tucked under her, displaying a perfect pedicure.

"I love you, Mom." I got up and pecked her on the cheek. "I'm tired and full, I ate too much parfait," I joked, so she wouldn't see the tears in my eyes. "I'm going to bed."

I slipped off my Chanel slippers and hung up my caftan. I wrapped myself in a St. Regis robe and took my hair out of its bun. I stood at the mirror for a long time brushing my hair. Finally I climbed into bed and snapped open the jewelry box. I could have worn the earrings and my mother would not have noticed. She hadn't been thinking about me at all.

Chapter Eight

*W*hen I woke up the next morning and peeked through the shutters, I saw the ocean was socked in with fog. Beach Boot Camp would be canceled. Max could spend the morning at Kids' Club playing Wii. My mother had God-knows-what saved on her TiVo and I didn't need to worry about her. I decided all I wanted to do was climb under the covers and sleep all day.

When I woke again it was almost five o'clock. My first thought was I was starving, but the hunger was quickly replaced by another emotion: fear. My mother was moving away, my marriage was over, and I had slept with another man. I, who thought when I exchanged vows with Andre ten years ago that "till death do us part" and "forsaking all others" actually meant something, had sex with someone else.

I checked my phone. I had two missed calls from Stephanie. I pressed delete. She would ferret out that I had slept with Edward and I wasn't ready for her critique. There was one missed call and a text from Edward. The text read: "Have surprise for Max. Can I pick you two up at noon tomorrow?" I smiled and texted back "yes." Then I got up, wrapped my robe around me, and hoped room service had left breakfast and lunch on the sideboard in the living room.

The fog cleared overnight, and Monday morning was crystal clear. I walked out onto the deck and sat down in front of a room service breakfast of sliced peaches and granola.

"Where are you off to today?" My mother had a *New York Times* spread out on the table and was eating an egg-white omelet.

"Edward says he has a surprise for Max. He's meeting us in the lobby." I wore a green cotton sundress, flat sandals, and the butterfly earrings. I had been rehearsing in the bathroom mirror what I would say if my mother noticed them ("they're my new good-luck earrings" was my favorite response), but so far she hadn't said a word.

"Do I have to come? I want to go surfing." Max sat across from my mother, eating spoonfuls of jam from a mini jelly jar.

"The surprise is for you. Plus, I never get to see you. You always have a surfboard leash attached to your leg." I shook my head.

"I didn't get to surf at all yesterday." Max pouted.

I finished my granola, wondering if it would be harder than I thought to tear Max away from the ocean at the end of the summer.

Max and I waited for Edward in the hotel driveway. Max had insisted on wearing boardshorts so he could surf the moment we got home.

A navy blue pickup truck pulled up and Edward waved. "Hop in," he said, motioning to us.

"You traded the Mini for a truck?" I asked.

"No, I'm borrowing Edward Junior's. Both sit up front with me," Edward instructed.

"What's the surprise?" Max asked.

"You'll find out when we get to the beach." Edward smiled.

It was odd sitting so close to Edward and not being able to touch him. My body remembered all the things he had done to me, and I wanted him to stroke me and kiss me, but Max was wedged on my other side.

We pulled up at Salt Creek Beach and Edward jumped out. He had a secret, very pleased look on his face.

"We're at the beach," Max said as he hopped out.

"I apologize for my impolite son." I looked hard at Max. "He didn't get to surf yesterday because of the fog, and he's a little antsy."

"Okay, Max, close your eyes," Edward commanded.

Max rolled his eyes like a bored eight-year-old, and then put his hands over his face. Edward opened the back of the truck and placed a yellow surfboard on the sand.

"You can open your eyes." Edward beamed.

"It's a surfboard," Max said cautiously.

"It was my son's first surfboard, and now it's yours." Edward smiled.

"My surfboard?" Max's voice rose a few octaves.

"Edward Junior picked it up from the house in Pasadena over the weekend. It's all yours."

"Why mine?" Max fell down on the sand and ran his hands over the fiberglass.

"Because from what I've heard, you are a champion surfer in the making. And to thank you for letting me borrow your mom now and then."

"Wow!" Max couldn't contain himself. "Can I surf right now?"

"Let me help you wax it up."

🦋 🦋 🦋

I found a towel in the back of the truck and spread it out on the sand. When the surfboard was gleaming with wax, Max picked it up like a young warrior and headed into the waves. Edward sat down next to me, took my head in his hands, and kissed me hard on the lips.

"Hello, sunshine, I've missed you," he said when he finally released me.

I let myself relax, snuggled in his arms. "I missed you, too."

"And I missed this," he said as he traced a path with his hands between my breasts, down my stomach, and between my legs.

"We're at the beach in broad daylight." I moved his hand away.

"I know." He took my hand and held it in his. "But I want you. Hey, you're wearing the earrings. Didn't the Wicked Witch of San Francisco protest?"

"The Wicked Witch of San Francisco has become the permanent guest of the St. Regis. She has other things on her mind." I smiled.

"What are you talking about?" Edward asked.

"My mother has decided she is going to stay at the St. Regis indefinitely."

"You're kidding. I thought she has a huge mansion in Pacific Heights." Edward frowned.

"I guess she has been really lonely in the house without my father. He was like Hamlet's ghost, lurking in every room," I continued.

"I can understand. It's good to be somewhere new." Edward nodded.

"She looks wonderful. She's not smoking. She's put away her Chanel suits and is wearing sundresses and sandals." I tried to keep my voice from cracking.

"You don't sound too happy." Edward stroked my cheek.

"I know I'm being a baby, but I'm going to miss her."

"Why not move here with her?" Edward's hand traveled to my thigh.

"She suggested that. But we belong in Ross." I let him push open my thighs. His fingers slid under my dress and caressed my panties.

"Because that's where your lothario ex-husband is?" He slipped his hand inside my panties.

"Because that's where Max's school is, and all his friends," I replied. I felt a tiny jolt as his fingers found the sweet spot inside me.

"Max loves the hotel, he's crazy about surfing. Laguna

Beach has excellent schools. You should consider it." He leaned forward and kissed me on the mouth.

"Max can't live in a hotel. He'll think it's normal to have people polish his flip-flops."

"Then rent a house, or you and Max can live with me." He pushed his fingers further into me. He opened me up, kneading me until I was wet and trembling. I closed my eyes and felt the delicious wave of an orgasm spread over me.

"You can't do that in public," I whispered finally.

"Yes I can." He sat up and looked at me. "I'm serious, Amanda." He was always smiling, joking. I had never seen him look so stern.

"Serious about what?" I straightened my dress.

"I haven't really dated since my divorce. What's the point? I'd done the courtship-marriage-children thing and it ended on a train in the Australian outback. But I find I just want to be with you. When I'm not with you I'm thinking about you. I want to give us a chance to get to know each other. I'm with your mother: stay here."

"You like me because I'm an easy lay," I said, trying to laugh.

"No, I like you because I might be falling in love with you," he said quietly.

"Oh." I sat up straight.

"It's a great life down here for Max," he said.

"I'm not very good at change. I've lived in San Francisco my whole life," I replied weakly.

"Sometimes change happens for us. Just think about it."

Max came galloping toward us, dragging the surfboard on the sand.

"Did you see how many waves I caught? This board is awesome."

"You're a star, just like your mother. How about if I treat you two to a burger and shake at Ruby's before I go to work?" Edward asked.

"Awesome! I'm starving. Did you watch me, Mom? This board goes so fast," Max prattled on. We got in the truck and Edward pointed out to Max the different surf breaks along the coast. I sat silently between them, trying to take in what Edward had said.

At Ruby's, I watched Max swallow a double cheeseburger, a side of onion rings, and an Oreo shake. I ordered a fruit cup and played with the grapes.

"Not hungry?" Edward whispered. His hand was on my thigh under the table.

"Not hungry." I shook my head. I felt too feeble to make a jokey comeback.

"Max, make sure your mom eats a good dinner tonight," Edward said out loud.

"Sure thing." Max nodded. He looked as if he had grown six inches in one afternoon. "Wait till I show Erin my surfboard." He finished his shake and wiped his chin with a napkin.

Edward drove us back to the hotel and the valets helped Max with his board.

"I have to work tonight. How about lunch at my place tomorrow?" Edward asked.

"Sounds delicious," I said, grinning.

"I'll pick you up at noon." He winked at me.

I walked into the lobby and out onto the balcony. I sat at a table overlooking the Grand Lawn and replayed the after-noon in my head. Sex on the sand, Edward saying he was falling in love with me. I was going to have to call Stephanie.

🦋 🦋 🦋

I decided to hold off calling Stephanie and give myself a week to think. The truth was I wanted to lie in Edward's bed, hot and sweaty, without Stephanie's advice running through my head. I gave myself over to five blissful days of possibilities and indecision.

Every morning Max collected his surfboard and headed off to the beach with Erin. My mother had her own new rou-tine: After a late breakfast she went to the salon and had her hair or her nails or her toes done. Then she took a few turns around the Grand Lawn and came back to the suite to watch *The Young and the Restless*.

Edward had to work each night so he picked me up at noon every day. The first day we made a halfhearted attempt to sit on the deck at his house and eat quiche and fruit salad. After a few bites, we both realized we'd rather be in his bed.

For the rest of the week we started in the bedroom. He would strip off my clothes, folding them neatly on the floor, before he undressed. Then he would lay me on the bed and lick my breasts, suck my fingers, cover my stomach with kisses. Only when I was dizzy with wanting him would he open my legs and slide into me. After we were both spent, we thought about eating.

We didn't talk about Andre or Max or his children. We didn't discuss what was going to happen at the end of the summer. But we did talk about movies, books, travel, the economy, the Internet, iPads, cars, pets, and roses. We talked and we ate and eventually we would clear away our picnic of fruit and wine and ham sandwiches, and make love again before he drove me home.

W W W

On Friday night, I lay on my own bed, feeling well satisfied but very confused. I watched the sun melt into a pink ball and wondered if I could just go on like this forever. School started in two weeks. I had missed several calls from Andre and Stephanie. My mother was so pleased with herself for making her decision to stay that she didn't grill me about how I was spending my days or what my plans were. Max's conversation was limited to the surfing vernacular he learned during the day.

I closed my eyes and let myself imagine what it would be like if Max and I stayed in Laguna Beach. We wouldn't live at the hotel, and it was too soon to move in with Edward. But what if I rented a small house on the beach, and Max could surf every afternoon after school? I would join the PTA and maybe help Edward and Sam out at the restaurant.

My phone buzzed. It was Stephanie. "Hello," I answered.

"Are you on the lam?" she asked.

"What?" I replied.

"I've been calling you for five days. I send you to Laguna Beach with a new summer wardrobe and you disappear. What's going on?" she demanded.

"My mother has decided to stay at the St. Regis indefinitely. And Edward asked me to stay here, too. He said he's falling in love with me," I said.

"Can I interpret your radio silence to mean you've been having sex with him for the last week?" Stephanie asked.

"Yes," I admitted guiltily.

"Is he good in bed?" she asked.

"Why do you want to know?" I laughed.

"Because if he's mediocre you're okay, but if he's really good you have a problem."

I thought about it. "Andre was so handsome, just looking at him was a sexual experience. But having sex was all about him. Edward makes me feel like I'm starring in my own porn movie. I didn't know you could have so many orgasms!" I sighed.

"So you do have a problem. I might have to come down and inspect him myself." She laughed.

"Can I really uproot Max just so I can see what happens with me and Edward?" I asked.

"It's not like you'd be moving to a farm in Kansas. Laguna Beach is a lovely place to grow up. And you'd be near your mother. What do you have in Ross? Besides me of course."

"All Max's friends, his school, his dad." I ticked them off on my finger.

"Have you heard from Andre?"

"He's been calling. The last time I talked to him he swore he's been faithful all summer and we should come home," I said.

"I wouldn't make any decisions based on that," Stephanie murmured.

"I wasn't going to," I said. "I've got two weeks, what should I do?"

"You haven't said how you feel about Edward, besides that he would direct a good skin flick."

"I'm not sure how I feel about Edward. I'm happy when I'm with him. He's funny, and he takes charge of things."

"Like a father?" Stephanie mused.

"Cut the psychobabble. You need to stop watching *Dr. Phil*."

"I want to hear all the sex details. Glenn's out of town again and I haven't had sex in days," Stephanie said.

"How is that going to help me make a decision?" I complained.

"It won't. But if I can't watch *Dr. Phil,* I need some distraction."

"Thanks for the help," I muttered.

"It'll come to you. Just don't make any decisions for at least an hour after orgasm. It might color your judgment."

🦋 🦋 🦋

I hung up and tried again to picture moving to Laguna Beach. I would have to find Max a new karate studio, a new pediatrician, a new dentist. He wouldn't know a single child at school.

I imagined him running along the beach with a dog, a black Labrador or a beagle. He'd bang into the kitchen after a long day surfing, and I'd feed him stacks of turkey sandwiches and gallons of milk. Edward would come over in the evenings and we'd sit on the deck, eating nachos and guacamole. Maybe we'd all go skiing in Bear Valley, or take the ferry to Catalina Island.

If we stayed in Ross, I'd never meet another man. By the time Max became a teenager he'd be sick of me. He would spend all his time at his friends' houses because if he brought them home, I'd be hovering around offering them snacks, and butting in on their conversations.

Andre would probably have some young babe installed in his house, and I'd see her at the post office every day. She'd cross the commons in tiny miniskirts and stiletto heels and the other mothers would whisper: "Poor Amanda, so sad."

I rubbed my eyes. My phone rang again. It was Andre.

"Hello," I answered.

"Amanda! I have wonderful news."

"Okay," I said.

"I got the restaurant covered this weekend and I'm flying down tomorrow afternoon to be with you and Max," he announced.

"We'll be home in two weeks! You don't have to come now," I protested.

"I need to talk to you, *ma cherie*, away from Ross." His voice dropped into a slow, sexy drawl.

"I don't want to talk to you," I said. I felt a pain creep into the back of my neck.

"You will, when you hear what I have to say. *À bientôt, ma cherie.*" He hung up.

I put down my phone. What could Andre possibly have to say to me that he hadn't made clear with his bevy of bachelorettes? I reached over and poured myself a brandy from the decanter on my bedside table. All that thinking had given me a headache.

I got up and went into the living room to put Max to bed. He lay on the sofa, Wii stick in hand, eyes glued to the screen. I sat down next to him and ran my fingers through his hair. I had to make a good decision for Max, not one based on sexual fantasies or my allergic reaction to Andre's mistresses. I lay my head on Max's forehead, wishing I was his age and had someone to make the decision for me.

Chapter Nine

I spent the next morning at the gym. I did thirty minutes on the treadmill, twenty minutes in the sauna, half an hour on the ballet bar, and capped it off with fifteen minutes of stomach crunches. By lunchtime I was sore and hungry, but still hyperventilating at the thought of seeing Andre again. I ordered my favorite goat cheese and fennel salad at the spa café. When the waitress placed it in front of me, I suddenly felt sick, and sent it back to the kitchen.

I left the gym and walked along the golf course. Andre had left a message he would be at the hotel by six p.m. I would say a quick hello, and send him and Max off to have dinner. Then I would hide in the Tranquillity Room until he brought Max home. I hadn't thought about where Andre would sleep. The thought of Andre staying at the St. Regis, even though there were 350 rooms, made me ill.

After three laps around the golf course, I felt better. I pictured Edward's crooked smile, I remembered his body on top of mine, I thought about how his fingers probed and pushed me. I walked over the bluff of the ninth tee and saw the ocean glistening like a giant infinity pool. I was not going to let Andre's presence disturb me.

My phone rang and I was relieved to see it was Edward.

"Good morning, sunshine," he said.

"Hi," I replied.

"I've missed you," he said.

"I thought you might have had enough of me," I laughed.

"I'm just beginning to get enough of you," he countered, "but I'm calling to ask a favor."

"Shoot," I said.

"Sam came up with an Early Bird Special for tonight that's a sellout. Do you think you could come help Gemma for a couple of hours? The crowd should be gone by eight p.m. We could cut out early and have a feast at my house. I promise to get you home by midnight."

"I can't come at six. Andre is flying down to see Max. I could be there by seven," I replied.

"Why do you have to be there? Just have your mother meet him." Edward's voice had an edge to it.

"I can't just let Max go with Andre without saying hello," I replied.

"Why not?" Edward asked tersely.

"Max hasn't seen him all summer."

"Max is eight years old. You don't have to pack Andre a diaper bag or give him a feeding schedule. Just tell your mother what time you want Max home. I'd really like you at the restaurant," Edward said firmly.

"It wouldn't be right," I said lamely.

"What's going on, Amanda? Do you want to see Andre?" He had that stern tone I had only heard once before.

"I don't want to see him at all," I replied truthfully. "I just think I should."

"When you figure out why you *should* see him, let me know. I'll be at work." He hung up.

I flipped the phone shut and shoved it in my pocket. This was our first fight. I walked back across the golf course feeling miserable and alone.

I sat down on a bench and closed my eyes. I wished I were sitting on the bench at Phoenix Lake with Max, throwing bread crumbs to the ducks. I wished I could rewind my life to pre-Ursula days. But that wasn't possible, because Andre had been cheating our whole marriage. I had to move forward.

Max was ecstatic that Andre was coming. He insisted on laying his surfboard down in the suite's foyer so it would be the first thing Andre saw when he walked in. He wore board-shorts and a surfing T-shirt and lined up ten bars of surf wax for Andre to inspect. I purposely allowed myself only fifteen minutes to get ready. I slipped on a Donna Karan bodysuit and skirt and Tory Burch flats. I brushed my hair, put in my butterfly earrings, and flipped opened *Vogue*.

The doorbell rang at six fifteen, and even before Max opened it I felt like I was riding up in an elevator and had left my stomach on the ground floor. Andre walked in wearing silk shorts, a navy blue shirt opened to the third button, and leather sandals. His skin was tan, and his hair was shiny black and curled around his chin. He looked like he had stepped away from the Cannes film festival.

"Amanda, *mon amour.*" He wrapped his arms around me and kissed me on the lips. "These are for you." He set down his bag, pulled out three wrapped boxes, and gave one to me, one to Max, and one to my mother.

"Andre, we don't want any presents," I said tersely.

"I haven't seen my family in almost three months. I should have a whole bag of presents."

"Cool, Dad!" Max unwrapped a Lego sailboat. I left my box unopened on the side table.

"Max, you've grown six inches! Grace, you look lovely, and my wife"—Andre took my hands in his—"is more beautiful than ever."

I pulled my hands away and grabbed my bag. "You two have a great dinner, I have to go."

"We must eat dinner together." Andre grabbed my hand and held it tightly. "You, too, Grace. My treat," he said to my mother.

"Thank you, Andre, it's lovely to see you," my mother said as she sat on the sofa, nursing her cocktail, "but I've already ordered room service."

"Amanda, come. What is the best restaurant in the hotel?"

"I can't, I have plans." I shook my head.

"Plans?" Andre asked.

"I'm helping a friend," I said, stumbling.

"Max, tell your mother she has to have dinner with us," Andre said.

"Please, Mom. Dad hasn't been here all summer!" Max begged.

"I really can't," I stammered, pulling away.

"Tell your friend you'll help later. Max, lead the way." Andre opened the door. "Grace, we will catch up after dinner. Thank you for taking good care of my wife and son," Andre called to my mother.

I found myself in the elevator with Andre and Max. I studied a chip on my nail while Max jabbered to Andre about surfing.

"And where did you get this new surfboard?" Andre asked Max.

"A friend of Mom's," Max answered innocently.

"You have made a lot of friends this summer." Andre stood close to me. "You'll have to tell me about them."

We got out of the elevator and Andre put his arm around me. I pulled away but he held me tighter and whispered in my ear, "Your body is so hard."

"Stop it," I hissed back.

"Max," Andre said, turning to Max, who was a few steps ahead of us. "Your mother and I are going to have a drink and watch the sunset before dinner."

"I have to go," I said through gritted teeth.

"Max, show me where we can have a drink," Andre insisted.

"Let's go to the pool bar. They have awesome shakes!" Max led the way.

Max was so happy to see Andre, I thought his smile would crack open his face. I felt myself deflating like a beach ball. If I left, Max would be heartbroken. One strong drink and I might be able to make it through dinner. I sat down at the bar and ordered a scotch and soda.

"You look gorgeous, coming here was a good idea." Andre put his hand over mine.

"Stop touching me," I said quietly.

"I lead a monk's life. All I do is work at the restaurant, walk home, and go to bed. I can't wait for you and Max to come home."

"I'm only having dinner with you for Max. We are getting a divorce and we're going to have to tell him."

Andre looked puzzled. "Why would we get a divorce? I adore you, we have the most beautiful son," he said, stroking my hand, "and you still love me."

"I don't love you," I replied in a low voice.

"You may say that"—Andre touched my face—"but your body says differently."

Max climbed up to the bar with his milkshake. "Hey, Dad, want to play Frisbee?" Max asked.

"Sure, I need to talk to your mother for a minute," Andre replied.

"I'll go borrow one from Kids' Club." Max set off across the Grand Lawn, leaving me alone with Andre. I took a swig of scotch.

"Amanda, I know what I did was wrong. I'm ashamed and I'm sorry."

"You are only sorry you got caught." I shook my head.

He took my hand and held it firmly. "In France, husbands have affairs and the wives don't care. It will never happen again."

"I can't." I shook my head.

"I will do anything you want." He put his arms around me and kissed me hard on the lips. His kiss was so familiar;

his mouth had the same sweet taste of coffee and mints I remembered. I felt for a minute like we had never stopped kissing.

"We're in public." I broke away from him.

"Then we'll go somewhere private." Andre stroked the back of my neck.

"We're not going anywhere."

He reached forward and kissed me again. "Amanda, we belong together. Let's have dinner and go up to bed."

"Are you crazy? I haven't seen you in two and a half months." I pushed away from him.

I ordered another scotch and soda. I needed the alcohol to create a plate of armor that Andre couldn't penetrate.

"My life will be an open book. You can visit the restaurant twenty times a day, you will never see me look at another woman," he said like a schoolboy pleading with his headmaster.

"You can't breathe without looking at other women," I said, and gulped my scotch.

"Give me a chance." He kissed the back of my neck.

Max came running up with a Frisbee. "Ready, Dad?"

"I'm coming." He jumped off the bar stool and took my face in his hands. He kissed me slowly, like a teenager on a date with his pinup fantasy. "As soon as I show your mother how much I've missed her."

"Yuck, you guys kiss too much." Max stood patiently with the Frisbee.

"Impossible," Andre smiled. "At dinner we will share a plate of oysters," he whispered in my ear.

I watched Andre and Max play Frisbee on the Grand

Lawn. Even though Max's hair had gotten blonder over the summer, they looked so much alike. They both moved gracefully, throwing and catching the Frisbee like natural athletes.

I took a small sip of scotch. It was having the opposite of my desired effect, and my feelings about Andre were teetering on a dangerous abyss. It would be so easy to believe him: to pack up and fly back to San Francisco, hang my clothes in our bedroom closet, and go back to being a PTA mom.

I grabbed a handful of cashews and chewed them slowly. I imagined having breakfast in our kitchen like we used to after Max had gone to school. Andre brewed organic coffee, and we drank it the French way: with real cream instead of half and half. Sometimes we shared a chocolate croissant. Our kitchen got the morning sun, and it was our time together, before Andre walked to the restaurant and I went off to a school meeting.

I knew, as I fantasized, what was wrong with this picture. Andre's days and nights at the restaurant included reaching under women's skirts, massaging their breasts, screwing them in his office, in the coat room, in the walk-in fridge. But what if he had changed? I knew I should be considering Edward, but he lay in some shut-off corner of my mind. All I could see was Andre running barefoot on the Grand Lawn, throwing Max the Frisbee.

Andre ran over to me and emptied his pockets on the bar. "I can't play with all this stuff weighing me down." He unbuttoned his shirt and laid it on the bar stool.

It was hard enough watching Andre run with his shirt on; I couldn't look at him bare-chested. I turned back to the bar. I fiddled with Andre's car keys, counted the change he spread on the bar, and picked up his phone. Andre had the same flip-phone I did. I flipped it open to see if he still had the picture of Max on his first day of school as his background. He had one new text.

Suddenly I was sober. Should I read his text? If I was going to trust him, shouldn't I start now? But if he was telling the truth, he had nothing to hide. I held the phone in my hand, thinking of the trouble I had caused myself by reading Edward's text.

Andre and Max were yards away, chasing each other around the lawn. I pressed read. "Hey lover, when are you back? I miss your chocolate croissants. Keeping bed warm. LOL MM." I snapped the phone shut like it was a piranha. Andre and Max seemed to be floating far away from me. I did the only thing my mind would let me do: I ran.

I ran up five flights of stairs, out the front doors, and into a town car that was parked in the driveway.

"Laguna Beach Tackle, please; 450 Forest Avenue," I said to the driver. Only when I rolled up the tinted windows and pulled away from the hotel did I exhale.

Later, I promised myself I would lie face down on my bed and cry. How had I let Andre's sheer beauty, the way his chest looked when he caught the Frisbee midair, stop me from seeing what a cheating, lying bastard he was? But I couldn't go up to the suite now. My mother would ask me what happened and Andre and Max would come to find me.

The town car pulled up in front of the restaurant and I froze. What if Edward was still angry with me?

"Could you wait for a bit?" I asked the driver.

I applied a new coat of lip gloss and stepped out of the car.

Gemma stood at the hostess booth, waving menus at a group of sunburned tourists.

"Hi," I said tentatively. "Edward asked me to help you."

"That would be great, we're mobbed." She nodded to the crowd.

"I'll just tell Edward I'm here." I walked toward the kitchen.

"He went home an hour ago, said he didn't feel well." Gemma stopped me.

"Oh, he didn't tell me." I felt foolish and out of place.

"I could really use you, if you have an hour," she said, and grinned.

I looked uncertainly at the men and women wearing fanny packs, picked up a stack of menus, and passed them out. I had nowhere else to be; I might as well make myself useful.

"I think I'm going to go." The crowd had thinned and I sat in the hostess chair. My feet ached, but at least I had shut my mind off for an hour.

"Hey, it was really swell of you. Edward will be pleased," Gemma thanked me.

I walked outside thinking if Edward was pleased, he probably wouldn't have gone home "not feeling well." I had ruined his night and mine by not listening to him. The town car waited at the corner.

"Where to, madam?" the driver asked.

I played with my phone. I flipped it open and sent Edward a text. "Done at restaurant. Can I come over?"

I sat back, waiting for a reply. I flipped open my phone: no texts. I leaned forward to tell the driver to go home, when my phone buzzed.

"Am home. Come over," Edward's text read.

The town car climbed the hill to Edward's house. I felt as nervous as the evening of our first date. Seeing Andre had destroyed my new confidence. I had behaved like a newborn puppy: innocent and looking for love in the wrong place.

Edward was waiting outside. He wore a blue robe over cotton pajama pants. His face broke into a smile when he opened the door of the town car.

"No Bentley tonight?"

"I had to make a quick getaway." I laughed.

"You can tell the driver to leave," he kissed me softly on the mouth.

"I have to get home for Max later," I mumbled.

"I'll drive you." He took my hand and guided me up the stairs.

"Gemma called and said you were a huge help," he said when we got to the living room.

"Edward . . ." I wanted to tell him how sorry I was for not listening to him, but he put his finger over my mouth.

"You don't have to say anything," he whispered. He put his arms around me and pulled me down to the sofa. He looked at me carefully, stroking my cheeks, brushing his fingers over my mouth. The pain and tension of the evening started to dissipate. I tried to wriggle out of my skirt but Edward stopped me. "Not so fast," he whispered. "I want to enjoy you."

He pushed me back on the sofa and lay on top of me. I could feel his heart beating, and he was hard underneath his robe. I lay back and let him kiss my mouth, my neck. He cupped my breasts and pushed them out of my bodysuit. He sucked my nipples, which sent shivers down my spine.

"Edward," I whispered again.

"Let's go upstairs." He got up and took my hand. We walked up the stairs holding hands, and when we got to his bedroom he laid me on the bed and kissed my knees, my stomach, my mouth. He peeled off my bodysuit and rolled up my skirt. Finally he threw off his robe, tugged off my panties, and slid on top of me and into me.

We came at the same time. It was so deep, so delicious, I felt different, not myself. I tucked myself under Edward's arm and closed my eyes.

"Gemma said you went home sick," I said finally.

"I'm better now." He grinned.

"Edward, I . . ." I started.

"How about I get some champagne? I think we deserve it." He got up, pulled on his robe, and treaded down the stairs.

I snuggled deeper into the bed. I was like a kitten that had just finished a warm bowl of milk. I rolled over onto my stomach and felt something small and hard dig into my flesh. I reached down and found my butterfly earring. I sat up, and felt my ears to see which earring was missing. Mine were both in my ears. I held the third earring in my hand, looking at it but not seeing it, until Edward walked back up the stairs.

"Ice-cold champagne, grapes, and caviar." He held a silver tray on his hands.

"Left over from your evening rendezvous?" I spat.

"What?" He was puzzled.

"Were you too busy fucking to drink the champagne?" I sat up. My whole body shook; my teeth were chattering and wouldn't stop.

"What are you talking about?" He put the tray on the floor and sat down on the bed.

"I'm talking about this." I dropped the earring into his lap.

"It's your earring." He picked it up.

"It's not my earring, because mine are in my ears. Whose earring is it?" I pushed back my hair like a madwoman.

Edward didn't say a word. I waited for him to deny everything, say he had no idea how it got there, maybe his son had a girl in his bed, but he didn't.

"I made a mistake," he said finally. "An old friend called while I was at the restaurant. An old fuck buddy, actually."

"A what?"

"Her name is Bethany. I met her after my divorce. She was recently divorced and we hung out a lot. We were fuck buddies. We had sex for fun, no strings attached. I'm not even attracted to her; she's one of those British rose types, pale skin and flabby thighs. I haven't seen her in years. She called in tears because her boyfriend broke up with her. She was sobbing, threatening suicide. She asked if she could come over and I said yes." He looked down at his hands. "I was angry at you. I knew when you saw Andre all the feelings would come back, and you would want to pack Andre and Max into a suitcase and fly off to be a happy family again."

I shivered and pulled the sheet around me.

"I know, because I wanted that with Julie. You always

think: This time it can be different; this time they won't hurt me. So I let Bethany come over, and she cried out her whole story and then she came up here. She used to like to fiddle with my things, arrange my bookshelves, tidy my dresser. I did buy another pair of earrings; they were going to be for Jessica and they were sitting on my dresser. I guess she put them on, I didn't even notice."

"You're missing the important part. You fucked her," I said.

He looked at me like he had just lost something valuable. "I did. She was here in the bedroom; we ended up in bed. I am so sorry, Amanda."

"How could you, you're my knight in shining armor, you're the good guy," I yelled at him.

"I am the good guy, I just made one bad mistake. I thought I was losing you."

"You didn't know anything. And you didn't wait to find out. You fucked another woman and then you fucked me an hour later. You're worse than Andre." I started to cry.

"I was an idiot. Look at me"—he took my face in his hands—"I want us to be together. I see that so clearly now."

"I want to go home." I grabbed my clothes. "I'll call the car."

"We need to talk, we can't just throw this away. I haven't met anyone in five years I felt anything for."

"There's nothing to talk about." I slipped into my bodysuit and zipped up my skirt.

"Amanda, please." He put his arms around my waist.

"I have to go." I kept my eyes on the ground.

"Let me drive you. I won't say a word." Edward pulled on sweatpants and grabbed his car keys.

We drove down the hill in silence. I hugged the edge of the passenger seat, trying to sit as far from Edward as possible. I tried not to think, because if I released the trapdoor that kept my thoughts shut, they would bury me. We pulled up at the hotel and I opened the car door.

"I'll call you in the morning. I know it's a shitty time to tell you, but I love you, Amanda." He leaned over and put his hand on mine.

"Good night, Edward." I got out and closed the door.

The lobby was full of guests laughing and mingling. Women wore strapless evening dresses and high heels. Men walked around with drinks in their hands, cocktail waitresses refreshed champagne glasses. I couldn't even nod or say hi to the hotel staff, I was so ashamed. I was a slut, an easy mark.

I sat in the quietest corner of the lobby lounge, in a giant velvet chair that made me invisible. I pulled out my phone and checked my messages. Andre had called three times asking where I was. His last message said he was staying at a motel on PCH and he would be over for breakfast. I sent him a text: "No need to come for breakfast. Save your croissants for MM."

I wanted to go upstairs and climb into bed, but I couldn't move. I felt like the heroine of a B movie who could see the train coming but couldn't get off the tracks. Twice down, game over.

Summer was ending. Returning to Ross would be a daily nightmare of stepping over Andre's women. I imagined them lined up on Ross commons, waiting to hop into bed with him. Staying in Laguna Beach would mean starting from scratch: new school, new house, new friends. In my exhausted state, that seemed an impossible task.

In my freshman year of high school the end-of-the-year party was held at my house. I was usually shy about kids coming over because they were in such awe of the gold-plated mirrors, the concert-sized baby grand piano, the wall of first editions in the library.

But I had nursed a secret crush on Chase Matheson for the last six months and I thought this was my opportunity. In the final weeks of school he showed an interest in me—he'd stop by my locker between classes, drop by my lunch table, walk with me to history. If I could get him alone for a few minutes, offer to show him the indoor pool or the fitness room, he might kiss me.

He gave me a bunch of flowers when he arrived. I went to the kitchen to put them in water, blushing that he was so thoughtful. When I returned to the foyer he had disappeared. I chatted with the other kids, the whole time wondering where he had gone. He finally reappeared through the doors to the garden, followed by Angie Bartholomew. Angie was a glamorous drama type; long red hair, green eyes smudged with black eye shadow, breasts too big for her body. When she had arrived at the party she was wearing a green shirt that buttoned up the front. Now, trailing behind Chase, it was buttoned up the back. I looked at her, looked at Chase, and ran up to my room. My mother found me crying on my princess bed, and made me go down and say good-bye to my guests.

I pulled myself out of the chair and headed for the elevator. I took off my butterfly earrings and put them in my purse. It was time to face my mother.

🦋 🦋 🦋

My mother sat on the love seat, flipping through *Architectural Digest*.

"Max said you ran off before dinner." She snapped the magazine shut.

"I did," I mumbled.

"He was very upset. He said he was playing Frisbee with Andre and you just disappeared. What's going on?" She wore a pink-and-white Burberry robe and satin Gucci slippers. Her skin without any makeup was smooth, and her hair fell naturally around her shoulders. I felt like Shrek having an interview with the queen.

"Andre started going on about how much he wanted me back. He'd never cheat again, he couldn't live without me."

"And?" She sat next to me on the sofa.

"I almost believed him. He's so gorgeous and he's my husband. I thought we could try again."

"You could," she said. "Max would be pleased."

"But then I found a text on his phone from a girl saying she was keeping his bed warm." I tried to be a grown-up and not cry like when Chase went off with Angie Bartholomew.

"Oh, honey. You don't need him. You can do so much better." She hugged me.

"But I can't do better at all."

"You've only been separated a few months and you're already dating," she said.

"Not anymore." I shook my head.

"Did something happen with Edward?"

I opened my purse, pulled out the butterfly earrings, and the whole story came out. Edward and I had started a serious relationship, he asked Max and me to live with him. He had given me the earrings. We got into a fight about me seeing Andre. And then tonight: going to see him, ending up in bed, and finding another butterfly earring in his bed.

"Oh, honey. He seemed like a lovely guy."

"That's the problem." I was almost hysterical. "I'm a bad judge of character. That's the one thing Dad always said. 'One doesn't judge a man by how much money he has, but by the strength of his character.' For so many years I believed in Andre. And then I met Edward and I thought he was kind, and solid, and he's even worse."

"All men have faults," she said uncertainly.

"Dad never cheated on you," I said.

"Maybe times were different then, different standards, less temptation."

"Only in your social circle. But I'm not a member of the San Francisco Junior League or the Friends of the Opera. Aren't there any men who don't wear a white tie on Saturday nights who can be faithful?"

Neither of us said anything. My mother got up and walked

around the room. She straightened the mini bar, fluffed up the sofa cushions.

"Maybe you should take a break from men for a while and do something for yourself."

"I love being Max's mom. But I don't want to be one of those single moms who pour all their energy into their kids: making three-course school lunches with homemade soup and a separate container for croutons."

"Remember the day your father and I told you he had liver cancer?" she said.

"Yes," I said, nodding.

"You came running down the stairs with your college acceptance letters. I'd never seen you look so happy, so sure of yourself."

"Mom, I was eighteen."

"Exactly, and your life was all about you. Before it became about taking care of your father, and me, and then Andre and Max. What do you want to do, for you?"

"You've been watching *Dr. Phil,* too." I sighed.

"Think about yourself for a minute."

I tried to picture a future without Andre, without Edward, with just me.

"You wanted to go to Parsons, and you didn't because of your father," my mother prompted me.

"That was fourteen years ago." I shook my head.

"Do it now. You're young, you have plenty of time to be the next Chanel."

"Just pick up and go to New York with Max?" I laughed.

"Why not?"

"I wouldn't be accepted. Andre is in California. Where would we live? Where would Max go to school?" I ticked the list off on my fingers.

"Let's put all that aside for a minute. Would you like to attend Parsons, try out the fashion world?" She sat down on the sofa.

I closed my eyes and pictured myself in a classroom, sketching a pantsuit or a fabulous coat. I imagined interning with a designer, learning how to cut and fit the perfect dress.

"Well, sure. But I can't just move Max." I opened my eyes.

"It would only be a trial period for one year."

"Andre wouldn't let me." I shook my head.

"He could move to New York, too, if he wants, work at a restaurant. But it seems Andre is pretty happy with his house and restaurant in Ross. He can visit Max every couple of months."

"I couldn't even get in to Parsons." I shook my head.

"They accepted you before. Stella Braden is a trustee, you know, my old bridge partner. I'll call her in the morning."

"But where would we live, and where would Max go to school?"

"Miriam Johnson's daughter lives in Manhattan, with her three children. I'll call her in the morning, too." My mother got up and put her hands on my shoulders.

"Let me do a little detective work," she said.

"Okay, I guess." I was suddenly so tired my eyelids flickered closed.

"Go to bed, honey. Let's see what I come up with."

Chapter Ten

I slept terribly. All night I lay under my thousand-thread-count Egyptian sheets, staring at the gold-and-yellow wallpaper, wishing it were morning. I fell asleep just before five a.m. and woke up sweating, with my sheets wrapped around me like a mummy.

My mother tapped on the door.

"Andre's here," she said, poking her head in. "He wants to take Max to breakfast."

"Fine, just tell him to drop Max off at Kids' Club after breakfast." There was no way I was going to see Andre again.

"He wants to talk to you," my mother whispered. I knew Andre was standing right outside the door, I could hear him talking to Max in French.

"Tell him I'll send him a text." I got up and locked the bedroom door.

🦋 🦋 🦋

I took my time getting up; I wanted Andre to be long gone before I went into the living room. I spent ages in my closet, picking out a dress. I finally settled on a peach-colored Juicy Couture terry dress, and platform sandals. Andre hated Juicy, he thought it was overpriced, and I had been avoiding wearing high heels since I met Edward. Today I was dressing for me. I debated whether to wear the butterfly earrings. I put them in my ears, brushed my hair into a ponytail, and looked in the mirror. I liked the way they sparkled; I kept them on.

"You look lovely," my mother said, when I walked into the living room.

Room service had left an array of breakfast foods on the end table: French-pressed coffee, whole-grain bagels, English muffins, jam, Vegemite, grapes, cantaloupe, strawberries, and a bowl of whipped cream. "Thank you for getting rid of Andre for me," I said, pouring myself a cup of coffee.

"I've been on the phone all morning." My mother smiled.

"And?" I spread jam on an English muffin.

"Stella gave me the home number for the director of admissions at Parsons. Lovely man, his father lives in San Francisco and is on the board of the Asian Art Museum. I think we actually met a few times."

"You know everyone." I smiled. My mother was proud of her endless society connections.

"Anyway, you're in," she said.

"You're kidding." I put down my coffee cup.

"I told him how talented you are, how you'd given up your space because your father got cancer. Parsons starts the week after Labor Day." She finished a piece of toast.

"You work fast, but what about Max?" I put the muffin back on the plate. Suddenly, I was too nervous to eat.

"Miriam gave me her daughter's number. Her name is Penelope. Penelope has a son who's nine and she sends him to a private school in the Village, just a few blocks from Parsons. She said it's very small, only twenty-five kids per grade. They wear uniforms; Max would look so good in a uniform," my mother mused.

"Should I phone the school? What's it called?" I was getting excited. I imagined being in New York in the fall, attending the shows during Fashion Week, spying Gwyneth Paltrow and Kate Moss and Katie Holmes whispering in the front row.

"I already did. The headmaster was very nice, sounded a little young. He told me a boy going into third grade just withdrew, his family is spending the year in Paris."

"There must be a waiting list." All good private schools had waiting lists.

"I told him I'm looking to expand my philanthropic ventures outside of California and I was very interested in elementary education. Max is in." My mother smiled. She was very pleased with herself.

"You mean you bribed your way in," I laughed.

"Look at it anyway you like," she said huffily.

"I'm sorry, Mom. I'm stunned. How did you do that in one morning, on the weekend?" I put some grapes and strawberries on a plate. At least I could try to eat some fruit.

"Aren't you thrilled?" she asked.

"I've never lived outside California. What will Max say?"

"Max will say the same thing he did when you told him

we were coming here: that it's a cool new adventure. Tell him you'll take him ice skating in Rockefeller Center. Times Square has a Nike store that's as much fun as Disneyland. It's New York, center of the universe."

"What about Andre?" I fiddled with my napkin.

"Did Andre ask your permission when he took all those women to bed? It's a year's course. You can reevaluate next fall. Maybe he'll move to New York and open a five-star restaurant."

"I thought the point was to get away from Andre." I shredded my napkin into little pieces.

"The point, Amanda, is to plan your future the way you want to live it."

I didn't say anything. Parsons. New York City. I remembered all the hours I spent in my mother's dressing room watching her get ready when I was a child. The rows of dresses, each on their own satin hanger: princess dresses, full ball gowns, strapless sheaths. And the colors: tangerine, ballet-shoe pink, emerald green. Even at the age of nine or ten, I didn't just want to wear those dresses; I wanted to make them. I wanted my label tucked on the inside.

"It sounds amazing, but it's so soon. How will I find an apartment?" I started to wrap my brain around the idea: Max and I could move to New York and I could attend Parsons. I felt like Alice in Wonderland.

"I made one more call." My mother looked so pleased with herself I didn't know what to expect. Had she called Mayor Bloomberg to see if Max and I could bunk at the mayor's mansion?

"I called the St. Regis in New York and booked you and Max a suite for as long as you need it." She beamed.

"The St. Regis in New York? That would cost a fortune." I shook my head.

"It was your father's favorite hotel. Look at it as a present from him."

"I can't see Max and me living in a hotel. What would his school friends say?"

"With the price of that school, half his friends probably have penthouses at the Pierre or jets that take them to Palm Beach for the weekend. It's Manhattan, Amanda. Lots of wealthy people have suites in hotels."

"Well, maybe for a bit. Until we find an apartment."

"For a week or a month or the whole year. You know how the staff here love Max, you'll have the same thing there." My mother poured herself a cup of coffee and stirred in milk and sugar.

She was right. Living at the St. Regis was like having a huge extended family; some staff member was always giving Max a bell cart ride, or a hot chocolate, or crayons and a coloring book.

"I guess you have it all figured out." I put the plate of fruit down.

"It's going to be so good for you." My mother hugged me.

"I think you're right." I hugged her back.

"I'm always right. Promise me one thing: I get first look at your debut collection. I want an Amanda Blick original before anyone else gets one."

"Deal. But I think it'll be an Amanda Bishop original. It has a better ring to it."

I didn't eat the English muffin or the fruit. I didn't even finish my coffee. I was amped on adrenaline and I thought I better put it to good use. At some point it would wear off, and the terror of what I was about to do—move to the East Coast, go back to school, try to have a career—would set in.

My first stop was the business center. I sat down at one of the computers and tapped out a long e-mail to Andre explaining that Max and I were going to New York. I wasn't going to risk calling him and hearing him purr: "*Mais, non, ma petite cherie.* You cannot do that. I adore you."

I explained that Max and I would come back to Ross for a few days to get our clothes, and at that time we would tell Max about the divorce. After I wrote the words I sat back in the office chair and studied them: "We will tell Max about the divorce." It sounded so final, and for the first time since Black Tuesday, I thought I would survive. The more miles I could put between us, the faster I would heal.

After I sent the e-mail, I felt a surge of confidence. I was really going to do this. The next step would be to tell Max. I thought about going to Kids' Club and blurting it out, but I needed it to settle first. I had to come from a position of "This is what we're going to do, and it's going to be great," rather than "What do you think, Max? Is this okay with you?"

I walked through the lobby, past families checking in, getting their complimentary sand buckets and kiddy backpacks. Kids ran down the hall ahead of their parents, excited to start their vacation. I felt a little wobbly. I had planned on working out at the spa, but I made a detour to the Balcony Bar. I needed a drink and a catch-up phone call with Stephanie.

I ordered a banana daiquiri, and looked out at the Grand

Lawn. It was a perfect day, there was a croquet game set up on the lawn, and two French bulldogs drank water from silver bowls.

"I can't talk long. I'm about to get kicked out of the playground. Graham put gummi worms in another kid's sand sculpture," Stephanie said when she answered her cell phone.

"What's wrong with that?" I asked.

"They weren't his gummi worms. They belong to the other kid. Personally, I think it shows his artistic bent. Pop playground art."

"How are you?" I sipped my drink, which tasted like a banana smoothie.

"Counting the days till school starts. We have a big calendar on our bulletin board. Every time I cross off a day, I feel like I'm one day closer to regaining my sanity."

"It sounds pretty good to me." I remembered the long afternoons at the park when Max was a toddler. He worked all day making me sand pancakes.

"Let me guess, you're at the beach sipping a mimosa?" Stephanie asked.

"The Balcony Bar, actually, with a banana daiquiri." I smiled.

"Don't rub it in. I actually thought about bringing a flask of rum and Coke to the park this morning. Okay, let's get to the good stuff. What's happening with Edward?"

I put my drink on the table and told Stephanie the whole story, right up to the part where my mother booked a suite at the St. Regis for Max and me. By the time I'd finished, the Grand Lawn, the ocean, and Catalina Island were all a blur because I couldn't stop crying.

"Rotten son of a bitch," Stephanie said when I'd finished.

"Edward or Andre?" I laughed, wiping my eyes with a St. Regis napkin.

"Both of them. All men who can't keep their dicks in their pants. I should tape Graham's dick to his underwear right now so he won't grow up to be a bastard."

"It's my fault. I should have listened to you." I shook my head.

"The only thing I was afraid of was Edward was going to bore you to death if all you two talked about was divorce and cheating spouses. I didn't think he'd cheat on you. Are the earrings nice?"

"The earrings are lovely," I laughed. "I'm wearing them."

"Good for you. Forget him but keep the earrings."

"What do you think about me going to Parsons?" I hesitated. I didn't know what I would do if she thought it was a terrible idea.

"Well, let's put it this way. You leave boring old Ross where the most exciting event is repainting the post office, first for a five-star resort on the California Riviera. Then, when you have a totally hard body and suntan, you move to Manhattan, where you'll probably hang out with Uma Thurman or James Franco. Everybody who's anybody lives in Manhattan and you're living at the St. Regis—"

"It's not sunny California," I interrupted.

"Wait, let me finish. And you're going to design school where you'll probably become the next Tory Burch and have your label in every Neiman's from here to Texas. Have I left anything out?" Stephanie said.

"Max. Is it okay to do this to Max?" I sighed. It was nice to have Stephanie's approval.

"As long as he doesn't become one of those teenage wankers on *Gossip Girl*. Who's that guy, Chase, with the evil smile but great hair? I'm kidding. It's going to be great for Max to leave the Ross bubble. Think how international his school will be. He'll probably have an Indian prince or Chinese genius in his grade."

"How do I tell Max?" I sounded wimpy even to myself.

"The same way you tell him to brush his teeth. I'm the mom and this is what we're doing."

"Poor kid." I thought about Max and his new attachment to his surfboard.

"If I can separate Graham from his Snuggly Blankie at night, you can do this. Piece of cake."

🦋 🦋 🦋

We hung up and I headed to the spa. I scheduled thirty minutes on the stair machine to work off the banana daiquiri, twenty minutes in the Jacuzzi to sooth my sore muscles, and fifteen minutes in the Tranquillity Room to rid myself of any lingering bad karma. Then I would pick Max up from Kids' Club, butter him up with a chocolate shake, and tell him our plans.

🦋 🦋 🦋

Max and I perched on stools at the Pool Grille, sipping our shakes. I watched women crisscross the Grand Lawn in outfits ranging from skimpy bathing suits that barely covered their butts to designer dresses, oversized purses, and four-inch heels. I found myself critiquing the dresses: One was too busy, another had competing patterns, a third was glorious—a floor-length safari-print caftan with a matching turban.

"It's been a great summer," I began, feeling as if I was on a job interview with the CEO of a Fortune 500 company.

"Awesome. Wait till I tell everyone about my new surfboard. Do you think we can go to Stinson after school and surf?"

"Stinson Beach has a lot of sharks," I faltered. I had to follow Stephanie's advice and just tell him. "Actually, Max, we're not going back to Ross," I said.

His expression wavered like he'd been hit in the stomach with a line drive. "Are we staying here?" he asked cautiously. "I guess it would be cool to surf every day."

"We're moving to New York, just you and me, for a year," I said firmly.

"What's New York?"

"You know what New York is. It's the busiest, most exciting city in the world. With a giant park that goes all through the city where you can see jugglers and magicians. And it's really close to mountains so we can ski on the weekends, and we can go out to Long Island and go sailing . . ." I knew I was babbling.

"I don't know anyone in New York. And what about Dad, and my school, and Grandma?" He was gasping for air like a fish that had been tossed out of its fishbowl.

"We're moving because I was accepted at a fashion design school and it's an incredible opportunity for me. Dad will come visit every couple of months, and Grandma is going to spend Thanksgiving with us. I haven't even told you the best parts." I hugged him tightly.

"Okay." His voice was wobbly.

"Grandma got you into a really cool school in the Village. It's very small so you'll get to know everyone, and they have a robotics class and their own organic garden." I had done a quick search on the Internet. Max had a passion for robots and he'd always wanted his own garden.

"Like building robots?" he asked.

"Yep," I said.

"Cool." He sounded interested.

"And the very best part is we're going to live at the St. Regis in New York. You're going to be King of the Hotel."

"I get to live in a hotel?" I could see endless bell cart rides dancing in front of his eyes.

"And drink St. Regis hot chocolate and roast s'mores in the fireplace." I was beginning to smile.

"Do they have a butterfly release?" he asked.

"No, but they have their own traditions. At Christmas they build a replica of the hotel in chocolate and display it in the lobby." I had researched the St. Regis as well.

"Do you get to eat the chocolate?" he asked.

"You'll have to ask the chef." I laughed.

"Wait till I tell Erin. She's never been out of California." He grinned.

"We're going to have a ball." I hugged him tighter. My mother was right. With the right encouragement, Max would see it as a big adventure. I just had to make sure I saw it the same way.

Chapter Eleven

*O*ur final week at the St. Regis passed in a blur of nervous anticipation. I spent half my time lingering on the Parsons Web site, learning everything about the school, and the other half trying not to think about our house in Ross, and Stephanie, and the rituals all the other mothers were doing to get ready for the school year. We wouldn't be lining up at the Panda Room to get Max's hair cut, or standing at the post office to see whose class Max was in, or bumping into everyone we knew at Staples when we were buying our school supplies.

I kept my anxiety to myself and every day regaled Max with a longer list of the fun things we would do in New York: watch a ball game at Yankee Stadium, eat a hot dog at Coney Island, rent a rowboat in Central Park. With all the information I ingested, I could get a job as a New York City tour guide. We even Skyped Penelope's son, whose name was Gunnar. Max and Gunnar discovered they had a mutual love for Wii Super Mario IV and Percy Jackson books. Gunnar showed Max the school uniform over Skype, and Max thought it looked like something you'd wear to Hogwarts. In other words, pretty cool.

Andre reacted as I expected, by calling and screaming there was no way I was taking Max to New York. I calmly told him it was only for a year and he was welcome to visit. I'd even buy him the plane tickets. He hung up in a fury and I spent an anxious night wondering if he could stop us, but the next day he called and said it might be good for Max to experience a big city. He suggested when Max was a teenager he might take him to France for a few months. I hung up, puzzled at his change of heart, but my mother let slip that she had asked Dean Birney to talk to him. I didn't ask my mother what Dean said, but I resolved to make sure we write in the divorce documents that Andre was not allowed to take Max out of the country.

The one person I avoided was Edward. I saw his name come up on my phone every few hours and I deleted his messages and texts without looking at them. Every now and then, when I walked the treadmill, I would see his crinkly smile, or remember what his chest felt like on top of mine, but I quickly erased the images and pushed the machine up a notch.

My mother and I took turns crying at the thought of leaving each other. We'd sit on the balcony sipping our cocktails, and I'd see her looking at me, and I'd start bawling. She would tell me to stop, she'd see us at Thanksgiving, and then she'd start crying. Eventually, we would stop, pour ourselves another drink, and watch the sunset.

🦋 🦋 🦋

We scheduled our departure for six p.m. on Saturday night, because Max wanted to go to the last monarch butterfly release. Our bags were packed, waiting with the valet. We left my mother in the suite, surrounded by boxes of Kleenex. I could hear the opening lines of *American Idol* when we walked down the hall, and I thought I heard my mother singing along.

Erin was waiting for Max in the lobby lounge to help Max catch his last butterfly. I took a seat at the bar and ordered a Lemon Drop.

"You know you really should eat something when you drink at midday," a voice behind me said.

I swiveled around. It was Edward, wearing Bermuda shorts and a Tommy Bahama flowered shirt.

"Hi," I said nervously.

"I hear they make a great steak tartar here. Can I order you some?" he asked.

"I don't think so." I swiveled back to the bar.

"Please, Amanda." He put his hand on my mine. "Let me sit down for a minute."

I took a deep breath. Max and I would be leaving in an hour.

"Okay, I guess," I said.

Edward sat on the stool next to me and ordered two glasses of champagne.

"I already ordered a drink," I said.

"Champagne is the only thing you should drink before six p.m. Anyway, we're celebrating." He smiled.

"What are we celebrating?" I kept my eyes on the bar.

"That I found you before you left."

"How did you know we were leaving?" I turned and looked at him.

"Bribed the bellboy. Don't be harsh on him, he's trying to put himself through college." He touched my hand.

"Oh." I sipped the champagne. It was cold and fizzy.

"Going back to Ross?" he asked.

"Yes." I nodded.

"Not to live with the dickhead, I hope. He doesn't deserve you." Edward nibbled a handful of cashews.

"Actually we're only going to Ross for a few days, to get our things. We're moving."

"Moving here?" Edward's face lit up.

I put down the glass of champagne. "No, to New York. I'm going to Parsons."

"Good girl!" Edward said. "How did you manage that?"

I told him how my mother got me into Parsons, found a private school for Max, and booked us a suite at the St. Regis all in one morning.

"Wow, she's impressive. I wouldn't want her working against me." He laughed.

"You should have seen her in her heyday. Once she organized a fund-raiser to save a neighborhood park in twenty-four hours. She got Wolfgang Puck to cater, Pavarotti to sing, and Mayor Feinstein to meet and greet. The developer who wanted to turn it into a skyscraper retired to Kansas. He was blacklisted in San Francisco."

"Amanda, I am so sorry for what I did. I can't think of anything else. I want to take a stun gun and shoot myself." His voice turned low.

"What's done is done," I said quietly.

"Give me another chance." He swiveled my stool so I was facing him. He touched my cheek and pushed my hair behind my ears. I remembered how firm and confident his fingers were. "Hey, you're wearing the earrings." He grinned.

"I like them," I said simply.

"Please, Amanda. You're new at this divorce thing, but I've been single for five years. I know how I feel about you, and I'm not going to feel that way about anyone again."

"Edward, I can't," I said.

"We can take it really slow. I have a good friend from law school who lives on the Upper East Side. "

"You hurt me so badly," I said, and shook my head.

He put his finger on my lips and kept it there. "It won't happen again. I'm not that kind of guy."

"I have to think about myself for a while. Just me and Max."

"Promise me one date. How about Thanksgiving? We could watch the Macy's parade together."

"My mother's coming out for Thanksgiving." I nibbled some peanuts. I was beginning to feel a little shaky.

"Perfect." He beamed. "I'll escort your mother. She shouldn't travel alone at her age. And as a reward you'll have one drink with me at the King Cole Bar at the St. Regis. That's where they invented the Bloody Mary."

"I know." I had read it on the Internet.

"I remember Max told me you're partial to celery." He smiled.

"I like celery." I nodded.

"Wait till you taste the celery in a St. Regis Bloody Mary." He put his hand on mine. "Please, Amanda."

I studied his pale blue eyes, his strong jaw, his nose, which looked more crooked when he smiled.

"Okay, one drink at Thanksgiving," I agreed.

He leaned forward and kissed me on the mouth, a long, slow kiss that tasted bubbly and salty.

A minute later, Max came tearing into the bar, his hands clasped around a butterfly.

"I got one for you. Take it, Mom, and make a wish." Max pushed the butterfly into my hands. I could feel its wings fluttering against my palms. It felt like a tiny heart beating.

I walked onto the deck, cradling the butterfly. The ocean glittered in front of me like a magic carpet. I opened my palms and stroked the butterfly's wings. Then I held it up high and released it. And made a wish.

Acknowledgments

Sincere thanks to my superb agent, Melissa Flashman, and to the fantastic team at St. Martin's Press: my editors, Hilary Teeman and Jennifer Weis, and editorial assistant Mollie Traver.

Thank you to my friends who have been there since the beginning: Ilana Weinberg, Traci Whitney, Patricia Hazelton Hull, Sue Rosenthal, Linda Burkhardt, and Laura Narbutas.

Most of all, thank you to my wonderful children: Alex, Andrew, Heather, Madeleine, and Thomas. And to my husband, Thomas.

1. Stephanie says that Amanda doesn't love Andre, she only lusts after him, because "he is completely unlovable." Do you think it is possible to love someone who has betrayed you?

2. Edward cheats on Amanda because he thinks she still cares for Andre. Do you think cheating is unforgivable no matter what the excuse, or should Amanda give Edward another chance?

3. Stephanie's friendship is very important to Amanda, yet they have little in common. What is the basis of their friendship? Is it important for women friends to have similar backgrounds?

4. When they are first dating, Andre says in France it is acceptable for men to have affairs and stay married. Should Amanda have taken that into account before she married him? Should she have reacted differently to his cheating because of his nationality?

5. Amanda comes from tremendous wealth, and one of her struggles is stopping Andre from feeling like a kept man. Do you think she is depriving herself and Max of a lifestyle they deserve? Do you think Andre's feelings of financial inadequacy contribute to his desire to cheat?

6. At the end of the novel, Amanda decides to take Max to New York for a year so she can attend Parsons School of Design. Do you think she is doing the right thing? Or will the move be detrimental to Max because he will be far from his father and grandmother?

7. How do you perceive Stephanie's marriage? Do you think Stephanie loves Glenn—or did she settle for someone who could take care of her? Do you admire Stephanie or think she sold out in order to have a beautiful home and stable family life?

8. Grace takes Amanda to one of the most beautiful resorts in California but for much of the summer she is unhappy. How does one's environment affect one's happiness? Does a person carry their problems wherever they go, no matter how gorgeous the surroundings?

9. Do you think one of Amanda's problems is that she married too young? Do you think there is a best age to get married? If so, what do you think that age is?

10. Could you see yourself marrying a man like Andre: handsome and sexy but with questionable morals? Why or why not?

St. Martin's
Griffin

Turn the page for a sneak peek at Anita Hughes's new novel!

Market Street

Available Summer 2013

Chapter One

*C*assie tore the edge of her croissant and looked out the floor-to-ceiling windows at Fenton's to the street below. Christmas was over, the post-Christmas sales were limping to a close, and men and women walked with their coats wrapped around them. The giant tree in Union Square had been carted away. The dazzling window displays in Gucci and Chanel—Cinderella slippers with real diamonds to wear to holiday parties, little black dresses accessorized with stacks of multi-colored bracelets—had been replaced with sensible January displays: rain boots, umbrellas, and floor-length winter coats. Even Burberry's window looked bleak. The sweet reindeer wearing a plaid sweater and socks had been exchanged for a faceless mannequin wrapped in scarves like a mummy.

"People in San Francisco don't know how to do winter," Cassie said, dipping her croissant into a white Limoges coffee cup. "They think California in January should be blue skies and seventy degrees."

"We could go to Mexico till March. Stay at Betsy's condo and sip sangria with pink plastic straws," Alexis replied, picking a petit four from the silver tray on the table and biting into it tentatively. She blotted her lips on the white linen napkin and stirred cream into her demitasse.

"Some people have jobs," Cassie replied, "or at least their husbands work. You don't just jet off to Mexico because the Christmas ornaments are gone."

"Carter would never miss me. He's too busy trimming trees, or whatever he does from six a.m. till midnight. We haven't eaten dinner together since Thanksgiving, and that was only because his mother insisted we join the family in Pacific Heights. You know old Betsy's on her second husband since Carter and I got married. I don't know how she keeps the place cards straight." Alexis tapped her long French nails on the edge of the coffee cup.

"Your husband runs a hedge fund, he doesn't trim trees," Cassie said, and collapsed in a fit of giggles. She dusted croissant flakes from her pants and glanced around to see if the society matrons sitting at the adjoining tables were listening.

"Trees, hedges, it's all the same to Carter. Money is the only kind of paper he knows. He does compensate well. I got some lovely baubles for Christmas," Alexis said, rolling her eyes.

"You don't have to pretend with me. We've known each other since kindergarten and even then you made rings out of Cheerios. Be happy Carter buys you jewelry."

"He does have great taste, he gave me the most beautiful sapphire necklace, with tiny diamonds like snowflakes. I just sometimes feel like a courtesan instead of a wife. Fling a necklace or a bracelet at her and bring her out to impress the Midwestern clients who want to invest in pork futures," Alexis replied, twisting her diamond wedding band around her finger.

"Carter loves you, it's just his way of showing it. Most wives would be envious," Cassie replied.

"I take it Aidan didn't shower you with jewels?" Alexis raised her perfectly arched eyebrows.

"Fuzzy socks, a cashmere scarf, gardening gloves, and packets of exotic vegetable seeds: fennel, purple spinach, and okra." Cassie counted the presents on her fingers.

Alexis picked up another petit four, eyed the layered chocolate, and put it back on the plate. "I've exceeded my caloric limit for the day. Lettuce and soy sauce for dinner tonight."

"You're the only person I know who loses weight over the holidays. I gained three pounds smelling the pumpkin pie." Cassie pushed the plate of mini desserts toward Alexis.

"Only because I swam forty laps before every holiday party and spent thirty minutes in the steam room each night," Alexis said, adjusting her skirt. She wore an emerald green miniskirt and a white angora wool sweater. Her blond hair was scooped into a high ponytail and tied with a green velvet ribbon.

"Oh, to have your own indoor swimming pool and sauna," Cassie said, finishing her coffee and putting her napkin on the table.

"You could have all that. As I recall you *did* have all that. You're the one who married the communist professor."

"Aidan is not a communist. He's a professor of ethics. Which means he doesn't believe in excess. We live well, just not in a three-story mansion in Presidio Heights with an elevator."

"If you'd gone to UCLA with me instead of Berkeley we would have found you a nice movie star to marry. I remember the day you packed your car and headed over the Bay Bridge. I thought, why is Cassandra Fenton, heiress to San Francisco's oldest, most exclusive department store, going to school in Berserkeley? I was right, you know." Alexis eyed her friend objectively. "Your Tod's are as old as my shih tzu and your Michael Kors jacket is vintage. Except it's only had one owner: you."

"I've never had your flair. You could shop at Target and come out dressed for dinner at Chez Panisse. I've always been happier wearing gardening gloves than opera gloves. I am happy, Alexis, and so are you." Cassie played with the cuff of her shirt, twisting off a few stray threads.

"What would we talk about if we didn't complain about our husbands?" Alexis shrugged, sifting through her purse for a tube of lip gloss.

"The homeless on Market Street? The lack of fresh water in Africa?" Cassie suggested.

"We could always talk about shoes." Alexis stood up and pulled her skirt down over her thighs. "Let's stop downstairs and see if there are any Jimmy Choos left on the sale rack."

Cassie followed Alexis to the escalator and surveyed the elegant floor displays as they descended to the third floor. The fourth level had always been her favorite; her mother used to treat her to high tea in the café on weekdays after school. Cassie had thought every third grader practiced their cursive on a linen tablecloth while sipping hot chocolate served by uniformed waitresses. Her mother would leave her in the café while she prowled the other departments, making sure cashmere sweaters were stacked in neat piles and salesgirls holding bottles of Chanel No. 5 were positioned in the aisles.

"Cassie, how nice to see you," said a tall man wearing a

navy suit as he took Cassie's hand when the escalator deposited them on the third floor. "You just missed your mother, she had to rush off to a restaurant opening. Fois Gras on Post Street. The *Chronicle* says it's going to be the next dining destination in the city."

"My mother's always rushing around." Cassie smiled. "I saw her on the way up. Derek, do you remember my friend Alexis?"

The man put on rimless glasses and looked closely at the two women. "Of course. The last time I saw you, you were being trailed by half a dozen bridesmaids collecting cosmetics samples."

"I'm an old married woman now," Alexis said, grinning, "with spending power."

"In that case, let me direct you to our newest jewelry line. I'm told all the thirty-somethings are wearing it." The man extended his arm and navigated through the aisles full of shoppers to a large glass case toward the front of the store.

Cassie and Alexis gazed at the glass like small children admiring Halloween candy. Rows of pendants, bracelets, and rings were displayed on a bed of crushed orange velvet. Cassie ignored the bracelets—they would be covered with potting soil within a day—but the pendants caught her attention: brightly colored stones on short filigree chains. She put her hand to her neck, imagining she was wearing one.

"These are right up your alley." Alexis tapped her nail on the glass. "That one would go so well with your eyes, Cassie. Try it on."

"Okay, just for fun." Cassie nodded. "Derek, could I see that one?"

Derek unlocked the case with an oversized gold key and

placed the pendant in Cassie's hand. "Your mother found these on a buying trip to Buenos Aires. They are *the* accessory on the polo fields this season."

Alexis watched Cassie click the pendant around her neck. The stone was turquoise and amethyst colored and made Cassie's eyes look like a powder blue sky.

"Take it home," Alexis insisted. "Tell Aidan you did your own post-Christmas shopping so he wouldn't feel guilty for getting you fuzzy socks."

"He didn't only get me fuzzy socks. But it is really pretty." Cassie leaned closer to the mirror.

"He can't complain about excess, it's not a diamond or a ruby. And you're supporting the South American economy. He'll be pleased." Alexis took a few bracelets out of the case and slipped them on her wrist.

"I don't need it," Cassie said uncertainly. She wasn't very interested in clothes; she usually pulled whatever was clean and pressed out of her closet, but she loved colorful jewelry. When she was a teenager her mother brought home bags of necklaces, earrings, and brooches, and Cassie was allowed to pick what she wanted. She still kept them in heart-shaped jewelry boxes and snapped on a hair clip or put on dangly earrings when she drove into the city for lunch.

"Would you two girls mind watching the display for a moment? I just saw Mrs. Benson go up the escalator. She's one of our best customers but she's almost deaf and she tends to scare the salespeople." Derek put the gold key on the glass.

"We'll do anything if you call us girls," Alexis said. She smiled, putting the bracelets back in the case and scooping up a selection of colored rings.

"I can't believe you're flirting with Derek. He's almost a hundred. He used to hold my hand when my mother sent me to sit on Santa Claus's lap. I thought Santa had spiders under his beard, and I'm terrified of spiders." Cassie unsnapped the pendant and laid it on the crushed velvet.

"Excuse me, I need to make a return." A girl approached the counter clutching a plain brown shopping bag. She had short blond hair cut in feathery layers around her face, and big brown eyes, like the dolls Cassie collected when she was a child. She wore a T-shirt emblazoned with Chinese letters and an army green bomber jacket.

"We don't work here." Alexis shook her head, stepping back from the counter.

"The store manager just went upstairs. I can try to find another salesperson for you; they're all busy taking returns. Post-Christmas hazard." Cassie smiled, seeing the girl's face fall. She clutched her shopping bag tighter. Her nails were painted neon pink and she wore a macramé bracelet around her wrist.

"Crap. My roommate gave me a ride. She's double-parked outside, probably going to get a ticket. The meter maids were circling like vultures around a Thanksgiving turkey. I don't know when I'll make it down here again. I never shop in Union Square, let alone Fenton's." The girl drawled the name of the department store as if it were a foreign language.

"We don't work here, but Cassie owns the place. I bet she can process a return for you," Alexis said, nodding at Cassie.

"My mother owns it." Cassie blushed. She felt like people had been saying that since she was seven years old, when her mother would dress her up in a Chanel suit and black patent

Mary Janes and guide her through the departments, introducing her to her best customers.

"Please, my roommate will kill me if she gets a ticket. It's her mother's car and she doesn't even know we borrowed it." The girl opened the bag and took out a red satin box imprinted with the trademark Fenton's signature.

"Oooh, one of these lovely pendants." Alexis picked up the box. "Why would you want to return it? These are going to be a must-have."

"To be honest, I could use the money. It was a present and I figured anything in a Fenton's box must be pricey. No offense." The girl looked at Cassie and clapped her hand over her mouth. "It's really nice, but I'm a student. I could use a bit of cash."

"Do you have a receipt?" Cassie asked awkwardly. She pulled her long bangs over her ears the way she did when she was nervous. She had tried manning different counters in the afternoons during high school—cosmetics, handbags, Godiva chocolates—but she had never felt comfortable taking other people's money. "You're giving them a bit of their dreams," her mother would coach her, but Cassie always felt the dreams came with a high price tag. She wondered how women could justify paying so much for elaborate gold boxes holding four pieces of chocolate.

"It was a present," the girl repeated. "But maybe you have the credit card on file. The name was Blake, Aidan Blake." The girl kept glancing around, as if one of the uniformed meter maids was going to appear and arrest her for double-parking.

"Excuse me," Cassie said.

"Aidan Blake, Professor Aidan Blake, actually, but I doubt it says that on the credit card. I guess physicians put 'doctor' in front of their names, but it would seem a bit silly for a professor to, wouldn't it?" The girl looked from Cassie to Alexis as if she was very interested in their opinion.

"Where did you get this?" Cassie held the box at arm's length as if it were a stick of dynamite.

"I told you it was a present. Do you think I stole it or something?" The girl stepped back from the counter. "I may not look like a Fenton's customer, but I'm not a thief. It was a Christmas present, from a friend," she finished, her round cheeks turning a light shade of pink.

"How do you know this friend?" Alexis demanded, glancing at Cassie, whose face had turned white.

"We don't give cash refunds, only store credit," Cassie said automatically. She gripped the side of the display case, pressing her knuckles against the glass. Every nerve in her body tingled, as if someone had set off a fire alarm only she could hear.

"You two treat customers pretty funny," the girl said, frowning. "I thought Fenton's was all about customer service. I've seen the ads online: 'Don't just walk the red carpet; take it home with you. At Fenton's every customer is a star.' Hardly." The girl pushed the box into the shopping bag. "Store credit isn't going to do much; what am I going to buy? A two-hundred-dollar pair of seamless stockings? A Marc Jacobs hairbrush? I'll probably never come to Union Square again, I'm obviously not welcome."

"Wait." Cassie exhaled, feeling like something heavy was sitting on her chest. "I'll give you cash. Here, give me the box."

"Okay." The girl stopped, eyeing Cassie suspiciously. "I want a full refund, I bet it was expensive."

Cassie opened the cash register and extracted three fifty-dollar bills. "Take these." She slid them over the counter.

The girl's eyes opened wide. She picked up the bills and crinkled the edges with her fingers. "I don't think it was that much. I mean, shouldn't you look up the credit card or look at the price tags on the other necklaces?"

"Take the money and leave." Alexis walked to the front of the case. She was almost six feet tall in her four-inch Prada heels and her body was muscled and lean from hours in the pool and on her bicycle. She stood so close to the girl she could see the brown roots at the top of her head.

"I'm leaving," the girl said, stuffing the money in her jeans pocket and moving away from Alexis. "You're lucky I don't go on Yelp or something. But thanks for the refund, I hope it doesn't all go to the meter maid."

Alexis walked back to Cassie and put her hand on her shoulder. "Breathe," she said quietly.

"I can't." Cassie's voice was like a robot. "I need some fresh air."

"You're not following her." Alexis grabbed Cassie's sleeve. "We need to sit down in private. Let's go to your mother's office."

Cassie followed Alexis to the private elevator in the back of the store, clutching the red Fenton's box that held the pendant. She felt any moment her knees would buckle and she'd crumple to the floor like an anorexic Victoria's Secret model. She closed her eyes as the elevator doors shut, wishing everything would stay black and the elevator would just keep going up and up and up.

"Cassie." Alexis poked her with one long fingernail. "Get

a grip. It can't be that bad. You've been married for almost ten years. There has to be an explanation."

"Maybe Aidan gave each student jewelry, instead of grades. Maybe he gave his whole lecture class gifts: polo shirts for the boys and necklaces and earrings for the girls. That would be so like him, don't you think? That sounds just like my husband, who believes material things have no relationship to one's happiness, and makes me do his family's birthday gift shopping. If it wasn't for me, he'd still buy Isabel My Little Pony every year, even though she's sixteen and lives with us half the time." Cassie was almost shouting.

"Cassie, stop." Alexis pushed the elevator button so the doors stayed open. "We need to think this through calmly, and we need a drink. I hope your mother still has that bottle of scotch under her desk."

Cassie nodded, biting her lip and pulling her bangs down till they reached her chin. She looked at herself in the smoky elevator mirror. Her mother always said she had the face of an angel: almond-shaped blue eyes, long dark lashes, a small nose dusted with freckles, and God's imprint, a dimple on the side of her mouth. The reflection staring back at her looked more like Snow White just after she realized she'd eaten the poisoned apple.

Cassie opened the door to her mother's office, smelling a mix of lemon Pledge and Chanel No. 5. The walls were papered in beige linen, and the wood floor was covered with a thick oriental rug. Vases holding bunches of lilies graced the coffee table, the end tables, and the fireplace mantel. There was a cherry desk, a Louis XIV chair, and a cream-colored sofa with throw pillows shaped like seashells.

"Your mother has the best taste, even where no one can see it," Alexis said as she admired the silk pillows.

"I'm not in the mood to discuss interior design." Cassie lay facedown on the sofa.

"Maybe she's Aidan's TA and he bought her the pendant to thank her for grading papers." Alexis opened the drawer under the desk and extracted a crystal decanter and two shot glasses.

"That would be such an ethical thing for a professor of ethics to do," Cassie moaned into the cushions.

"Cassie, sit up." Alexis dropped onto the sofa, holding a shot glass in each hand. She kicked off her heels and tucked her stocking feet under her legs. "Drink this, quickly," she said as she put the glass under Cassie's nose.

Cassie drank the scotch in one gulp. She felt the alcohol burn the back of her throat, and her eyes stung. She blinked and held her glass out for another shot, promising herself she would not cry.

"That's the girl who wrote love notes to Father Chatham senior year, and signed Sister Agnes's name." Alexis nodded approvingly, refilling Cassie's glass.

"Sister Agnes was in love with him"—Cassie threw back the second shot—"the whole school knew. Every song in chapel was a love song."

"I think those were called hymns to God." Alexis grinned. "Honestly, Cassie, I know Aidan looks like a lion, king of the jungle, and all those sophomoric undergrads hang on his every word, but has he ever given you a reason to doubt him?"

"No," Cassie said, and shook her head, choking back a hiccup, "but he's never given anyone a red Fenton's box. The only thing he buys for me at Fenton's are scarves, because my skin is so sensitive I break out if it's not true cashmere."

"Fenton's does carry the best scarves; I should get more. Maybe on the way down we can check and see if they have any new colors." Alexis rubbed her finger along the edge of her glass.

"You can have the ones Aidan bought me for Christmas, if I don't use them to strangle him."

"I know you've been married much longer than me," Alexis said, pouring herself another shot, "but it could be completely harmless. A silly misunderstanding."

"This isn't one of those old black-and-white movies where the hero gives the heroine a gift and it's intercepted by the wicked stepsister." Cassie leaned back on the pillows.

"A few weeks ago I found a cigar in Carter's blazer pocket. Not that I snoop, of course, I'm not that sort of wife." Alexis put her glass on the rug. "But I felt this long, hard thing in his pocket, like a small penis."

"How is this relevant?" Cassie interrupted.

"I was really angry; I hate the smell of cigars, it stays in the sheets forever." Alexis plumped the pillow with one hand. "He said he didn't know how it got there and I didn't believe him. I withheld sex," she said, sucking in her breath, "until he told the truth."

"Carter without his nightly pillaging? He must have climbed the walls." Cassie tried to smile.

"It turned out one of the guys at work put a cigar in every-one's blazer. Invitation to a bachelor party."

"I hope you gave Carter some sex before he went to the bachelor party. Who knows what might have happened."

"I'm serious, Cassie. All you have is circumstantial evidence. Don't you watch *Law & Order* or *The Good Wife*? Circumstantial evidence is never going to carry a conviction."

Cassie opened the red Fenton's box and stared at the offending pendant. The stone was light brown on a thin gold chain. She turned it over to see if there was a card or a note enclosed.

"How many times have you told me Aidan gets a dozen Facebook friend requests a day from students and deletes them all, unread," Alexis pressed on. "And what about the fresh pizza that showed up at your front door with a note written in haiku? Aidan threw it away even though it was from Guido's."

"You're turning things around. Aidan gave this to that girl." Cassie waved the box in the air like a red flag.

"It might have ended up in her hands a number of ways."

"Like how?" Cassie sat up straight. The shots had made her brain sharper, instead of numbing the pain.

"That's my point. You have to find out how, and you can't jump to conclusions until you do."

"Do you want me to hire a detective, like that guy on *CSI: Miami*?"

"David Caruso? I don't know what all the fuss is about, how can anyone with red hair be sexy? Do you believe in your marriage?" Alexis asked.

"Yes." Cassie nodded, blinking to stop the tears from spilling down her cheeks.

"Then take the box and show it to Aidan, let him explain it."

"What if he can't?"